THE EARL OF MORREY

The League of Rogues - Book 14

LAUREN SMITH

Lauren
SMITH
TIMELESS ROMANCE

This book was previously published in 2014 by Samhain Publishing. This is a republication of the original version.

ISBN: 978-1-952063-30-5 (e-book edition)

ISBN: 978-1-952063-31-2 (print edition)

Excerpt from the *Quizzing Glass Gazette*, September 10, 1822, the Lady Society column:

MY DARLING LADIES,

I have returned to bring you the most delicious gossip. It must be noted that the existence of a certain club has recently reached my attention, one called the Wicked Earls' Club. Only the most wicked of titled earls are said to be members. Naturally, my mind has run away with thoughts of a most dangerous nature. Who belongs to this club, and do you already know them? Is the polite earl you danced with last night at Lady Allerton's ball all that he seems? Is there more to the tall, dark-haired gentleman who tipped his hat as he rode past you in Hyde Park this fall?

. . .

I AM MIST. I AM MOONLIGHT. I AM THE SMOKE OF AN extinguished candle. I am the shadow you do not see, but only feel . . .

Adam Beaumont, the Earl of Morrey, let the words of his private mantra flow over and through him until he believed them to be true. As he moved through the crowded ballroom of Lady Allerton's home, the words worked a subtle magic. They rendered him nearly invisible to the husband-hunting ladies prowling around him, their matchmaking mamas leading the hunt. Given that he was an unmarried, young, and attractive gentleman with a title, that was quite a feat. If the *ton* knew what sort of man he truly was, those young women and their mothers would not be so eager to snare him.

He swept his gaze over every face in the packed ballroom, seeking that cunning gleam in a pair of eyes or an overly observant glance in his direction. He listened carefully for clever discussions designed to collect information best kept hidden.

A loaded pistol would have been a welcome companion tonight, but he could not conceal such a cumbersome weapon on his person. No, the only friend he carried tonight was the slender dagger pressed flat against his chest beneath his waistcoat. He dared not risk a dance, lest the blade dislodge and become a danger to him.

If only the *ton* knew what sort of man stood in their midst. A man whose job was to end any threat to the Crown. An agent of His Majesty who worked to keep the monarchy safe, as well as to protect the kingdom from foreign threats. He was the knife in the dark that claimed the life of anyone who came here to do his nation harm. It was a burden Adam had never wanted, but he had been given little choice.

Many thought that wars started and ended on the battlefield, but Adam knew the darker truth. Wars began in drawing rooms and ballrooms, where men let down their guard and become targets for spies and assassins. He'd learned that after losing his friend Lord Wilhelm. It had been two years since he'd watched a French spy take the life of his dear friend.

John Wilhelm had struggled with a French assassin on a bridge over the Thames. Adam had been too late to stop the man from plunging a knife into John's back, but John had taken the murderous bastard with him over the bridge and into the dark, swift waters below. Adam had rushed to the spot where his friend had gone and leapt over the side into the water himself. The fall had nearly killed him, and it had been for naught. He'd searched the water for what felt like an eternity before finally crawling up the bank and collapsing in exhaustion.

As he lay gasping for breath, a man Adam had seen once or twice before at social engagements had emerged from the darkness and rushed to help. That was the night Avery Russell, the man who would become London's new spymaster a year later, had recruited Adam to the Court of Shadows.

After the previous spymaster, Hugo Waverly, died last year, Avery had taken control and restructured the spy network. Many of the older spies had retired, and fresh blood like Adam had been brought deeper into the ring. Adam promised himself he would have his revenge upon John's killers, for as Avery had taught him, French agents worked in pairs, a master and his loyal left hand. Adam did not know which one had perished in the river with John, the master or the left hand, but he would someday find out. Becoming a spy was his penance for being too late to save his friend that night.

A quiet voice broke through Adam's dark thoughts. "Morrey?"

James Fordyce, the Earl of Pembroke, his new brother-in-law, came to his side. He was a fellow member of the private Wicked Earls' Club and had recently married Adam's half sister, Gillian. He and James had a passing acquaintance through their membership in the Wicked Earls' Club. There were only a handful of members he'd been close enough to get to know in the last few years.

Adam hadn't been particularly active in the club or pursuing any rakish wickedness of late. He'd been preoccupied with matters of England's security.

But that didn't mean England had been the only

matter on his mind. He'd been searching for his long-lost half sister who'd been working as a lady's maid in London, and that had brought him deeper into James's circle of friendship, for which he was grateful. He trusted the man with his secrets in ways he couldn't trust anyone else.

"Pembroke, good to see you," Adam replied.

James had been the only one to notice him tonight. One of the few who were able to see past Adam's ability to disappear into crowds whenever he wished to.

"Is Caroline with you? Gilly was hoping to see her." A silent question lurked in James's dark eyes, as if he wanted to ask what had Adam on edge.

"No, not tonight." He had convinced his sister Caroline that there would be other balls this week to attend. Once he'd informed her that he had a mission to fulfill tonight, she'd understood the dangers and thankfully had remained home.

"Should Gilly, Letty, and I leave?" Pembroke asked as he and Adam stepped deeper into the shadows at the edge of the ballroom.

"Yes, I would if I were you, but be calm about it—let no one suspect anything. Tonight the *devils* are among us." It was the warning he had devised with Pembroke to let the other man know when danger was close at hand. Pembroke was not a fool. From the time they'd first met, James had sensed that Adam was more than merely a titled lord searching for his long-lost half sister. So without putting James too much at risk, he'd let the man know that he worked for the Home Office in some secretive capacity, though he never went into details unless lives were at stake.

"Right. Well, I see Gillian but not Letty. She must have gone to one of the retiring rooms. I'll go and fetch her."

Adam was only partially listening. He'd caught sight of a woman leaving the ballroom, with another woman upon her arm.

Viscount Edwards's wife, Lady Edwards, the woman he was to protect this evening, was leaving the safety of the ballroom with a dark-haired woman whose face he could not see.

"Find your sister and go, quickly," he said to James before he slid through the crowds now gathering in rows to begin a dance. The pair of women vanished at the doors on the far end, and Adam's fear spiked. Lady Edwards was in grave danger. Her husband had lately been an ambassador to France, and Avery had recruited her to be a spy while she was on the Continent, as he and the Home Office worked in connection with the Foreign Office. She had memorized a verbal cypher that she was to give Avery this very evening, and it was Adam's duty to make sure no one silenced her before she could relay it.

Adam reached the partially open doorway leading out of the ballroom and stepped into a dark corridor. He pressed himself against the wall and moved swiftly from door to door, checking for the presence of Lady Edwards and her unknown companion.

"Hold still. Do not move," a soft, alluring voice said close by. "Be very still, Lady Edwards, lest I prick you. We wouldn't want that."

Christ, he was too late. Some foul French wench likely had a stiletto blade pressed to Lady Edwards's throat.

Adam's hands curled into fists as he moved toward the doorway where he'd last heard the voices. He reached up to undo the first two buttons of his green waistcoat and slid his dagger free. Still concealed by the edge of the doorframe, he drew in slow, steady breaths.

"Be still, I say!" the feminine voice commanded. "I don't wish to hurt you."

Lady Edwards began to beg. "Oh, please, do have mercy on me. I—"

Adam didn't wait another second. He shot around the doorframe and into the room, running straight for the feminine figure in a dark-blue silk ball gown. He caught the woman around her waist with one arm and jerked her back against his chest while he held his dagger to her throat.

"Make a sound and you will not live to regret it," he warned in a harsh whisper. The woman in his arms gasped and went stiff with terror.

"What?" Lady Edwards spun around. Her hands flew

to her mouth. "Lord Morrey, what are you doing?" Her blue eyes were wide with fear.

He gave the spy in his hold a tighter squeeze, and she wriggled in his arms. "Saving you, my lady."

"She's not a spy!" Lady Edwards insisted in a frantic whisper.

"She had you at her mercy—I heard her," Adam said.

"Don't be silly. My hair came undone. She was putting the pins back." Lady Edwards held a pair of jeweled hairpins up for him to see. Diamond-studded pins glittered in muted lamplight as the reality of the situation sank in.

He'd made a grave error.

Still holding the woman captive in his arms, Adam slowly lowered the blade. Her breath quickened as though she'd been too afraid to breathe the last few seconds. As he released her, he caught her wrist to keep the woman from fleeing until this matter was settled, and she was sworn to secrecy. She turned to face him, and this time *he* was the one who forgot to breathe.

Letty Fordyce, James's little sister, a beauty he had admired—*desired*—from afar these last few months, was his frightened captive. He released her wrist, and she pulled free. She retreated to the safety of Lady Edwards.

"Lady Leticia," he greeted in a gruff rumble barely above a whisper.

The dark-haired beauty held a hand up to her neck and gazed at him in terror.

"Oh, Letty, I'm so sorry." Lady Edwards grasped the young woman's shoulders and tried to soothe her.

"What . . . ?" Letty stared at him. "Why?"

"We haven't time," Lady Edwards said to her. "Morrey, have you seen Mr. Russell?"

"I haven't. I fear something may have happened to him."

"I must give you the message, then," Lady Edwards murmured.

"No, not me. I am no messenger," he reminded her. "I was only meant to protect you."

He was not one of those spies who played with coded messages and costumes on missions. He was a harbinger of doom, a hand of death for those who tried to harm his country.

"He must be told *tonight*, Morrey," Lady Edwards said.

"What are you talking about?" Letty had finally found her voice. "Why did he hold a knife to my throat?"

"I'm sorry, Letty, dear—not now. We haven't time—"

A creak on the wood floor outside the retiring room made Adam spin around. A pistol barrel, half-illuminated, was aimed straight at them.

He launched himself at the two women, tackling them to the ground.

The crack of the pistol made him flinch as he hit the floor with the women beneath him. A moment later, he rolled off them and leapt to his feet, blade at the ready, but whoever had fired upon them had fled. He charged into the corridor, seeking any sign of where the assailant had gone.

The crowd in the distant ballroom soon turned to chaos as someone screamed about a pistol being fired. Half a dozen men ran in his direction, and Adam ducked back into the retiring room. Letty seemed to have collected herself and was assisting Lady Edwards up off the floor. Letty was pale, but she wasn't weeping or fainting dead away. She was no wilting rose, and for that he was glad.

"Did you catch them?" Lady Edwards asked as she brushed out the wrinkles in her gown.

He shook his head. "A crowd is gathering, searching for whoever fired that pistol. You must go at once, my lady. We cannot be seen together."

The lady spy nodded and rushed to the open window that led into the gardens outside. Thankfully, they were on the first floor, and Lady Edwards could drop three feet onto the grass outside. She gathered her skirts and slipped through the opening, vanishing into the darkness beyond.

"Godspeed, my lady," Adam said as he closed the window behind her. Then he turned toward Letty.

"Lord Morrey, what—?"

"Lady Leticia, I'm sorry about this."

"About what? What just happened? Why did you hold a knife to my throat?"

"I'm sorry about the fact that I have to kiss you now. I cannot be seen in here alone, not if I wish to avoid being connected to that pistol."

Letty's eyes widened as the sounds of the men in the corridor grew louder. "Why can't you be seen alone? Wait . . . kiss?"

He swept Letty into his arms, holding her tightly to him. And he claimed her parted lips with his. She drew in a shocked breath as he kissed her soundly.

Lord, the woman tasted sweet, too sweet. At any other moment he would have gotten drunk on her kiss. But he kept his focus on the closed door, waiting for the moment it would burst open. When it did, he purposely held Letty a moment too long, making sure the men who'd entered the room saw the girl was quite clearly compromised.

"Good God, it's Morrey!" one man said. Another man called out for Adam to let the girl go.

Adam stepped half a foot back from Letty, his hand still possessively gripping her waist, implying that they had been about to make love. Then he faced the men and dropped his hold on the poor young woman whose reputation he had just put the proverbial bullet through.

"Morrey, what the bloody hell do you think you're doing with my sister?" James demanded. He started toward Adam, vengeance in his eyes that Adam knew would likely end up with his face a bloody mess if this matter was not resolved.

"I . . ." Adam struggled for words as he pushed Letty behind him, keeping her well out of harm's way, lest her brother take a swing at him. He'd given Lady Edwards a chance to escape, but now he was to face an entirely different peril that *he* could not escape.

"We heard a pistol go off," a man said in confusion. Adam recognized him as Jonathan St. Laurent. "We feared something had happened. We thought it came from this room."

"I can't say I heard anything—I was rather preoccupied," Adam said with a rakish grin. He'd become a good actor in the last two years, showing only what he wished and hiding what he needed to.

"That much is clear," Jonathan snorted, his gaze fixed on Adam's chest.

Adam reached up to touch his waistcoat and realized the two buttons he'd undone to free his dagger were still out of their slits. It painted the situation with Letty in an even worse light because it looked as though he'd been in the process of removing his waistcoat.

"We should let Pembroke handle this," another man in the party said. "She is his sister, after all."

"Yes, leave him to me," James growled. "Continue your search."

The other men left the room, leaving James alone with Adam and Letty.

THE EARL OF MORREY

Pembroke closed the door, trapping Adam in the room with him and Letty. "Morrey, what the bloody hell happened?" James demanded, his eyes straying to his sister, who stood nearly silent behind Adam. "I thought you told me to leave because you were up to something dangerous, and then I find you kissing my sister. I expect there to be a damn good explanation for this."

Adam saw the hurt and fury in James's eyes. He had every right to assume the worst. Adam would have, had he been in James's place.

"There is, but I cannot explain here. It may not be safe," Adam replied.

James rubbed his closed eyes with his thumb and forefinger. "You're telling me that what happened tonight was connected to . . . ?"

"Yes." Adam saw that what he was carefully conveying to James was finally sinking in. "And you know what it means for her." He nodded his head toward Letty.

"I know . . . but I can help her weather the scandal. It doesn't have to end the way you expect. I won't force that upon her, not if she doesn't want it."

"Unfortunately, I think you must." Adam kept his tone quiet. "I'm the only one who can protect her. She's been seen, James. Before the night is through, she'll have been made as one of mine, and she will not be safe."

James's eyes widened and then narrowed as he looked

between his sister and Adam. Yes, the man was finally coming to understand what Morrey was saying.

"Then we must make a few decisions, mustn't we?"

"We must," Morrey agreed.

"The sooner the better, I suppose?"

"Yes. I'll go to the Doctors' Commons tomorrow. We can tell everyone we had a secret understanding and plan to marry within a few days."

"It will be enough." James sighed heavily. His reluctance to agree to this plan was obviously still strong.

"Wait—marriage?" Letty suddenly seemed to realize what they were speaking about.

"Yes, you and Morrey. Immediately." James glanced at Adam, an apologetic look in his eyes.

"James, you can't—"

"Letty, after what happened tonight, there are reasons that require you to comply with this decision. You know I would never want to force this, but you must trust me. This is the only way forward that keeps you safe."

"Safe? Safe from *him*? This man just held a knife to my throat!"

James shot a startled glare at Adam, renewed worry and anger apparent in his expression. "What?"

"A misunderstanding. I thought she was the threat I'd been sensing. Then the real threat revealed itself and fired. That was the pistol you heard from the ballroom. Whoever took that shot, they saw your sister's face clearly and likely knew that she'd been talking to Lady Edwards."

"Christ." James began to pace the floor of the retiring room. Then he looked at his sister again. "Letty, I've never asked you to obey me for any reason, but that changes tonight. You must trust me now when I say you *will* marry Morrey. All will be explained to you when it's safe."

"James, you cannot ask this of me—please. It isn't fair. You know what I want, and this isn't it." It was such a soft plea, a little sister asking her older brother for his love, his trust, his protection. Adam watched in dread as James had to deny his sister what she needed by a simple shake of his head. No decent brother could form words to deny such a plea, and James was a good brother. All he could do was deny her with his actions.

"Yes, it is unfair," Adam agreed, turning Letty's attention away from her brother. "And for that I'm sorry, Lady Leticia, but it must be done. Do not blame your brother for this. It is my fault. I bear the blame for it."

"No." She shook her head violently. "How can I marry you? I barely know you!"

"Many couples marry knowing each other for less time than we have," Adam said, keeping his tone gentle. It was clear Letty was still in shock. "Pembroke, allow me to have a moment with her."

"I should stay." James's overprotectiveness would have amused him at any other time.

15

"Just a moment is all I need."

"Very well," James allowed. "But only a moment. My sister has been through enough tonight. I would like to get her safely home before more daggers or pistols come into play." He stepped outside.

Adam grasped Letty's hips again, pulling her toward him. The blue silk of her gown was soft beneath his palms, filling him with desire. Yet she wasn't affected the same way he was. She was trembling, though he could hardly blame her under the circumstances.

"I will explain all that has happened tonight when I can, when it's safe. Please know that I'm sorry for how this came about. I will be a good and loyal husband to you. I swear it upon my life."

Tears gathered in her lovely dark-brown eyes. He reached up and brushed one away.

"Do not cry, please," he begged. "It will be all right. I promise."

Then he stole a soft, lingering kiss from her lips. The sort of kiss he wished he'd given her that first time. She went still in his arms, but not stiff with terror as she had been earlier. He nuzzled her cheek and held her close. The poor innocent creature, barely twenty, a full decade younger than him, was to have her life upended all because she'd sought to help Lady Edwards fix her hair. When he moved his face back to look down at her, all he saw was dazed confusion.

"There, there," he said, his natural need to comfort intensified for this beautiful young woman.

"Do you *wish* to marry me?" she asked him.

"I had no thought to marry. Not in a long while. But I am glad it will be to you." It was the truth. He had abandoned the idea of such things the night John had perished. But now Letty had need of his protection, and this was the only way he could be there to protect her at all hours. He felt like a bastard for having a small flare of happiness that a beauty with such a soft heart would be his. From the moment he'd laid eyes upon her, he'd had a fleeting rebellious thought that she would have made him a wonderful countess. Now she *would* be his countess, and he could not shake his sudden excitement and gratitude at the thought.

"Lord Morrey—" Letty began, but the door opened, and her brother came back inside.

"I have your cloak, Letty. We need to leave. I found Gillian. She's waiting out front." James held up a cream-colored cloak lined with blue silk that matched her blue-and-gold gown. Letty allowed her brother to slip it over her arms, and she buttoned it up with trembling hands.

"Pay a call on us tomorrow, and we'll discuss the ceremony and the matter of Letty's dowry." James held his hat under one arm and nodded brusquely at Adam.

Adam nodded back and watched the pair leave the retiring room. Once he was alone, he searched the chamber until he spotted the small hole in the wall where the bullet had struck. He retrieved his dagger and dug the bullet from the wall. He chipped at the hole, scratching it until it looked like the damage to the wall had been done by something else.

He searched the room until he found a chair about the right height, and then he pushed the tip of the chair into the hole. Now it looked as if someone had simply shoved the chair into the wall at an angle, causing the damage. The last thing he needed was proof of what had happened in this room. He needed London society to think that he simply had been lost in passion with Letty, not thwarting a French assassin.

He slipped the bullet into the tiny pocket of his waistcoat and left the retiring room.

Given the tight crowd now at the front door, Adam surmised that there had been a mad dash upon the poor grooms to fetch coaches and horses. Lord and Lady Allerton were attempting to oversee the mass exodus from their home.

"I don't understand it, Henry," Lady Allerton murmured to her husband. "A pistol? Why would anyone . . ." She trailed off and wrung her hands in her red satin skirts.

Adam slipped between pacing gentlemen and packs of gossiping ladies until he made it to the front of the line. The next groom who rushed up the steps of the Allerton house was breathing hard and caught Adam's summoning wave.

"Bring around my coach. The one with the Morrey crest." He knew all the servants of great households like the Allertons were trained to recognize the crests of the noble houses for occasions such as these.

"Yes, my lord."

Adam moved out of the hot crush of the crowd and waited outside for his coach to be brought forward. He donned his cloak and climbed inside the vehicle once it was in front of the Allerton house. Then he sat back in the darkness for an instant before he realized something was wrong.

He lunged forward, his dagger pressed against the man's throat. He would have laughed in triumph at discovering this hidden man, but he felt a second blade pressed against his own throat.

"Easy, Morrey," a familiar voice chuckled. Adam relaxed, and the weapons were lowered.

"Russell, what the bloody hell are you thinking, sneaking into my coach?" He sat back in his seat and tucked the knife in his waistcoat. Avery Russell did the same. Adam pulled one of the curtains away from the window so that he could better see the spymaster. "Did you find Lady Edwards?"

Avery nodded. "Barely. I saw her escaping from the window after the gunshot. I feared I was too late. We had but a moment to speak in the garden, and I received the message."

"You almost were too late." Adam leaned his head

back against the cushioned wall of the coach. "Tonight was a disaster."

"No one was hurt, and Lady Edwards gave me her message," Avery mused.

"No one is hurt, but I'm now to be married."

Avery's eyes widened. "What?"

Adam explained how he'd attacked Letty, and how he'd seen to it that Lady Edwards had the chance to escape safely. Then, to keep suspicion off himself, he'd kissed Letty publicly, making it look as though they'd met for a secret romantic assignation.

Avery fought off a grin. "You're to marry Pembroke's sister?"

"Go ahead and laugh," Adam grumbled.

"I'm not laughing at you, or her. Just the ludicrousness of the situation. Letty is a sweet girl, very intelligent, but not suited to a life of danger," Avery said with more seriousness.

"I know, but what can I do? The spy who fired upon me tonight had a good look at Letty's face. They'll assume she's working with me or Lady Edwards. Pembroke won't be able to guard her as well as I can. She'll be safer being married to me."

Avery was studying him now. "Marriage won't be enough. She'll need you as a protective shadow until we can discover who attacked you at the Allerton ball."

"I plan to be that shadow," Adam agreed. "I only dread knowing Letty will hate me for it."

"I believe Letty is due more credit than you would give her." Avery tapped the roof of the coach with a fist, and it rolled to a stop.

Adam glanced at the darkened street. "You're leaving here?"

"Like you, the shadows are my friends." Avery stepped out into the waiting gloom and soon vanished.

Adam called out to his driver to continue home. He had much to think on and much to plan, including the last thing he'd ever expected to plan—a wedding.

❧ 2 ❧

"**M**arried," Letty Fordyce muttered for the tenth time as she, Gillian, and James walked up the steps into their townhouse.

"Letty, perhaps we should have that talk now," her older brother said.

A footman removed her cloak and took her gloves as she turned to glare at her brother. "Talk? James, what is there to say? I barely know the man! What's more, he grabbed me from out of the shadows and held a knife to my throat! Then he just kissed me like . . ." Letty couldn't finish.

"Yes, well, I trust you when you say it happened, I do, but there's more to discuss than . . . knives and kisses."

"What could be more important than that?"

At this, Gillian spoke up. "Letty, my brother is

involved in matters that require the utmost discretion. Please allow James to have a moment to explain."

"Yes, that's all I ask."

Gillian put her arm through Letty's in a show of support as James gestured for them to follow him to his study. Once inside, James closed the door and spoke in a low voice.

"We could not speak of this at the Allertons' house— it was far too dangerous."

"Speak of *what*? I am tired of all this secrecy and whispers!"

Tonight had been both terrifying and confusing, in turn. All she had done was go to the retiring room to help Lady Edwards with her hair. Then Lord Morrey had gripped her from behind and held a knife to her throat. Letty had been frightened, until she discovered it was Lord Morrey. Then he'd pulled the blade away, yet still held her captive by her wrist. A strange and unexpected flare of heat had begun in her lower belly at still being in his grasp. Before she could even process what any of that meant, the misunderstanding had been followed by a very real attack on them by an unknown assailant.

But she had found herself drawn, *clearly* against her better judgment, to this new and dangerous side of Lord Morrey. She had always thought him undeniably hand-some, with his dark hair and flashing gray eyes, and there was such an intense seriousness to him that had been a mystery to her. Letty had seen a different part of him tonight, and she found she liked this new, dark side to the gentleman who had been the focal point of so many of her more stirring dreams at night.

"Morrey is a spy," James said, still using that hushed tone.

"A spy?" Letty echoed the word, still baffled. "If he is a spy, why would you and Gillian know about it? It seems as though that would rather be kept a secret."

"Yes, I quite agree, but when I married Gillian, the man took me into his confidence and told me about it, at least in broad strokes. He did not want me to worry, should something happen to him. He wanted me to know that whatever befell him was in the course of his duty to the Crown. I asked his permission to tell Gillian, and he agreed I could, knowing he could trust his sister with the knowledge of his occupation."

"A spy," Letty muttered. It didn't make sense, his secrecy and veiled discussions with Lady Edwards about messages and the way they'd been attacked. She'd been in such a state of shock that she hadn't yet fully processed what had happened to her this evening.

"His duties are not what you would expect. They are far more dangerous," James added even more quietly.

Letty waited for her brother to continue.

"He removes threats of a human sort." James seemed to be wording this carefully, and it did take Letty a moment to unravel the meaning behind it.

"You mean he's an assassin? He kills people?" she uttered in horror.

"If he must, but only those who attempt to harm others, such as the person who tried to harm Lady Edwards," Gillian added. "Please believe me, Letty— Adam meant you no harm with his actions tonight. I'm not in agreement with James that you should marry him, but I do ask that you believe me when I tell you he wouldn't have hurt you."

She now understood why he had grabbed her, how he'd thought she was the threat to Lady Edwards, but it was all too much to take in. Still, against her better judgment, she would give Lord Morrey credit this evening for being the gentleman Gillian insisted he was.

"He did save my life," she conceded. "When he saw the pistol at the doorframe, he shoved me and Lady Edwards to the floor and shielded us." Letty would have to make peace with the thought that she was soon to marry a man who took the lives of others, yet had *saved* hers.

"Morrey is a good man. Since Gillian and I married, I've come to know him better," James added. "Marriage to him will protect you."

"From what? I am not a spy," Letty argued.

Her brother crossed his arms over his chest. "Whoever fired that pistol has great reason to believe you *are* a spy. You were standing in a room with *two* spies— speaking to them, in fact. It's not as though you can just disappear to the country for a spell and be safe. You might as well have put your face on every paper and declared yourself working for the Home Office. But if you marry Morrey, he can help keep you safe. He has special skills and talents suited precisely to that duty."

Letty looked to Gillian, her only supporter in this matter. "But James can keep me safe, can't he? You know I fear scandal, but I won't bow to it and wed simply because society dictates it must be so."

Gillian glanced at her husband before replying. "You know I agree, Letty. But James is right—your reputation is nothing compared to the danger you will face if these spies believe you are important to their ends, which I'm sadly certain they will. My brother wouldn't have suggested marriage if he didn't think it was necessary. He never planned on marrying, given the dangers, but now—now he must . . . and you must. Surely marrying Adam isn't such a terrible fate. He is a good man, a kind man, a fair man, and he'll keep you safe." Gillian touched her stomach and looked at James. "If it wasn't for Gabriel, we would do our best to protect you here, but our son could be put in danger if someone intent on harming you came into this house."

A crushing sense of guilt settled on Letty's shoulders. Here she was demanding that James protect her, when she should be thinking of James and Gillian's new babe. Gabriel would indeed be in danger if someone came here looking for her.

"I am a selfish creature," she said, acid eating away at her stomach. "You're right. Gabriel must come first. I am a grown woman. I can take care of myself. James, I will move out of this townhouse tomorrow and find another."

"Nonsense," James said. "I'm not going to simply buy you a home to run away to. I am putting my foot down, Letty. You'll marry Morrey. Do you understand?"

Letty clasped her hands in front of her, staring at the floor. James had never spoken to her like this, like a child needing to be chastised for bad behavior. She wanted to yell and tell him she wouldn't marry anyone unless she chose to, but she also knew he was right.

Marrying Morrey was the intelligent thing to do. The last thing she wanted was to be seen as a fool which meant she must accept the situation. She was going to be married to Lord Morrey.

And it wasn't as if she hadn't daydreamed about that. Ever since they had met, she'd been bewitched by the quiet intensity of his eyes, the sensuality of his full mouth, and the soft but deep rumble of his voice. The man was a mystery cloaked in an enigma clouded by riddles.

"Please, Letty, you can trust my brother to take care of you. I know this all came about suddenly, but give it time. It might yet be the best thing to happen to the both of you," Gillian said. Letty saw hope burning in her sister-in-law's gray eyes, eyes so like Lord Morrey's.

"Gillian . . . is he the sort of man who could . . . could come to love me?"

Letty had few desires in the world that mattered to her so much as to be loved. She had been blessed with looks and a well-to-do family. Her circumstances had made it possible for her to wait to marry. She was fortunate enough that she could wait to find a gentleman who would, in fact, adore her, and whom she could adore in exchange. It wasn't so silly as wanting to be loved for the sake of *needing* adoration—it was more complicated than that.

She was a smart woman, and she lived in an age where women were barely above possessions in a man's eyes. But she clung to the hope that someday her children, especially her daughters, would live in a better time, one where women were equals. Where they would be valued for their thoughts, their knowledge, their education, and not just their looks, money, or birthing abilities. She held her desires for that particular future close to her heart, never letting anyone know.

"He will come to love you." Gillian clasped her hands, squeezing them. "He knows your value, Letty."

Gillian had once been a lady's maid, and she knew better than most that women held value. She understood what Letty had meant.

Letty faced her brother again. "Very well. I will marry Lord Morrey the day after tomorrow."

James's shoulders drooped in relief. He came over to her and placed his hands on her shoulders.

"Thank you. I know what this means to you to accept this situation, and I thank you for doing it. It makes me feel like I haven't failed you, to know that you'll have the best protection, better than what I can give you."

This—this was the brother she had grown up with. The man who cared about her, who truly did see her value and believe in her. He was acknowledging that though he'd commanded her to marry, it was still within her power to refuse. Her acceptance had been the right thing to do, and he was proud of her for it. This, above all else, made her want to cry. She was putting away her childish dreams of love and equality with a husband in order to protect her family. It was what women had done for centuries, and she wouldn't be any different.

"You had better go to bed, my dear. You've had a trying evening,and have a long day ahead of you tomorrow." James kissed her forehead before Letty left the study and headed to her bedchamber. As she climbed the stairs, she tried to arrange the crowded thoughts that tonight's events had caused. If she was to marry Lord Morrey, she must be a better master of herself, especially her emotions. But tonight—tonight she couldn't do that. She wished to curl up in her bed and cry like a child, and she hated herself for that weakness.

Her lady's maid, Mina, was laying out a nightgown and a robe de chambre.

"Good evening, m'lady," Mina greeted her. Mina was from Scotland and had been her mother's lady's maid. Since Letty's mother had passed away, Mina had become almost like a second mother to her. Her dark hair, now threaded with gray, was pulled back in a comfortable but unfashionable bun.

"Mina," Letty said, her voice suddenly breaking as fresh tears filled her eyes.

"What's this now, love?" Mina came around the bed to take Letty into her arms.

"I am to be married in two days," she said.

"Married? What? To whom?" her maid asked, stunned.

"To Lord Morrey." Letty sniffed, feeling the damnable tears coming.

"Oh, my poor dear. Let's sit, and you can tell me all about it."

Letty and Mina sat at the foot of her bed, and she told the maid all that had transpired at the ball and afterward, even the part about Morrey being a spy.

"But you must keep it all a secret, Mina, please." Letty knew she shouldn't be telling servants something like this, but she had to talk with someone about it, someone aside from James and Gillian.

"I have never once betrayed you, my lady, and I won't start now." The maid gave her a gentle nudge. "Let's get

LAUREN SMITH

you undressed. Shall I bring you a glass of milk and a few biscuits, perhaps one of Cook's tarts if there is one left?"

"Only if it's not too much trouble." The hour was late, and she had heard the clock chime in the corridor. She didn't want to keep her maid up very late.

"For you? Nothing is ever too much trouble." Mina clucked her tongue in a motherly way and worked at the laces on the back of Letty's gown. Once Letty wore only her nightgown, she pulled on the robe de chambre, leaving the floral-patterned robe open, not bothering to do up the tiny pearl buttons. She eased into her bed, the sheets a little cold, but she would soon warm up with the steady fire burning in the hearth across the room. Mina returned with a glass of warm milk, along with a few biscuits and a raspberry tart served on a blue china dish.

"Now, tuck in and rest. We'll have much to plan for on the morrow." Mina kissed her forehead, much like she had done when Letty was a child. She hadn't done that in a very long time. It made Letty want to cry. She'd been a grown woman far earlier than other girls her age, having to care for a mother whose memory had faded until it was no more. And now—now she felt like a very small girl who was facing the world far too soon.

"Good night, Mina," Letty said softly.

Now left alone with her thoughts, Letty replayed the events of the night over and over, trying to puzzle out her reactions, especially to Lord Morrey. When the man held a knife at her throat, and later when she was nearly shot, she ought to have been terrified. And while she had been afraid, the reason she'd trembled as Lord Morrey held her in his arms was because of something else. It was another sort of fear entirely, which made no sense at all.

Letty finished her milk, licked the sugar from her fingers, and set the plate and glass on the nightstand. She got up and cleaned her teeth before climbing back into bed and blowing out the candle. She watched the smoke coil in the moonlight from the windows. The light and smoke seemed to merge, forming a mist that enthralled her. It made her think of Morrey. He was like mist, smoke, and moonlight, a mysterious dream.

Could a woman marry a man like that and be happy?

A FEMININE FIGURE DRESSED IN A DEEP-BLUE SILK gown with a black velvet cape wrapped about her walked down the narrow mews behind Twinings tea shop. She held her breath against the stench that lingered in the still night air around her. The stagnant smells brought back memories of home, far across the English Channel.

She moved quickly through the shadows, careful to keep out of sight. Dangerous men prowled the streets like wild dogs, and while this woman could take care of herself, she was loath to tangle with anyone tonight. Her fingers gripped the hilt of a pistol, ready just in case.

Soon she reached a private room at a certain coaching inn that belonged to the man she'd come to see. She knocked on the door and listened for the command to enter. Only then did she step inside and pull the hood back to show her face.

"My beautiful Camille," a deep voice purred in delight. "How did you fare in your task this evening?"

Her master, the man she knew only as the Lord of Shadows, sat in a chair by the fire.

"Bonsoir, monsieur." She curtsied deeply, her eyes cast to the ground.

"That wasn't an answer."

"The English lady spy is still alive. I could not get her alone to force the message from her lips. But I did find out her name. It is as you suspected, Lady Edwards." Camille waited for her master's wrath. She had failed him as his left hand and would most likely be punished.

"Tell me what happened."

She took a seat by the fire and told of how she'd gained entry to Lady Allerton's ball. She explained locating the woman she'd been sent to torture for the message and then dispose of when no one was around.

"You know how these English ladies are—they are *never* alone. They always travel in flocks like twittering little birds. Lady Edwards left the ballroom with another woman. I followed them, but a man came between me and my target."

"How?"

"I do not know, monsieur. I had memorized all the faces in the ballroom, of course, but I did not recognize him. He seemed to materialize out of the shadows." Camille was proud of her uncanny memory. She could recall any picture or diagram and could even remember every word ever spoken to her. She'd once been a lowly stage actress in Paris, barely surviving on the coins tossed at her feet after each performance.

But *this* man had been sitting in the front row at her last performance. He had not tossed a coin. He had, with quiet intensity, met her gaze as he left a letter, sealed with wax, at her feet. She had retrieved it and opened it later that night. It had given her instructions, told her how to find him, and he had closed it with the following words: *Someone with your talents can be a master of her own fate.*

She had been afraid to go at first, but she had no future, and in the end, natural curiosity and hope had driven her into this man's arms and his bed. But she had not regretted it. The master was a wonderful lover, and he did indeed see her talents for what they were. He gave her power, a future with money and nice clothes, and a life beyond anything she'd ever imagined. All she had to do was obey him whenever he gave her a mission.

"Tell me more of this man." The Lord of Shadows had risen from his chair by the fire and began to pace.

"He was tall, as tall as you, dark-haired, eyes the color of the sky before a winter storm." Camille thought the man beautiful, perhaps even more beautiful than her master, but she would never admit that.

"You like his eyes?" the monsieur inquired curiously.

"Yes. They are intense, a mixture of violence and gentleness. They confuse me, monsieur."

"Did you notice anything else about this man?"

"He wore fine clothes, and yet until he came between me and my target, I had not seen him at all at the ball. Someone of his appearance should have stood out to me."

"What happened when you went after Lady Edwards?" Her master drew her back to her narration of the events.

"He reached the retiring room first. He attacked the woman who had accompanied Lady Edwards. I think perhaps he thought that second woman was me, but then he released her and spoke to them both in hushed tones. The two ladies seemed to be well acquainted. I believe Lady Edwards's companion may also know the message. They were speaking to each other, and they were there when the man joined them, all of them whispering. I believe Lady Edwards shared the message with them. This other lady must be greatly important."

"What makes you say that?" the master inquired.

"When I fired at them, the man sought to protect both ladies, but he covered this other woman more, shielding her completely from me. I wonder if she might be the one with the message and Lady Edwards is but a decoy."

"Interesting. I hadn't considered that. Avery Russell might be clever enough to try that. It's entirely possible. I simply hadn't thought to give Avery enough credit for it. Maybe he is surpassing his own master in talent. Waverly was distracted in his later days by his own personal vendettas. Russell won't have that same problem. In time, he might become even more cunning than Waverly."

Camille listened to her master talk as her thoughts drifted to the League of Rogues, the group Hugo Waverly had had a vendetta against. She had seen them many times in the last few months. They were handsome, reckless, and seductive, each of them—though none of them were spies. It puzzled her and her master that the previous English spymaster had spent so much of his time chasing them from the shadows. Worse threats faced England. Threats like her and her master.

"Did you recognize the woman? The one with Lady Edwards?"

"Yes. She is the sister of Lord Pembroke."

"Oh, yes. I recall the fellow," her master said and stopped pacing. "Let's leave Lady Edwards for now. I can have someone else deal with her. This other woman, Pembroke's sister, warrants closer scrutiny. I need to get her away from her brother and find out what she knows. Then we can arrange an accident."

"Yes, monsieur," Camille agreed. "What must I do?"

"Come closer, my dear, and I will tell you." Her master beckoned her to join him in the shadows.

⁂

IT WAS WELL AFTER MIDNIGHT WHEN ADAM RETURNED to his townhouse on Half Moon Street. But as he expected, Caroline had waited up for him. She rushed down the steps toward him, wearing a robe over her nightgown.

"Oh, Adam, thank God," she said, embracing him.

He held his sister in his arms for a moment before letting go. Like his trusted butler, Caroline knew of his secret work—he couldn't keep that from her.

"What happened?" she asked.

It never ceased to amaze him that she could so easily read him, whereas so few others ever could. Perhaps it was because they had both grown up relying upon each other while looking after their mother when they were so young. Other men might have pushed their sisters off on governesses and eventually husbands, but he couldn't do that to Caroline, not after all she had been through.

"Russell was waylaid, unable to make his rendezvous."

"How is Lady Edwards?"

"Safe. He found her in the gardens after she made her escape. I'll never know how that man always ends up in the right place at the right time." He shrugged out of his cloak and handed it to the butler, Mr. Sturges. The man was a former infantry officer and not much older than Adam. He was as capable as he was trustworthy.

"Avery's like a cat with nine lives," Caroline said. "But never mind about him—tell me what happened."

Adam headed for the drawing room. Caroline followed, after asking Sturges to send in some food and a bit of wine. Collapsing into a chair by the fire, Adam rubbed his face, feeling the weight of all that had happened tonight starting to settle more heavily about him.

"Everything was a bloody mess. I followed Lady Edwards, thinking a French spy had discovered her importance to Avery's ring, but when I grabbed the woman with her, it turned out to be Pembroke's sister."

"Letty was with Lady Edwards?"

"Yes, and that was where everything went wrong. She was merely trying to help the woman fix her hair. I held the poor girl at knifepoint." He still couldn't erase from his mind the look of terror he'd seen in Letty's eyes.

"Oh, Adam, you didn't," Caroline sighed. "She must've been very frightened."

"I'm afraid it gets worse. The real spy was also there and fired upon us, so I tackled both women to the ground. And then I gave chase but couldn't catch the spy. When I returned, Lady Edwards had to escape, and I had to keep my cover."

"Oh, heavens. What did you do?" Caroline asked.

Adam didn't immediately reply, knowing that what he said next would change his life—and in some ways, Caroline's as well.

"Congratulate me, sister. It seems I am to be married in two days." Adam tried to smile, but his sister simply stared at him.

"Married? To whom? Lady Edwards is already married."

He shook his head. "To Letty. I had to kiss her as some men from the ball heard the gunshot and burst into the room."

"*Had* to?"

"To throw off suspicion as to what was truly happening."

Caroline raised an eyebrow.

"But . . . I do admit that perhaps I wasn't thinking as clearly as I should have been when I made my decision."

"Oh, Adam," she sighed. "Are you very unhappy?"

"Unhappy? No, not exactly. *Worried* is what I am." He smiled ruefully. "The fact is, I do like Letty, have since the moment I met her when we were searching for Gillian."

"You like her?" Caroline's eyes brightened with a glimmer of joy.

"I do. She is so sweet, so innocent. Yet she is also intelligent and brave. She is what I would have sought in a bride, had it been safe to marry after I started working for the Home Office. But after . . ."

"After John died, you couldn't put a woman in danger," Caroline finished, stark pain clear in her eyes. "And now in order to protect a woman, you must marry her."

"It's quite the irony, isn't it?" He sighed heavily.

Adam's quest for vengeance was not only due to the loss of his dear friend, but also for his sister, who'd been in love with John. The two had planned to marry, but he'd died two months before the ceremony. The shadow of John's death had turned Caroline into a ghost herself in some ways, and Adam wished he could do something to give his sister her life back. But Caroline's broken heart would either mend on its own or it would not, and Adam was helpless to do anything but watch.

"If you are to marry Letty, then she must be told . . ."

"She knows part of it already. I will pay a call on her tomorrow, and after I speak with James, I will tell her the rest. I will have no secrets from my wife."

Caroline bit her lip. "But what if she isn't strong enough to know about your secret life?"

"I know she is. There were no hysterics after that shot was fired."

"Well, she may have been a bit shocked. Not everyone reacts the same way to such things. I think when you see her tomorrow, you should ask her if she was well the rest of the night."

"I suppose you are right. I've lived the last two years in such relative danger that I forget how it can be for those unused to it." He rubbed his temples and let out a long, weary breath.

"You ought to go to bed," Caroline said. "We have a busy day tomorrow."

"We do." He needed to be up early to obtain a special license, and then he ought to see to the wedding arrangements.

"Should we arrange for it to be at St. George's?" he asked Caroline.

"You could, but might it not be better to take her to Chilgrave?"

"You think I should?" Chilgrave Castle was the ancestral seat of the Morrey family. Adam loved the estate, yet he hardly spent any time there these days. A wedding might be a good reason for him to stay at the castle for a spell. It would be safer for Letty as well.

"The rectory there is very lovely. Quite romantic, I think. If you let me go on ahead tomorrow, I could have it all arranged and the castle ready to host guests."

"Thank you, Caro." Adam meant it. His sister was a true gem. It filled him with a deep sorrow that she had not yet found another man to give her heart to after losing John.

They stood and embraced each other. Adam gave her an extra squeeze as he murmured his thanks again.

"Now, off to bed with you. I'll send some cutlets and wine upstairs," Caroline said.

Adam exited the drawing room and climbed the stairs, his steps now heavy with weariness.

So, they would open Chilgrave Castle for the wedding. It did sound rather lovely. Part of his staff stayed there, and he had enough money to keep them employed, but they had little work to do. Hopefully, it would cheer them to open the house and shake off the dust and let the masterfully gilded rooms gleam again and be filled with the sounds of life. He could perhaps pretend to have a normal life for a while.

Dudley Helms, his valet, was waiting in Adam's bedchamber when Adam entered. Sturges followed behind and set a tray of cutlets on the table before bowing and leaving. Adam began to unbutton his waist-coat, while his valet prepared his nightclothes

"And how was your evening, my lord?" Helms asked as he removed the waistcoat and helped Adam with his sleeves.

"Filled with the unexpected, Helms. You'll be hearing from Sturges tomorrow officially, but I am to be wed in two days."

"Wed? I assume congratulations and not condolences are in order?" Helms teased.

Adam laughed. "Yes, congratulations, certainly."

Helms removed the cuff links and Adam's pocket

watch before placing them in their boxes for safekeeping. "And who is the bride-to-be?"

"Lady Leticia Fordyce."

"Ah, Lord Pembroke's sister. What a wonderful choice," Helms replied with warm honesty. "The staff will be quite happy, my lord, if you don't mind the boldness of my saying that."

"Not at all. You think they will be happy?"

"They will," Helms said with a twinkle in his eye. "Mrs. Hadaway has been wanting babes in the nursery for years."

Mrs. Hadaway, the Chilgrave housekeeper, would indeed be glad. She was a cheery woman and had a genuine smile never far from her face.

Adam bid his valet good night and had a bit of the meat, chasing it down with some wine. Then he forced himself to bed. Tomorrow would be a challenge. His entire life was about to change. Sweet Letty would soon be his wife.

3

Letty was as nervous as a cat during a thunderstorm. Every time a carriage rolled past the townhouse, she flew to the window, expecting to see Lord Morrey heading up the steps toward her door.

"Letty," Gillian laughed. "Do try to sit down."

"But it's nearly ten o'clock," Letty said. "Half the morning is gone, and he did say he would call in the morning, did he not?"

Gillian rolled her eyes. She sat on a settee, reading a book with one hand and holding her baby, Gabriel, in the crook of her other arm. Like his parents, their baby was utterly perfect and completely well behaved. He slept on, unaware of the two women talking.

"He has to procure the special license first. Give the poor man a bit more time."

"Time, yes," Letty murmured, still peeping out the curtains. A coach with the Morrey crest had just stopped in front of the steps.

"He's here!" She sprang toward the door. "I have to go. I should—"

"Letty," Gillian said firmly. "Go out into the gardens for a bit, and remember to breathe. We shall come find you once the men have talked all the business of money and other matters."

"You don't think *I* should be involved in that?" Letty challenged.

"You know I do, but I think you're a bit frantic this morning. Breathing the cool, crisp air of the gardens might calm you."

Gillian was right. Everything about Lord Morrey had Letty feeling edgy and out of sorts. Quite frankly, she didn't know what to do with herself. She collected her shawl and hastened from the drawing room just as the butler answered the door. She had no time to go outside unseen, so she ducked into the nearest doorway to wait.

From her hiding place, she was able to see Lord Morrey step inside and remove his hat and greatcoat. He wore a dark-blue coat and biscuit-colored trousers, which molded to the masculine perfection of his long, lean legs. She had seen many men wear pantaloons that were skintight, but only the best well-built men were able to carry off such a fashion. Morrey looked even better than the statues in a museum, not that she had ever *officially* seen many of the nudes, which were considered highly improper for a young, unmarried lady to look upon.

Her mind quickly strayed to other thoughts: how he'd gripped her so tightly last night, yet without hurting her; how he'd held that blade to her throat with such skill that she'd been unharmed; how he'd continued to grip her even after he'd put the knife down. She remembered his eyes. Those twin silvery pools had locked on her eyes, holding her captive as easily as his hands had. Her body flashed with a sudden heat, and her heart pounded hard at the memory. This dark and dangerous man was to be her husband in but a handful of days.

It made her wonder if Lord Morrey's body would be like the statues she'd seen. The male body was both fascinating and confusing at the same time. But as she watched Morrey linger in the hall, his dark hair falling in his eyes, she wondered, *How would he look without his clothes?*

"Adam, thank you for coming." Gillian joined Morrey in the entryway, carefully embracing him in a hug while still holding Gabriel in one arm. She then showed him into the drawing room. Letty breathed a sigh of relief as she sank deeper into the room she'd escaped into, the library. It was a better distraction than the garden. She collected a few volumes on economics and tucked herself into a nook at the back of the room. Surprisingly, she managed to lose herself in the texts for a little while. But the sound of voices soon drew her attention.

She recognized the voices of James and Morrey as they entered the library. She started to rise, but then halted as she realized she couldn't slip past the two men unseen. She remained hidden, unable to avoid hearing their discussion.

"I thought it would be a bit nicer to discuss things in here. My office is cluttered at the moment. We'll sign the documents in there when we need to. Do you have the special license?" James asked. The sound of the men settling in chairs accompanied this question.

"Yes," Morrey replied.

"Excellent. Now let us talk finances first. Letty has a dowry of five thousand a year."

"If you recall when you married Gillian, I offered you the same for her." Morrey sounded amused. Letty wished she could see his face.

"I remember, and I only grudgingly accepted, which means you will too."

Morrey chuckled. "Well played, Pembroke. I will accept, but those funds will be entirely within Letty's control, for her use and pleasure."

Letty's heart gave a leap at hearing that. She hadn't been sure before what sort of man Morrey was, and if he would allow her any independence, especially financial.

"Very good," James replied. "Now about the wedding . . ."

"I think I'd like it to be in the small church by Chilgrave Castle."

"Not St. George's?" Her brother sounded surprised.

"No. Too open, too dangerous. Chilgrave is off the beaten path. It's safer. Besides, I have a personal connection to the place."

"So now we come to the heart of this matter. What the *devil* happened last night, Morrey? I know you cannot tell me about the mission itself, but you must explain how Letty became entangled in this mess."

There was a heavy silence, then a long, weary sigh.

"I was to protect Lady Edwards last night while she waited to deliver a message. I had been warned that French agents might try to silence her. The message was only in her head, not upon paper. Had she been killed, she would've died with that precious intelligence trapped inside her." Morrey paused, and Letty realized she had stopped breathing as he spoke. "The French are clever. They use female spies to their advantage, far better than we do, at least until Russell took over from Waverly. I saw a woman walking with Lady Edwards away from the crowd and feared the worst. I realized too late it was your sister. As Lady Edwards and I sorted out the mess, the real French agent fired upon us. Lady Edwards was able to escape out the window, where she eventually met her contact, but while she escaped I needed to maintain my cover. I did the only thing I could think of."

"By kissing my sister . . ."

There was an uncomfortable pause. Letty could only imagine the looks being exchanged.

"I admit, my judgment was . . . clouded. But in the moment, it seemed the wisest course."

"Yes. I understand the logic. You countered one outrageous act with another. No one there would have imagined that the two events were connected. I must say, however, that I'm still displeased."

"I quite understand, James. Your sister deserves to be wooed by a gentleman who is mad about her. I could not woo her, but the truth is I am quite mad for her."

Letty covered her mouth to keep the sound of her gasp from escaping. He was *mad* for her? That forbidden flutter of excitement filled her lower belly again.

"Oh? Are you?" James sounded surprised. "I had no idea you had a tendre for Letty."

Morrey gave a soft chuckle, and Letty desperately wished she could see his face again. She clutched a book to her chest as she strained to hear his response.

"From the moment I first saw her, I was captivated, but in my line of work it is unwise to marry. It is simply too dangerous. Either her life is threatened, or she faces a future where her husband does not come home and she may have to live forever with a lie about the circumstances of my death. I couldn't do that to a woman. So I closed off that part of my life and buried any affections I felt for any woman I was interested in."

"Until last night," James asserted.

"Yes. Last night forced my hand, but I won't deny that it does give me joy. But now Letty faces a danger that never should have been placed upon her shoulders."

"What can be done to keep her safe?" James's voice grew slightly louder, and Letty knew he was moving closer to the bookshelf she hid behind.

"She should remain at Chilgrave for the foreseeable future. My staff, both in London and Chilgrave, were hired for their abilities to deal with the risks my employment creates."

"Will you stay with her?" James's tone held a hint of worry and a bit of warning that endeared him to her even more.

"I will be with her as often as I can, but there will be times I must be called away. She will have the utmost protection in those circumstances," Morrey promised.

Her brother let out a sigh. "I cannot help wishing that I could protect her. After losing our mother, we were both adrift. Gillian has helped me navigate the rivers of my grief, but I worry over Letty being alone."

"I understand, Pembroke. Believe me, I do. I'm still very much a stranger to Letty, but I will be present for her and give her anything she needs, within my power."

"Give her love, Morrey. *Give her love.* It is perhaps the most crucial thing of all."

Yes, Lord Morrey, give me love, she thought.

Letty bit her lip as unexpected tears burned her eyes.

Now was not the time to turn into a silly watering pot, but James was right. The death of their mother, the cruel fate of watching her memories fade at so young an age, had been awful. It had left scars upon Letty's heart that would never fully heal.

"Let's draw up the paperwork, and then you may have a moment with Letty."

"Thank you."

She waited a full thirty seconds for them to leave before emerging from her hiding spot. She screeched as a hand suddenly clamped over her mouth and pulled her back.

An instant later, the person holding her cursed. "Not again."

"Lord Morrey?" Letty mumbled through his fingers.

"Lady Leticia," Morrey sighed, then uncovered her mouth and turned her around to face him. "What on earth are you doing hiding in here?"

Letty, stunned by the sudden thrill she felt being manhandled by Lord Morrey, could only blink up at him.

"I . . . ," she stammered as she lost herself in his storm-cloud-gray eyes.

"You mustn't do that around me—*never* spy upon me. I can feel it, like a tingling at the back of my neck. I feared you were someone else."

Finally, Letty found her tongue. "Someone like a French spy?"

Morrey's gaze turned stormier. "Yes, exactly like a

French spy. What did you hear from your little hiding place?"

Letty pursed her lips together, refusing to tell him that she'd heard, among many things, his confession that he was mad for her.

A worry line creased his brow, and then he seemed to relax a bit. "Understand me, Letty—my instincts must never be tested. You understand? I usually act automatically. I could have hurt you."

Morrey still held her waist, their lower bodies pressed together. The contact of his legs against hers through the thin barrier of her skirts left her dizzy and excited.

"Your eyes," he said softly.

"What about them?" Letty dared to ask.

"Your pupils—they're quite large." He cupped her face, his thumb brushing over her lips. "That only happens when one is very frightened or very . . ." He didn't finish.

"Very what?" she pressed, fascinated by the way his own pupils seemed larger as he leaned close to her.

"Very aroused." The sensual and completely scandalous word set fresh fire to her blood.

"You mustn't speak of such things," Letty whispered, but she actually *did* want him to continue saying such wonderfully exciting things.

Morrey continued to study her. "Well, now. You aren't what I expected."

"What did you expect?" she asked, her breath coming a little shallow.

His eyes grew stormy again, but rather than frighten her, it excited her. "I expected you to be unable to understand me. That your fear would be too much to cope with. But a bit of fear arouses you, doesn't it?"

Shame flooded her face with heat. He was right. She had never been in a position before where she'd been truly afraid like she had been last night. It was as though she was waking from a very dull dream, and she was starting to understand who she truly was.

"Lord Morrey . . . ," she began, but she failed to say much more.

His eyes focused on her lips, and his gaze stoked the growing fire within her.

"I must be a gentleman," he said to himself. "At least until we are married." He gave her waist a small squeeze. "And then, if you wish it, I can teach you all the things I know about pleasure, about the wildness of it, the rough excitement, the games of cat and mouse we might play. I can give you what your eyes tell me you need. Do you understand?"

She could only stare at him blankly. His words didn't fully sink in.

"You don't understand, not yet, but I'll teach you, *my wild one*." Morrey leaned down that last breathless inch, his warm breath fanning over her face. She could see each of his long dark lashes, and she desperately wished he would seize her for a kiss.

He cupped the back of her head, his fingers twisting in the strands, and her knees buckled at his easy control of her body. She felt helpless, yet she craved it with a hunger she'd never experienced before. Morrey's heavy-lidded eyes gazed down her body. He made her feel excited and erratic, like a summer storm. How was it possible to want him and yet fear that same wanting?

"Your brother will be waiting for me, wondering where I am, what I'm doing—or more importantly, what I'm *wanting* to do." His lips barely caressed hers as he spoke, not quite a kiss.

Strangely emboldened by all that he'd said, she breathed in the scent of this beautiful man and tilted her head back. "Then let him wonder." She hoped he would give her a kiss that satisfied all the teasing he'd done in the last few moments.

He shook his head, his lips brushing over hers again, enough to taunt her, but not satisfy, then stepped back. A breath of cool air swamped her heated body, and she leaned back against the bookcase to regain some of her balance. Morrey leveled her with a dark, intense look. Then, without another word, he left.

Suddenly, she could breathe again. She leaned heavily against the bookshelf, trying to make sense of all that had happened in the last few minutes. Of three things, she was sure:

Lord Morrey was a dangerous man.

He frightened her.

And she desired him.

ADAM CAREFULLY READ OVER THE MARRIAGE agreement while he tried to ignore James's gaze upon him. He finally lifted his eyes to James and arched a brow. "Done."

"You took your time," James replied. He was doing his best not to look worried.

"I met with Letty in the library after you left. I had a word with her before coming to you." There, he'd let James worry about what *that* meant.

James crossed his arms over his chest. His frown deepened. "Did you?"

Picking up the pen nearest him, Adam scrawled his name in the appropriate spot on the marriage settle-ment, then passed the paper to James, who signed beneath him.

"So, it is done." James blotted the paper, then folded it up. "I will have my solicitor prepare a copy for your records. Then I'll have my banker begin the transfer of funds, to give to Letty at your discretion."

"Thank you. Now, if you have no need of me, I shall leave for Chilgrave so I may have time to prepare for the wedding tomorrow."

"That suits me. I will have Gillian help Letty pack her trousseau. We shall arrive at Chilgrave this evening, if that suits you."

"It does." Adam shook James's hand, then paused in the doorway. "Since I've already had a brief discussion with Lady Leticia, I will not need to speak to her again until this evening."

"All right." James stood and followed him to the door. "Safe travels."

Adam collected his coat and hat before heading to the waiting coach. Once inside, he let out the breath he'd been holding, and he couldn't resist replaying that moment in the library with his future bride.

He had suspected someone was listening to him and James. He wasn't sure who he had expected. He had certainly not expected to tug sweet, innocent Letty into his arms a second time. He also hadn't expected her reaction to the encounter.

Lord, the fire burning in those lovely brown eyes had driven him half-mad with lust. She had no understanding of her reaction—that was painfully clear. But he could teach her. She was a woman who would enjoy excitement in the bedchamber. She would enjoy playing games and would embrace lovemaking.

He realized now that he was a damned lucky man. But he also knew that he would have to be careful with her. A woman as innocent as Letty could easily become frightened and confused by her own passions.

The coach took him to his townhouse first, where he and Caroline discussed his plans at length. After the wedding, Caroline could return to London if she wished; indeed, he nearly insisted on it, because the farther away she was from Letty the safer she would be. This way, he would only have to worry about protecting one woman.

"Adam, you know I can take care of myself, and it is my duty to protect my future sister-in-law. I adore her, and this must be so frightening for her. Having another woman to confide in would help her." Caroline had stiffened her spine and raised her shoulders. Yes, he wouldn't win this argument at all.

"Very well, you may stay and guard my new little wife, Caro."

His sister's usually solemn face turned impish. "I am so excited, Adam. Truly, she is so sweet and clever. Your babies will be beautiful."

Caroline had a fondness for children, and for a moment, Adam was lost in a daydream of what those children would look like, and how completely devoted he would be to them. It was something he had not thought of since John had been murdered.

But perhaps it would be possible. If he could keep Letty safe and protect her, they could have such a future. All that stood in his way was finding and removing the threat against her. He needed to formulate a plan with Avery Russell.

Russell was one of the few spies in England who

knew the larger picture when it came to spycraft. Most had only bits and pieces of information, in order to keep their mission as a whole safe. If he had to guess the nature of the French threat, he would wager that the Bonapartist struggles were at the heart of this.

It was a bloody relief that Napoleon Bonaparte had died, but his supporters still gave the French royals plenty of problems. Normally, England was glad to have France preoccupied with its own problems, but Napoleon's overthrow of the monarchy had ruffled the feathers of every decent Englishman.

Rebellions, uprisings, the killing of kings—England had done it before and had no wish to do it again. A country undergoing rebellion was a country *exposed*, a country that could be easy prey for others. Whether it was France, Spain, or any of the other power-hungry nations of Europe, all would happily prey upon the British Isles if they sensed weakness.

Adam had never been ignorant of politics, but after John's death he'd been thrust into the forefront of a battle that was fought in the shadows. With whispers, coded messages, and stiletto knives flashing in the dark, everything had become so tangible, so very real and threatening that Adam had trouble sleeping most nights.

"Adam, are you happy about this? Truly?" Caroline's question broke through the darkening spiral of his thoughts.

He reached across the drawing room table and touched her hand.

"I believe I will be. There is just so much that weighs upon me. I worry for your safety and Letty's. I cannot help but wonder which path is safer for her: to be my wife or to send her away somewhere the French cannot find her."

"There is likely no place to send her where French spies could not find her, Adam."

"I'm not so sure about that. There are some rather wild and unexplored places in the far north of Scotland where she would be safe."

Caroline shook her head. "Oh, you cannot mean to take her to see Uncle Tyburn?"

Their uncle, a robust old man, was a Highlander through and through. Although he had been born long after the dreadful events at Culloden, he still held true to the old ways, as dangerous and illegal as that could be.

"Tyburn would be safe. He has an old castle surrounded by flat land that has been cleared of forests. He can see a person coming for miles, as long as it's daylight or the moonlight is bright enough."

"Why don't we put Tyburn as a very last option. Letty is *very* English, and I'm not sure if dragging her through the pitted roads of Scotland to spend time in the fierce, frosty Highlands would be ideal for your honeymoon."

"You have a point," Adam conceded, then rose from

the table. "I must be off for Chilgrave. Do you wish to come early with me or travel with Letty?"

Caroline seemed to debate this a moment. "I believe I shall come with you. There's much to do to make it a welcoming place for a bride and for a wedding reception to be achieved tomorrow. As much as I adore you, Adam, you are still a man and quite incapable of planning a proper wedding."

Adam laughed. "Very well, I concede on that as well." He went to seek out his valet, and then it was time to leave. He could not shake the feeling that danger would still come, even to the sanctity of Chilgrave Castle, but he hoped that whatever evil followed he would have the strength to stop.

4

etty and Gillian arrived on Bond Street just as the shops opened. They needed to get what Gillian deemed the necessities for her meager trousseau, and after a spot of lunch that wasn't nearly long enough, they were whisked back home to finalize their packing.

Before Letty could catch her breath, Mina was helping her into her carriage dress, and she was boarding the coach for a two-hour ride to Chilgrave Castle—a place she'd never been before but, by the next night, would be the mistress of.

Was it all real? Was she to see her future home tonight, or was this some fantastical dream? There had been no amorous glances across a roomful of chaperones or flowers delivered to her door; all the things she knew and had come to expect of such moments were absent.

She'd longed for a proper courtship. Romantic interludes of the sort her mother had told Letty about when she was just a young child. Most young ladies began their courtship dance at balls or card parties in the assembly rooms. She had begun hers at knifepoint.

Letty's parents' marriage had been a love match, which was not as rare a thing as some made it out, but for her parents it had been unexpected. Because theirs had been a love match, they'd spent their entire marriage sharing a suite of rooms and the same bed. They shared their lives with each other, and rarely had they ever spent time apart. Letty had learned later on as she grew up how rare that was, even for couples who married for love.

As the buildings of London gave way to green fields and trees and idyllic villages, Letty found herself ever more silent as Gillian and James spoke with her. She answered in monosyllables as her mind churned with thoughts of her uncertain future as the Countess of Morrey.

As they reached Chilgrave Castle, she saw it at first from a distance, a square fortress with circular towers at each of the four corners. The design was simple, but the strategy behind it was clever. A wide moat separated the castle from the land surrounding it. A long stone bridge stretched across the water to the castle, which loomed eerily in the fading sunlight. It reminded her of the sort of castle a child might try to build in the sand on

Brighton Beach, but this castle could not be washed away by any wave. If any part of the structure were to crumble in some distant future, it would only be because of the long march of time.

"What do you think, Letty?" Gillian asked. "I've been here a few times. It seems quite austere outside, but inside, it is a proper home."

Letty kept her gaze upon the structure. "It is certainly daunting." The coach drove over the narrow bridge to pass into the courtyard. Castles like this had been built during the time of Edward III, the royal age of castles. But that era of time, like many others, had faded.

"You'll find it's quite nice," Gillian said again. "Most medieval castles were built strictly for military fortification. When the ancient Morreys had this castle built, however, they sought to reconcile the military purpose with the prospect of a lord and lady living comfortably within. The courtyard is not made of stone, but rather full of lush gardens and a fountain. I hope you'll find it as beautiful as I do."

Letty was used to a sprawling estate that ambled over rolling hills, a place where she felt able to run free. Despite Gillian's assurances, Chilgrave felt closed off, a stone cage. She shivered at the thought.

The coach rolled to a stop, and a fleet of footmen met them as the three of them exited the coach. Their valises and trunks were removed and carried inside after them. Letty watched as her two dark-blue painted trunks were hoisted up between a pair of servants and hauled out of sight.

My entire life, packed away into two trunks. My silk gowns carefully folded, my jewels blanketed in velvet pouches. My favorite books wrapped in cloth and stacked neatly to one side. Will my small life have a place here in this vast gray structure?

"Welcome!" Caroline Beaumont came down a narrow stairwell to greet them. "I trust the ride wasn't too unpleasant?" Caroline rushed to her half sister first. "Gillian!" And the two embraced each other.

Gillian smiled. "Caro, it's so lovely to see you!"

"How's my little nephew?"

"Fine, fine. Gabriel is with his nurse while we stay for the wedding. You must come back to London and see him soon."

"I shall. He's such a little dear. So beautiful." Caroline sighed dreamily. Then she turned to Letty, her joy still evident. "Oh, Letty, I'm so happy to see you again!" She hugged Letty with the same enthusiasm.

"You look quite worn out. I imagine today was hectic. Why don't you come in and freshen up for dinner. Then you can go straight to bed and rest."

"Thank you, Caroline, we would like that. Letty and Gillian have barely had time to eat all day." James chuckled. "All that shopping and making preparations."

"I can imagine." Caroline squeezed Letty's hands and gestured toward the stairs. "Follow me."

Caroline tucked her arm in Letty's, the warmth of the gesture waking Letty from her maudlin thoughts.

"We have a lovely room all prepared for you," Caroline said.

Letty walked through the gatehouse that formed the front door for the main part of the castle and up the winding staircase Caroline had come down. Rich tapestries hung from stone walls, making the medieval castle feel warmer and more welcoming.

"Where is Lord Morrey?" she asked Caroline.

"Adam will be here shortly. He was in his bedchamber, seeing to a few things. He and the housekeeper got a bit dusty when they were up in the attics earlier this afternoon."

Letty wrinkled her nose in confusion. "The attics?"

"Yes. I believe he was looking for the Morrey coronet. It was our great-grandmother's. We put it away when she died. It's perfectly splendid, and you may wish to wear it for tomorrow's ceremony."

Letty liked to think that she was above being excited over jewels, but the thought of a coronet did give her a girlish flash of excitement that made her feel extremely foolish. She had graver concerns than pretty diamond coronets. Like the fact that a French spy was likely looking for her.

They entered a wide hall. The stone walls had been covered with wood and papered over with an expensive and lovely emerald wallpaper. Crown moldings painted with gold decorated the ceiling, bordered by Grecian scenes that would have rivaled any Wedgewood china. Between portraits of past Morrey ladies dressed in flowing gowns and dashing men in their bright, brilliant doublets, there were tall mirrors lined with vines covered in gold plating. It was not at all like the outside of the castle. The interior had a gilded, glorious atmosphere, each room exuding a warm decadence. Gillian was right—it was rather lovely.

"James, Gillian, you have the bedchamber here." Caroline opened a door and showed them into a beautiful bedroom with a dark-red coverlet and red brocade hangings. "I'll have a footman meet you here in half an hour to escort you to dinner."

"Thank you," Gillian said.

"Letty, your room is at the end of the corridor. It's in the west tower. It has a lovely view. One of the best rooms, in fact."

The room Letty was to sleep in had painted walls the color of a winter sky. Opposite the bed in the circular room was a bookcase built into the wood-paneled walls. The natural white posts of the bed gleamed in the firelight. It was large for a tower room. The four-poster bed was made from white birch tree wood, roughly hewn. The black knots in the wood were like a dozen eyes staring at her from the pale faces of the posts, but even that was strangely beautiful. The coverlet on the bed and the bed hangings were a shimmering frosty-green color.

"Well? What do you think? Adam thought you might like this room. It will be your own personal room, even after you're married."

At this, Letty faced Caroline. "I'm not to share my husband's room?"

A deep voice came from the doorway. "You certainly may . . ."

Letty and Caroline turned to see Lord Morrey, standing tall and handsome in buff trousers and a burgundy waistcoat. The firelight played with him the way a lover might, caressing his features and illuminating his silver-and-gray eyes.

"Oh, Adam, why don't you say hello to Letty? I need to run down to the kitchens." Caroline flashed Letty a knowing smile before hastily leaving the bedroom.

For a second, Letty wavered as she faced the man who had, less than twenty-four hours ago, held a knife to her throat, kissed her, and become engaged to her. The whirl-wind that was Adam Beaumont was making her dizzy. She straightened her shoulders, rallied her remaining strength after the trying day she'd had, and met his gaze.

"Good evening, Lord Morrey," Letty breathed. She still felt nervous around him, especially thinking of that moment in the library and how fear and excitement had mingled together in his presence.

"Adam, please. I cannot have you calling me 'Lord Morrey,' even though tomorrow I will become your lord and master." There was a sensual teasing to his words that dashed the rebellious retort that flew to her lips.

"Adam," she said softly, and Adam came deeper into the room.

"Yes?" He reached her, their bodies only a few feet apart now.

"I do like this room. However, my understanding of marital relationships was that we would share a room. My parents shared a bedchamber, as do James and Gillian, and that was my expectation. I acknowledge I do not have a large amount of experience to draw on, and we will be married to each other rather quickly. What do you think our arrangement ought to be?"

"What do *you* wish our arrangement to be?" he countered with a hint of playfulness.

Letty bit her bottom lip. "I want to . . ." She fisted her hands in her skirts as she studied him, and he leaned casually against the doorjamb, blocking her escape. Not that she was sure she wanted to escape.

"Say it. Say what you *desire*. You need never fear telling me what you need. Do you understand?" The playfulness in his tone was gone, and that brooding intensity of his that left her breathless had returned. His stare ensnared her, rooting her in place.

She sensed he was telling her something deeper, something more profoundly intimate, but she didn't yet quite understand.

"I would like to share a bedchamber with my husband—with *you*."

"I sense some hesitation," Adam said as he continued to stare into her eyes. He reminded her of a cat her mother once had, a Russian blue beauty with green eyes that could peer into one's soul. The cat would stare at her, unblinking, and she had been convinced the feline could read her every thought. Adam shared that same trait.

"Are you surprised? You frighten me a little. The way you held that knife, the way you look at me . . . You must know I've never been with a man in any intimate way. I have no experience with this. That is why I hesitate." She lowered her voice when she spoke of intimacy, not that anyone could hear her. They were quite alone for the moment.

Adam's gray eyes studied her, unlocking something inside her, something that made her feel weak at the knees, yet she held her ground, even as his gaze seemed to burn her skin as it roved over her body. He reached up to catch a loose curl that fell against her throat. The whisper of his fingers against her skin sent her head spinning, her blood humming.

"I will endeavor to make us friends as well as lovers." He leaned in just enough that she inhaled the scent of him, and her body hummed with a feminine awareness.

Friends and lovers, not merely husband and wife. A

marriage, she knew, could have a profound meaning and connection between two people, or it could be a piece of paper and some muttered words that bound two unhappy souls together until one of them died.

"Are you afraid of me?" Adam asked as he lifted her face to his.

"No . . . Not exactly," she said, surprised at the ease with which she could answer him when he spoke in that commanding voice. It was true. She didn't fear him. She was nervous and more than a little anxious, but not afraid. She was worried about what being a wife to him would entail, especially in the bedroom. She had experienced a great range of emotions in the last day, and she'd accepted that the life she'd wanted, the life she'd planned for, was not going to happen. She had longed for marriage, but under such different circumstances.

Yet when she was alone with him, as she was now, he seemed to cloud her thoughts until all she could think was that she wanted him to keep touching her, how the danger and excitement of that touch sent wild thrills through her.

"*My wild one*," Adam sighed as he cupped her cheek. "You deserve bouquets, boxes of sweets, presents as well as passion. I've given you none of these, but someday I will remedy that. You can have it all, the gentleman and the rogue at your beck and call." He stroked his thumb over her bottom lip. She exhaled as she lost herself in gazing at this gorgeous man.

"The gentleman *and* the rogue?" she asked.

He smiled a wolfish smile. "A man who can give you sweetness when you want it." He threaded his fingers into the hair at the nape of her neck, tugging just enough that she felt completely in his power. "And a rogue's brazen roughness when you need it."

Something sharpened inside her, like a sense she hadn't known she'd possessed. It heightened everything about that moment until she felt something pulse hard between her thighs.

Adam was not a brute, but she could tell that every inch of him was full of power, radiating a raw, primal strength. His face, while almost predatory in his handsomeness, was not without gentleness. Gazing upon her wild lion she knew she could trust him to protect her rather than devour her. He continued to hold her gaze, neither of them speaking. Her thoughts spiraled with dark, carnal images, and she wondered if he was thinking the same, given the way he looked at her with such heat. Then he blinked, breaking the spell, and she drew in a shaky breath.

"We should go to dinner," he said. "Unless you still need a moment?"

"I . . ." She pulled her thoughts away from him and nodded. "I'm ready to go down."

He stepped back and offered her his arm. Letty walked with him into the corridor, running her fingertips over the wood panels on the walls.

Adam took her down a different set of stairs, this one made of wood, not stone. Crouching lions sat on the banister, silently roaring at passersby. They were fine heraldic beasts, their front paws clutching shields that bore a unicorn and a Scottish thistle. Evidence of the ancient line of Morreys was everywhere.

The dining room was far more intimate in size than Letty had expected. No grand medieval roughhewn table with a pack of wolfhounds lying by a roaring fire, waiting for meat off a trencher. No, this room was small but elegant.

"It isn't what you expected, is it?" Adam teased.

"No—I mean, yes. I mean . . ." She ducked her head, too embarrassed to say what she had actually expected. She was still thinking of that moment when he'd grasped her hair and held her captive, and she thought of his promise—to give her the gentleman *and* the rogue, whenever she wished. Letty swallowed hard and did her best to focus on their conversation.

"Most of the older furniture has long since been removed and replaced with modern styles. We do our best, even out here in the country, to keep the castle updated." His tone was still light, but she heard the pride in his words.

He had every right to be proud. The marble fireplace was vast and exquisitely carved, the table was made of a beautiful mahogany, and the walls were cream accented by gold wainscoting. Mahogany doors leading in and out of the room on both sides were a clear contrast to the pale cream walls. Green velvet backed the chairs surrounding the table, offered a comfortable place of repose, rather than the harsh high-back chairs with no cushions that she was accustomed to in typical dining rooms in London.

Gillian, James, and Caroline had already gathered around the fire and were in quiet conversation.

"Ah, there you are," Caroline said as they entered. "We wondered if you had gotten lost."

Letty smiled at Caroline, glad to see Adam's sister truly was happy that she was here.

"Well, shall we eat before our cook becomes overanxious?" Caroline asked.

Adam chuckled as he seated Letty beside him. "Mrs. Oxley is most particular about her food not going cold."

"Is she a very good cook?" Letty knew that some old country households with families who didn't visit that often and did very little entertaining, had cooks who were perfunctory at best, as they often had other duties in addition to cooking fine meals.

"Quite good, actually, but she threatens to quit every Christmas, so be ready for that."

"She threatens to quit?"

"Yes, she thinks she will retire and go live with her son in London, but then she changes her mind in a matter of days, usually on Christmas Eve, and returns to the kitchens, bellowing out orders. It is rather amusing, once you become acquainted with her. She might seem prickly at first, but you never will find a better cook. I don't care what our friends in London say about their fancy cooks from France. Mrs. Oxley has them all beat."

Adam flashed her a smile, and Letty's stomach flipped in excitement.

"So, shall we talk wedding plans?" Gillian asked the table at large.

"Oh, yes," Caroline said. The two women began to discuss Letty's wedding as though she wasn't even in the room.

She listened to Caroline and Gillian plan her life. She could have interrupted them, demanded things to be done as she wished, but she was tired. The last few days had robbed her of her strength. Right now, she did not feel she could be even remotely active in the planning of her wedding.

"Letty, what do you think?" Adam asked, drawing her out of the thoughts circling in her head. She tried to focus on the soup in front of her, which had gone a bit cold.

"Whatever they decide is fine with me."

"It is *your* day," Adam reminded her. "You should make the most of it."

He met her gaze and held it. She wished she knew what he was thinking behind those fathomless, mercurial eyes. Most of the young men of her acquaintance were so easy to read, easy to understand. They discussed their lands, their horses, their favorite sports or gambling, and occasionally—when they thought she couldn't hear, of course—their mistresses.

But Morrey—Adam—was nothing like those men. Whatever thoughts ran in his mind would be serious, dangerous, and most likely *fascinating*. He had been right about her—she was drawn to him and excited by the sensual promises he made. The man was clearly knowledgeable about all manner of sins of the flesh, and she was going to be married to this prowling wolf who could likely devour any maiden he liked at his leisure. The thought didn't frighten her, however. Quite the opposite, in fact, if *she* was the maiden to be devoured.

"Letty, I *know* you've thought about this." James faced Morrey with a soft, brotherly smile. "She's been planning this since she was a child. She used to marry off her dolls."

"James!" Letty hissed in mortification, her smile wilting and her blood boiling.

"Well, it's true—" James began, but he suddenly winced and glanced under the table. Gillian glared at him, and Letty suspected his wife had kicked him in the shin, though not hard enough, in her opinion.

Morrey caught Letty's gaze again. As he lifted his goblet of wine to his lips, he smiled at her, but this smile was not a sweet expression. It was enticing, seductive, intimate, as though they were together in some private secret.

"James and Adam are right," Gillian said. "Letty, you must tell us what you wish. Let us start with flowers. Chilgrave has a lovely hothouse."

"Oh, well, I do like orchids," she admitted, knowing that orchids were rare and also quite scandalous, given the way they resembled certain parts of a woman's body, but she couldn't deny that she liked them.

"Orchids . . . Well, that is a bit unorthodox," Caroline said. "But we are having a small country wedding, so perhaps it's all right to do as we wish."

"If my bride desires orchids, then my bride will have them," Morrey said, and she didn't miss the possessive tone to the way he said "*my bride*."

This truly was nothing like she'd imagined her wedding would be. As a girl, she'd envisioned a large crowd, hundreds of flowers by the altar, and a handsome young man with laughing eyes and a warm smile waiting for her to come to him. She had not imagined a dark-haired, serious, enigmatic man whose kisses could erase all rational thought.

"Orchids it shall be," Caroline said. "I assume you brought your trousseau?"

"Yes," Letty said. Her London modiste, Madame Ella, had worked a veritable miracle in just one day.

Letty relaxed a little more now that she felt she was to be included in the wedding planning. Yet she couldn't get her mind off Morrey, or his seductive gaze. He watched her for the entire meal, and when it was over, he was there to escort her to her bedchamber. They soon stood alone in the corridor together, just outside her bedroom.

"Thank you, Lord Morrey."

"You really must start calling me Adam. More importantly, you must learn to stand up for yourself." He tilted her chin up to face him. "I know there is fire in you. I see it in those lovely, innocent eyes. You must let that fire burn. Do not let it go out. I have no desire for a meek, submissive wife. I want the woman I met at the Allerton ball. You faced danger without fear that night." When she opened her mouth to protest, he continued. "You were my equal. Never cease to be that version of yourself."

She looked to him, mystified. He wanted her to be . . . what? She wasn't quite sure. She bit her lip and would've looked away if not for the spell of his gaze.

"Lord Mor—Adam, I'm afraid I don't understand."

"You will." He traced the seam of her lips with his thumb and leaned in to whisper, "I shall dream of kissing you tonight."

He stepped back and seemed to vanish in the shadowy corridor.

She would dream of him kissing her too, and it left her only that much more confused.

5

A
dam was up before dawn, pacing in his chamber long before his valet arrived to help him dress. He did his best to rein in his thoughts, wondering how he should proceed, not only with a new wife but also with a virgin. The carnal track of his thoughts quickly strayed to those of her general safety and whether the measures he'd taken would be sufficient. He knew how easily a man's throat could be slit in the dark, or how a shadow could slip past and into a place it didn't belong if one was not careful.

A knock on his door halted his pacing. "Come in, Helms."

His valet entered. The two of them shared a bit of small talk, with Helms teasing him about the wedding. The man was a godsend, humorous and lighthearted whenever Adam became too serious. He always seemed to know when Adam's mood needed a bit of lightening up.

Helms ran a brush over Adam's shoulders, removing imaginary specks of dust. "There, my lord. You cut a fine figure today."

"I shan't shame the House of Morrey today, I suppose," he mused, and Helms grinned.

"Certainly not. If you wished to compare who looks finest, I wager you could go a round or two against your ancestors in the portrait gallery and certainly win."

Adam chuckled. The portraits in the gallery had always been a source of jesting between them. Helms was quite insistent on keeping Adam dressed fashionably, while Adam sought to dress conservatively so as not to attract attention. More than once Helms had reminded him that his forefathers had embraced the bolder modes of fashion.

Once appropriately attired in his wedding clothes, he retrieved the black box he had removed from a trunk in the attic. Inside was a lovely coronet studded with sapphires and diamonds. He opened the box to look at the glorious item again.

The last woman to wear this had been his great-grandmother. His grandmother and mother had dared not wear it. An old family legend said that any woman who wore the coronet must be brave—brave enough to die for love.

Shortly after they had been married and she had first

put it on, his great-grandmother had saved his great-grandfather from a deadly stable fire. As a result, Adam's mother and grandmother had been far too superstitious to wear the coronet, not wishing to tempt fate. So the coronet had sat in a trunk gathering dust—until now. But, knowing that Letty had faced death once with him already, Adam felt she could wear it without fear. He wouldn't allow anything to happen to her.

Box firmly in hand, he stepped into the hall and entrusted it to a maid to deliver to his future bride.

James stepped into the corridor just as the maid passed by. He came over to clap Adam on the back. "Ah, there you are. Feeling squeamish?" he joked.

"Not exactly. Just worried."

James frowned slightly. "Not about my sister, I hope?" He fell into step beside Adam as they walked down the corridor toward the stairs.

"No, toward her, I have no doubts, other than concerns about her safety. Spies have a way of turning up around every corner, and the last thing I want is someone shooting my wife on the steps of the church."

James clasped his hands behind his back as they continued on their way. They soon reached the gatehouse door and waited for the grooms to bring their horses so they could ride to the chapel.

"Get her into the coach quickly. I suppose that's about the only thing we can do. I understand your worries, but if you wrap her up in blankets and never let her do anything, she'll lose her joy for life and so will you. You'll need to find a balance between protection and freedom."

"Easier said than done."

He and James rode to the small chapel abutting his estate to see to the last-minute details of the ceremony. A dozen footmen had already arrived and were arranging vases of orchids around the alter. Bouquets of flowers adorned each pew. His staff had done commendable work in such a short amount of time.

It struck Adam that he was about to get married. In the last few days, he hadn't let the gravity of the situation truly settle upon him. He'd been treating this more as a mission, a problem that needed to be solved, and not yet thinking of how much his life was truly going to change.

This was no temporary arrangement. This would be permanent. He could say he was marrying for his country, and he had even considered ways to escape once the danger had passed, for Letty's sake.

A vicar could be bought off, a signature signed incorrectly, and an annulment achieved a few months later, so long as the marriage had not been consummated. He would bear the brunt of any scandal, and Letty would be free to continue her life as before.

But the truth was he wanted Letty, and his loyalty to his country had merely given him an excuse to at last claim that which he desired. He only hoped she felt the same way about him. Everything about their private moments together seemed to indicate it.

The vicar met them just inside the entryway. "Welcome, my lord."

Adam shook the older man's hand. "Everything looks well."

The vicar's spectacled eyes twinkled. "Your servants have been quite dedicated to the decoration of God's house. I believe it will please your bride."

The exotic floral scent of the orchids filled the room. It made him think of Letty. "I certainly hope it will."

"She will love it," James promised. "She adores flowers—but not in the way most women do, mind you. She genuinely enjoys the cultivation of them. She was always in our hothouse, meeting with our gardener to discuss herbology and flowers."

"That is good to know. I too enjoy growing things. I will be sure to take her to the hothouse." Adam would take pleasure in showing her all the plants and rare flowers he cultivated. "James . . . would you stand with me as my groomsman? I had not even thought to select one yet."

James chuckled. "I'd be honored. I'm not a bachelor, though. Isn't that one of the traditional requirements?"

"I suppose it is, but I don't particularly have the urge to chase down a bachelor at the moment. I don't suppose the vicar will mind."

Adam and James helped set up the last few vases of orchids before they heard the guests starting to arrive.

"Are you ready?" James teased, despite the serious nature of the question.

"I suppose so. It's all rather strange, to think that shortly I'm to be leg-shackled. I'm not complaining, mind you. I merely hadn't thought I would ever do it." He had given up on that future two years ago when he'd committed himself to this dangerous path. But now here he was at the altar, ready to swear his heart, body, and soul to a young woman he barely knew in order to protect her.

I must have faith that this is the right choice.

⚜

LETTY STOOD STILL, HER HEART BEATING FAST AS Caroline retrieved the Morrey coronet from its box. She bowed her head a little to allow them to nestle the glittering diadem into her artfully styled hair. Gillian, who stood next to Caroline, gave a little gasp.

"What? What's the matter?" Letty asked in sudden panic.

"Nothing. You look absolutely *beautiful*, Letty. Come see." Gillian pointed to the tall mirror that stood in the corner of the room.

Caroline beamed at her. "She's right. Go look."

Letty stepped up to the mirror and saw a stranger. This woman wore a high-waisted pale-blue gown with a delicately beaded bodice and a long flowing skirt draped over with a sheer silver netting, studded with hundreds of tiny pearls. Two white gloves stretched up to the stranger's elbows, and a shimmering coronet sparkled atop her head. She looked royal, like a princess of some fairy court.

She did not look like herself.

Gillian placed her hands on Letty's shoulders. "Are you all right?"

"I feel so strange. Not at all myself."

"That's to be expected," Gillian said. "Marriage is a union of two souls and two bodies. It's natural to feel displaced. But you will find yourself again. Hold fast to who you are, and you won't be lost."

"Were you lost?" she asked Gillian.

Gillian's gaze was soft and thoughtful as she gave Letty another gentle squeeze of the shoulders. "Not as such, but the feeling of almost losing myself was there. If your brother hadn't been so steadfast in his love for me and not wanting to change me, I easily could have been drowned by my own doubts and become something I wasn't."

"We mustn't delay too long," Caroline cut in gently. "The guests will have arrived, and the vicar will be waiting."

"But . . ." Letty blushed. "I didn't even have a chance

to speak with my mother before she passed. I don't know what to . . . what to *expect* tonight."

Caroline and Gillian exchanged looks. "We should wait until after the wedding breakfast to speak of this," Gillian said. "You have enough to worry about right now with the ceremony."

"I have a reason to worry? No, *please*. You must tell me now. I cannot wait that long." She needed to have some idea of what to expect tonight with Lord Morrey. His brief yet incredible kisses had left her overanxious.

"We'll tell you in the coach," Caroline said decisively as she ushered Letty from the room.

The morning was crisp, and Letty was thankful to see an enclosed coach waiting for them when they reached the door. Before she had a chance to savor her last moments at Chilgrave as an unwed woman, she was bundled into the coach and driven to the chapel.

Her companions attempted to avoid her gaze as they spoke about the flowers they'd sent over to the chapel with the footmen early that morning. Letty was not to be deterred, however, and was grateful for the privacy of the coach so she could speak freely to the two other women without worrying that anyone might overhear.

"Now, tell me."

Caroline's face reddened. "You start, Gilly. I shouldn't know about any of this."

"It's all right." Gillian covered her half sister's hand with her own, giving it a comforting squeeze. Letty realized that something must have happened to Caroline, yet she had never breathed a word of what it might be. Gillian seemed to know the secret, but they were siblings, after all. It was only natural that they share such things. By comparison, Letty was practically a stranger to Caroline.

"Right, well, you know that a man's member is . . . well . . ." Gillian's face was red now too.

"I've seen statues," Letty assured her.

"Yes, well, a man's member is not that small when he is interested in a woman. During lovemaking, it increases in size and becomes hard like the shaft of an arrow. Only . . . well, much *wider*, of course."

Letty drew in a breath at the thought. That was a bit frightening.

"And then, you see, after some preparation, a woman is able to take that shaft into her body. Some men thrust only once or twice, but it usually takes more for them to achieve satisfaction."

Letty paled. That sounded positively dreadful.

"What she means," Caroline injected, "is that there is a rhythm a man and a woman can find together if they try. It might hurt a little at first. Some women experience very little pain, but others . . . It can be a bit more, but it does fade. Ask for him to hold still, until the burning between your thighs disappears. But with a bit of practice, our bodies can stretch to accommodate them inside us. You might be sore after the first time, but that is quite normal. If you feel yourself becoming anxious, just kiss him. That's quite important. You need to focus on how it feels to be *with* him, to kiss and caress him. That's the only way you can calm yourself that first time and ensure your pleasure."

Putting aside worries about pain, she focused instead on what she thought was more important. "What is the pleasure like?" She had heard something about what the exquisite power of that final passionate moment between a man and a woman could be like. But she did not see how a body could feel the depth of what she'd heard described in those giggled whispers.

"Your body feels out of control, and the sensations . . . It's hard to explain, but don't be frightened by it," Caroline said. "I thought I might die the first time I felt it."

"But don't be fooled by that," Gillian added. "Embrace it, even if it scares you."

Letty remembered all too vividly how Lord Morrey had spoken of their coming union and the way that she'd responded to him, how her slight fear of him had played some role in her arousal. No doubt he knew exactly what to do with her tonight. That thought reassured her. It also worried her.

"If you are frightened, you can always have a bit of warm brandy right before," Caroline suggested. "It soothes one's nerves."

Letty took all of this in, more mystified than before

as to what to expect. Yet she knew one thing with certainty—she would be having that glass of brandy tonight.

When the coach stopped before the small church, a footman helped Gillian and Caroline out first, then assisted Letty. The two other women would share the role of bridesmaids today. One handed her a small bouquet of lilies and white roses, while the other smoothed out Letty's veil. Her veil had been attached to the tips of the coronet and trailed down behind her. The lace was sheer, almost as finely spun as a spider's web.

"There," Caroline said. "You're ready." The two women then walked ahead of Letty into the church to take their seats.

She stood alone at the end of the aisle, staring straight toward the altar where Lord Morrey and her brother stood. She thought for an instant of the embarrassing secret James had shared the other day, of how she used to marry her dolls off as a girl. But to her it had never been about a woman becoming a man's possession or tying her identity to a man. It was about finding a companion, a partner she could share her secret dreams and innermost thoughts with. The person she would have children with, and they would raise them together. A person who would belong to her as much as she would to him.

And now the time had come for her to live out the first part of her dream. Marriage began upon the wedding day; this was the beginning. Now she was to be married to a man who'd promised to be what she'd always hoped for in a husband, a man who saw the *real* her.

I know there is fire in you.

Letty inhaled slowly, watching Lord Morrey just as he watched her. He cut a rakishly handsome figure in his dark-blue coat and gold waistcoat with white breeches. The lilies and wild orchids around him reminded her of how he'd insisted she would have what she wished for their wedding. It said much about the kind of man he was.

This man would be her husband if she was brave enough to take a leap of faith, and that leap began with the smallest of steps down the aisle.

Just one step.

The step she took was almost a half step, uncertain and hesitant, but the next was stronger. By the time she reached the altar and lifted her face to gaze upon Adam, she was confident of her decision.

His gaze searched hers, as though he sensed the battle she had fought at the entrance of the church. She smiled at him shyly, and the solemn, serious Lord Morrey suddenly winked at her.

The vicar cleared his throat and began the service. Letty was more aware than ever of Lord Morrey's hand touching hers as they spoke their vows and when he slipped the ring on her finger, which matched the coronet resting upon her head. That awkward feeling of having all the eyes of their guests upon her faded a bit as she focused on the singular sensation of Morrey touching her. Not for a moment did she feel his attention lay anywhere but on her, providing a lovely sort of romantic magic she hadn't expected, at least not so soon. It made the weight of her vows that much stronger and that much more meaningful.

"Let no man put asunder what God hath joined together," the vicar continued on.

Letty thought of this enigma of a man who would soon share with her the mysteries of the bedchamber. A spy, a dangerous man, a man who seemed to understand more about her than she understood about herself. And now he was her husband.

The ceremony ended, and Morrey tucked her arm into his. The possessive husbandly gesture was strangely comforting. At first, she kept her distance, only their arms touching as she came to terms with being married so suddenly. But as the crush of their friends came toward them, she leaned closer to Morrey, relying on his strength as they faced everyone gathered at the front of the church to speak with them.

"Congratulations!" Audrey St. Laurent kissed her cheek and whispered more softly, "Remember, *you* are in control. Do not let your husband think he is in charge." She winked at Letty, who could only stare at her.

Be in charge of Lord Morrey? It simply wasn't possible. That man was out of her league when it came to control.

They made their way through the small crowd and over to the Morrey coach that waited outside. Morrey opened the door and grasped her waist, lifting her up. The crowd behind them cheered, and a few of the League of Rogues tossed out suggestive comments about where Morrey should have put his hands, which earned a sharp bark of "Silence!" from James, which only resulted in more hoots and good-humored laughter.

Once inside the coach, they sat opposite each other, both stunned that they had indeed gone through with the whirlwind marriage. Letty could still feel the heat and gentle pressure of his hands on her waist, even though he no longer touched her. Morrey held out a hand to her as the enclosed coach rolled into motion. Letty gazed at the offered hand, that shyness returning. Then with a steadying breath, she accepted his hand, uncertain what it was he desired.

"Come sit by me." He pulled her gently, and she acquiesced. She pressed against his side as he put an arm around her shoulder, feeling so warm. Her gloved hands turned over fretfully in her cloak before she hesitantly reached for his other hand, which rested on his thigh. He turned his palm up, and his fingers closed around hers, warm, gentle, firm. Her trembling breaths calmed as she felt blanketed by the safety of this man beside her.

They were silent for most of the drive back to Chilgrave. She wished she had the ability to know what he was thinking. The longer she looked at him, the more he seemed to become aware of her focus.

"Are you all right?" he asked.

She nodded, still staring at him.

"What is it?"

"I . . . it's very silly," she said, and turned her face away. But he caught her chin and turned her back toward him.

"Tell me." His voice was commanding, but gentle rather than stern.

"It's . . . well . . . I wish to know what you are think-ing." She waited for him to laugh at her for such a silly thought.

"You wish to know my thoughts?"

She nodded.

He looked confused for a moment, and then his expression turned to one of amusement. "At the moment they are quite a lot. I'm worried Mrs. Oxley hasn't had time to prepare the wedding breakfast. I'm thinking of how I must meet with my estate steward this afternoon, and I'm worried about Lady Edwards, as well as the other men and women who work alongside me in London. And last, but certainly not least, I am thinking of you." He brushed his gloved fingertips over her cheek.

"Me?" Letty was even more curious and a fair bit anxious to know what those thoughts were.

"Yes. I have a wife now. You will take precedence in my mind from now on. I'm occupied with thoughts of caring for you, protecting you, especially from any dangers that may result from the grave error I made at Lady Allerton's ball."

At this, Letty put a hand on his knee, silencing him briefly.

"I've been thinking about that. I was stunned at first to find myself in a forced marriage, but if you hadn't come after me, well, whoever fired that pistol would have succeeded in their goal of silencing Lady Edwards, and likely me as well. So you see, if you hadn't done what you did, I'd be dead rather than married, and I do prefer marriage infinitely more than being deceased."

At this, Morrey—*Adam*, she reminded herself—chuckled. "Marriage to me is preferable to death? Thank heavens for that."

Letty, emboldened by his laugh, nudged him in the ribs with an elbow. She had the sudden urge to embroider those words upon a handkerchief for him. She did love to tease and be teased. She hoped, in time, she would discover that Adam had a teasing side as well.

"You know very well what I meant. You also know that I find you . . ." She stalled.

Lust darkened his eyes. "Yes? How do you find me?"

"I . . . I find you quite handsome. Very charming. And more than a little intimidating . . ." Each time she spoke, he shifted closer, and she instinctively retreated each time toward the corner of the coach, until he effectively caged her in with his body. It was done so subtly, yet with such clear purpose that she marveled at how he'd directed her so easily to move where he wished without even touching her. Their new sensual predator and prey position made her blood hum in fevered excitement.

"Do you wish to know how I find you?" he asked, his voice lower now. His laughter had been replaced with a tone of silken seduction that left her with no doubt as to what he planned to say, at least in generalities.

"I find you sweet, innocent and love the way you blush when I touch you. Yet I see that carnal hunger in your eyes, and I get lost in thoughts of all the wicked things I wish to do to you." He tilted her head up as he lowered himself until their mouths were but inches apart. "I dreamt of you last night, just as I said I would." His voice softened into a whisper against her skin, and her mouth ran dry as her lower belly began to fill with a heavy warmth.

In one fluid motion, he pulled her onto his lap so that she sat across his thighs, his hands exploring her lower back, the heat of his palms warming her through the fabric of her wedding gown. She trembled at the feel of being held so tightly in his arms. Their mouths hovered so close, and only when she closed her eyes did his lips press to hers. His kiss was persuasive, coaxing, as he lured her deeper under his sensual spell. His tongue flicked against the seam of her lips, and she hesitantly opened to him.

"That's it, love—*open to me*," he whispered against her mouth. He sounded so sinful. So erotic. She pressed closer, and his arms tightened around her. She felt trapped, and she loved the thrill of it. Audrey might have advised her to control her husband, but Letty liked it when Adam was in control. At least in this. She felt safe, even with the hint of fear that accompanied him. It was what made him impossibly alluring.

"You taste sweet. As sweet as can be," he said before kissing her again.

She arched into him as his hands began to roam over her body. She wanted him to touch her everywhere. Wriggling on his lap, she felt something hard beneath her bottom.

"Easy, sweetheart," he said, and chuckled as he kissed her throat. "You'll be the death of me."

"Did I hurt you?"

"Far from it. In fact, I think you should—" The coach stopped, and Adam cursed softly. "Bloody wedding breakfast."

"Couldn't we simply tell the coachman to drive around a bit longer?"

At this, her husband laughed. She *loved* the sound. For such a serious man, that simple sound changed him completely.

"Oh, sweetheart," he said again, the endearment

falling easily from his lips. "I am sorely tempted to do just that, but we've caused enough scandal as it is. Besides, when I claim your body, I would rather not be rushed. And once you understand why, you will be grateful I exercised some measure of restraint at this moment."

He gently set her on the seat beside him, and they smoothed out their clothes.

"Thank heavens I didn't muss your hair," he said as he opened the door. A flustered footman assisted her down. It must have been clear to the young man what had been going on inside, and that was why he hadn't dared to open the door.

Adam and Letty now entered their home for the first time as husband and wife. She had hoped to feel suddenly in command of Chilgrave, yet it didn't feel as though anything had changed inside of her. She still felt like a guest who would eventually be asked to pack up her valise and leave. But that wasn't going to happen. She was here to stay. This was her new home. She and Adam had a few moments to collect themselves in an adjoining drawing room, where she hastily sipped from a glass of champagne before they entered the dining room to greet their arriving guests.

The dining room was decorated with lilies and orchids, lending the feel of a garden to the beautiful dining room. The table was laden with a dozen small bridecakes, and the scent of oranges filled the air. Mrs.

Oxley had outdone herself, offering a host of other dishes for the guests and champagne poured into slender flutes.

"Heavens," Letty whispered at the sight of the festive spread.

Adam smiled fondly. "Though she can be grumpy, Mrs. Oxley does love weddings. I can only imagine how thrilled she was to finally be the head cook at one. Usually she volunteers to cook for the villagers nearby when weddings occur there."

"That's lovely." It delighted her to know that the servants in her new home were so caring and kind.

Adam retrieved one of the bridecakes and cut out a tiny piece. He held it out with his fingertips.

"I wouldn't want you to miss this," he said. The intimate gesture made a low heat burn in her belly as he placed a small bite of cake between her lips.

"It's quite good," she said as she swallowed the sugary bite. "You should have some too." She reached for the cake, but the sound of guests arriving halted her. Adam offered her a soft smile when he saw her disappointment.

"We'll have plenty of time for that later." They met their guests, and she did her best to embrace her new role as Countess of Morrey. As Adam's wife.

She and Adam split apart to better greet the guests. She still snuck glances at him every few minutes, and she was delighted and a little shocked to see that he was watching her with the same interest.

At one point, Adam was surrounded by a group of tall, rakish men. She knew them to be the League of Rogues, and she giggled at the sight of him. Whatever the men were telling him must have shocked him to his core. He looked suddenly as though he'd lost his footing and ran a hand through his hair, murmuring a reply to the group that made them all burst out laughing.

Audrey and Gillian now stood next to Letty. "What the devil do you think they are talking about?"

"I'm afraid to know," Gillian replied as she noticed her husband was among them.

Audrey sighed in disappointment. "It makes one very angry that one cannot simply transform into a potted plant so that one could sit close by and listen unobserved."

Gillian, who'd been taking a drink, and Letty, who'd been about to take another bite of bridecake, stared at her before both women started laughing. The bit of cake on Letty's fork dropped to the carpet between her slippered feet.

Gillian pressed two gloved fingers against her nose and looked as though she might sneeze. "Heavens, some champagne just went up my nose."

"And now I've ruined the carpet. Poor Mrs. Hadaway —she'll have to have it scrubbed."

By the time the guests had all departed, only Caroline remained behind with them in the dining room. Even James and Gillian had to return to little Gabriel.

"Letty, would you like to rest a bit? I'm sure you could use a bit of food and drink too. You scarcely had a moment to breathe, let alone eat," Caroline observed. "What do you say? I can have Mrs. Oxley send a tray to your room."

It sounded heavenly, but Letty sought to catch Adam's eye, wondering what he might prefer. It was half past three in the afternoon, and she remembered he had mentioned he needed to meet with his steward.

"My lord—Adam," she corrected herself. "Are you still intending to meet with your steward today?"

Her husband sighed. "I'm afraid I must. Now that I'm to live at Chilgrave for the foreseeable future, there are some changes that need to be made to the estate."

"Should I go with you?" Letty suggested. She wished to be a part of his life, and especially to be involved as Chilgrave's new mistress. Not all men allowed their wives into the sanctum of estate stewardship, and she hoped Adam wasn't one of those.

"You look tired. Rest today, but next time you'll come with me to meet Walpole."

"Promise?" Letty reached out to touch his hand.

His silver-and-gray eyes softened again. "I promise. We are partners from now on."

"I'm glad to hear you say that," Letty admitted. "I

wasn't sure if you were the sort of man who would allow his wife to be involved in estate matters."

"If you know nothing else about me, know that I believe a wife is her husband's equal, no matter what the laws of England say." There was no hint of deception in his voice, only honesty.

"Well, you had better go if you plan to be back in time for dinner," Caroline said.

"You're right—I must go. And you must rest." Adam headed for the front door, still wearing his wedding clothes. Letty followed behind, a sudden sense of concern for her husband forming a pit in her stomach.

"Adam, you'll be careful?"

"Yes, I will. As will you," he reminded her, and she nodded, wanting desperately to say something or do something more before he left.

Adam pulled Letty to him and kissed her hard before letting her go. "I will be back as soon as I can."

With a whirl of his cloak, he left to mount his horse before the front steps and then rode away from her on their wedding day.

6

Adam dismounted outside the village of Hemsley and took a moment to stretch his legs as he made his way to the office of his steward, Henry Walpole. It gave him a moment to once again reflect upon the new direction his life had taken.

I'm married.

He smiled at the memory of Letty standing beside him at the altar. She'd looked so dazed, as dazed as he'd felt on the inside, that he'd felt compelled to flash her a wink to get her to smile. Then he'd lost his control in the coach on the way back to Chilgrave, but knowing she was his, finally, a bride of his own—he'd gone a bit mad to kiss her and hold her. Then he'd seen the way she'd responded to his more commanding side, the way she'd let him give chase to her, and how her pulse had beat and her eyes had been wide and full of an excitement that matched his own.

I'm a bloody blessed man to have a wife who embraces passion as she does.

A sudden tightness in his breeches made him wince. The hour-long ride to Hemsley had done little to ease his amorous thoughts. He ought not to be thinking of bedding his wife, not when he still had business to settle. The sooner he was done here, the sooner he could get back to properly bed her.

Adam passed the reins of his horse off to a waiting groom and approached the small stone building that served as Henry's office.

A man of Adam's age got to his feet, shoving aside a stack of papers he'd been sorting on his desk. "My lord!"

"Henry, how are you?" Adam asked.

"Excellent, quite excellent. I wish you congratulations. The village has been abuzz with the news of the new Lady Morrey."

"Thank you. I'm sorry you could not come."

"As am I. But the urgent missives from London kept me away."

Adam took a seat opposite Henry as the man pulled a stack of letters out of a pile and handed them to him. Underneath the letters from Adam's bankers and solicitors in London were other messages of a more serious nature.

Henry was not only his steward for the Chilgrave

estate, but was also his contact with Avery Russell whenever he was here. Henry had proved trustworthy, and Adam had brought him in to work with the Home Office two years ago.

Adam reviewed the documents and cursed. There had been another attempt upon Lady Edwards's life. The reins of the horses on her private coach had been cut, and she and Lord Edwards had nearly perished in a carriage crash. The letter relayed that Avery had sent the pair of them to take refuge in Ireland in order to hide them on an Irish estate until it was safe to bring them home. French spies rarely visited Ireland. The distrust toward foreigners there extended not only to the British but also to the French, and the French were far easier to notice.

"I'm beginning to believe Lady Edwards, like Avery Russell, has nine lives," he told Henry. It was something Caroline had always said of Avery, and now he was quite certain it applied to the daring lady spy as well. He could only imagine the shock on Lord Edwards's face when he'd learned of his wife's activities in France.

"I quite agree. Thankfully, Lady Edwards has the devil's own luck." Henry settled into his desk chair and folded his hands over his stomach while he waited for Adam to finish reviewing his estate correspondence, as well as the missives from London from both the Home Office and Whitehall.

"I need you to send a message to Avery. Tell him I'm

increasing security at Chilgrave. If he plans any unexpected visits, have him come to you first."

"Of course. And what are these new security arrangements?"

"I wish for you to find some local able-bodied and sound-minded men who will be loyal to the House of Morrey. Men who won't drink themselves into a stupor or fall asleep while on duty. I want regular patrols in the forest around the edge of the estate, and double them at night and just before dawn."

"Anything else?" Henry inquired.

"I also want more grooms in the Chilgrave stables and increased pay for the staff. Anyone who believes they aren't making enough may be willing to sell information, perhaps even access to my wife."

"You truly think she's in danger?"

Adam nodded.

Henry sighed. "Bloody French. Can't even have a proper honeymoon without worrying some French fellow will stab you in the back."

"Yes, you'd think a country of romantics would have more respect for such matters. However, we have enough to worry about." Adam tapped the letter from Whitehall on his knee. "Thistlewood is back in play."

Arthur Thistlewood was a man determined to overthrow Parliament. He was an anarchist who believed the government and the Crown were only out to oppress. If he could not overthrow Parliament, he would attack it with everything he possessed.

"Christ, will we never be rid of that fellow? What has the Home Office to say?"

"Well, Edward Shengoe has infiltrated the group. Apparently, the conspirators have formed a group called the British Patriotic Benevolent Association."

"Charming of them to throw the word *benevolent* in there."

Adam smirked. "I thought the same. Mr. Shengoe sent the Home Office a copy of the group's rules and their statements and sentiments. They are meeting mainly in various pubs in Spitalfields, Bermondsey, and West Smithfield."

"That's rather provident of them. They're being more cautious this time," Henry mused.

"Yes, well, most of them have spent a great deal of time in a jail cell. No one wants to end up on the gallows like Jeremiah Brandreth and his men for their revolutionary antics."

Adam had not been employed by the Home Office in 1817, but he remembered that awful day at Friar Gate jail in Derby when the hanging of Jeremiah Brandreth and his comrades had occurred. Several thousand people had packed the streets outside the jail. Adam had struggled to get his horse through the crowds and had finally given up. He'd caught sight of the scaffolds, and as if drawn by some hand of fate, he had moved closer, not knowing that the men who were to die that day would change his fate.

A group of sheriff's officials sat on horseback, armed with javelins, protecting the back of the scaffold to prevent any last-minute rescue attempt. Jeremiah Brandreth, the so-called Nottingham Captain, was the first to climb the steps to stand beneath the trio of nooses. His cool stare upon the crowd unnerved Adam.

"God be with you all, and Lord Castlereagh too!" Jeremiah called out, standing resolute. The executioner removed a black silk handkerchief around his neck and replaced it with a noose.

The next man, William Turner, was less accepting of his fate. He cried out, "This is all Oliver and the government. The Lord have mercy on my soul!" The prison chaplain, in an attempt to disrupt this, placed himself between the two prisoners and the crowd.

The last man, Isaac Ludlam, climbed the steps, his lips moving over and over in fervent prayer, but the chaplain prayed louder, drowning out the doomed man's voice. The Lord's Prayer was recited, and then the executioner placed a cap over each man's head.

At half past, the lever was pulled, and the three traitors dropped. Brandreth and Turner died quickly, but Ludlam kicked and struggled for several minutes. Adam's stomach knotted, and he covered his mouth at the horrific sight.

"It is a dark day when a man's voice is silenced simply

because he disagrees with those in power," a man standing beside Adam said.

"I agree," Adam replied. "They were traitors, no question, but when a country loses its ability to have discourse, it drives men to commit treasonous acts. Who then is at fault? The man or the country who silenced him?"

"Indeed, that's the difficulty we face," the man replied solemnly, then held out a hand and introduced himself. "John Wilhelm."

Adam shook his hand. "Adam Beaumont."

Adam had had no way of knowing then that this first meeting with John would change his life. The easy friendship between them had only deepened over the next few years as John had fallen in love with Adam's sister, Caroline. John had been murdered just a few months before they were to be married.

So often, Adam replayed that first meeting in Derby. Had John known then that his work at the Home Office would cause his death and compel Adam to follow in that same line of work? Would it have made a difference if Adam could step back through time and warn his friend of what lay waiting for him on that lonely bridge at midnight?

Adam gave a shake of his head, clearing his mind. The past needed to stay in the past.

"Henry, keep me informed as to your progress in

finding men to patrol Chilgrave and let me know if Avery Russell intends to visit."

"Yes, my lord." Henry collected the papers of a dangerous nature, now that Adam had reviewed them, and tossed them into the nearby lit fireplace. The flames soon consumed the documents completely. If anyone were to break into this room now, it would simply appear to belong to an estate steward.

"Congratulations again, my lord. Do try to enjoy your honeymoon." Henry's tone was once again teasing.

Collecting his hat, Adam stood and headed for the door. "I will endeavor to do just that."

❦

"Do you remember that childhood game girls used to play with cherry stones or flower petals?" Letty asked. She and Caroline had just finished dining. The dinner table had felt empty with only the two of them there, so they'd chosen to sit close together by the tall fireplace.

Caroline grinned. "It's been ages since I thought of that. My nanny taught it to me. How does it go again?"

"Tinker, tailor, soldier, sailor, rich man, poor man, beggar man, thief," Letty recited. How often had she tossed cherry stones and counted them with these words? Little girls used to predict their future husbands this way. It was a silly child's game, but for some reason it came back to her today.

Caroline rested her chin in her hand, a bemused smile on her lips. "Whatever made you think of that?"

"Well, it seems that I want to keep changing the lyrics to *Tinker, tailor, soldier, spy* . . ."

Caroline winced at Letty's replacement word. "He didn't choose this life, you know," she said quietly. She had dismissed the footman a short while ago. There was no chance of their hushed conversation being overheard.

"How did it happen?" Letty asked. "I need to know. I need to understand."

Caroline played with her wineglass. "I suppose I can tell you. It's almost as much my story as it is Adam's."

Letty took a gulp of wine and waited.

"In 1817, Adam was passing through Derby, and he witnessed three traitors being hung. It was there that he met Viscount Wilhelm . . . John." She paused as she used the man's given name.

"They formed a fast friendship, but unbeknownst to Adam, it was John who had exposed the three traitors and had them arrested. He worked for the Home Office, you see. John continued in his secret labors, but he and Adam continued to be the best of friends. Adam has always been reserved, even before working for the Crown. He does not easily let people into his circle. But once you win Adam's trust, he is loyal to you beyond measure."

"Lord Wilhelm . . . The name sounds familiar." Letty couldn't quite place it, but she knew she'd seen or heard it somewhere before.

"Two years ago, John and Adam were to meet for dinner, but John never arrived. Adam went in search of him and found John fighting for his life on a bridge with another man." Caroline's voice grew tremulous, and her grip on her wineglass made her knuckles turn white.

"What happened?" Letty whispered.

"Adam witnessed John's murder. John fell into the river and never resurfaced. Adam dove in after him, but the effort nearly killed him. John's body was never found." Pain flashed in Caroline's eyes.

Letty put a hand on her sister-in-law's arm. "Oh, Caroline. Was Lord Wilhelm the man you had an understanding with?"

"Yes. I loved him more than anything." She touched her abdomen and turned anguished eyes upon Letty. "I was carrying his child when Adam told me he was gone. My grief was so great that I became ill and lost the baby, a girl. She was so small, but I held her in my arms. She was the only thing I had left of him, and then she was gone too."

"And Adam?"

"Adam was never the same. He was broken. When the Home Office came to interview him about that night, something happened. I'm not sure whether they recruited him or he volunteered, but the next I knew he was working for them."

Letty gave Caroline's arm another squeeze. "I'm so sorry about the baby. If I had known, I would never have asked."

"It's all right," Caroline assured her. "You're family now, and I do want you to know us better, even sad matters of the past." She looked away toward the fire.

"This is a crusade for him, isn't it? To find John's killer? That's why he continues to do this work."

Caroline nodded. "I know James probably told you that Adam has a more lethal position with the Home Office, but that doesn't mean he's a ruthless killer. He's more of a guardian than an assassin, but unfortunately that means claiming the life of an enemy sometimes. It weighs upon him greatly."

Letty couldn't begin to imagine the gravity of such a burden.

"He takes much upon himself, so you must give him time to open up," Caroline advised. "But he will. I know he cares about you."

"He said he does, but I wonder how that can be when we've known each other so short a time." Letty leaned in, a new excitement replacing her sorrow at the story of John Wilhelm, at least partly.

"Yes, he told me himself that he liked you the first moment he laid eyes upon you."

"And I was there trying to discredit Gillian. How could he have possibly liked me then?"

"You weren't there to discredit Gillian. You simply wanted answers. You did not know who she was, and so you sought to protect your brother. Trust me, I know the sentiment well."

They both fell into silence. Letty finished her wine and blushed. "Caroline, I'm still anxious about tonight . . ."

"You need not be. Why don't you go on upstairs and have the servants prepare a bath?"

"That isn't a terrible idea," Letty conceded and bid Caroline good night.

Half an hour later, she was sinking into a large copper tub, the hot water enveloping her. She giggled a little, then hiccupped. She'd had far too much wine at dinner tonight. It was not at all what she had intended.

No, that wasn't true. She had intended to be a little freer with her libations in preparation for her wedding night. The prospect of pain terrified her, and she wasn't sure she would be up to her wifely duties after all.

She reached up to touch her hair and giggled again as she realized she was still wearing the extravagant coronet from her wedding. In all of her troubles today, she'd gotten quite used to the weight of the jeweled headpiece and had forgotten it was still on her head.

Letty sat up in the bathtub and started to remove it, but a deep voice stopped her.

"Good evening, lady wife."

She glanced over her shoulder and went rigid as she realized her husband was standing in her bedchamber, and she was not a dozen feet from him, completely naked. She could feel his eyes upon her in such an exposed and vulnerable state, and it sent her pulse racing.

"Er . . . ," she stuttered. "Would you mind terribly averting your eyes while I remove myself from my bath?"

"You've turned shy now?" Adam teased as he drew closer.

"Oh, please, you mustn't tease me," she said in mortification.

"She says this to me while wearing nothing but a coronet and a blush before her husband." Adam gave a long-suffering sigh, but his eyes were bright with teasing.

"I was waiting for you," she said, trying not to giggle.

Adam knelt by the tub, his eyes fixed on her face. "Well then, I have arrived, and you need not wait any longer. Stand and I will help you put this on," He held up her robe. The glint in his eyes had softened, and she felt a warmth in her chest that made her giddy with joy.

Her face was on fire as she rose and he slipped the robe about her arms, then over her shoulders. Before the fabric could touch the water, he grasped her hips and raised her out of the copper tub, setting her down on her feet next to him.

"I rather like this," he said. "My countess wearing

nothing but her coronet. The diamonds make your eyes sparkle." He brushed a damp lock of her hair back from her cheek.

"I quite forgot I was wearing it. I'm so sorry."

"Tut, tut. What's this now? No apologies. As I said, there is something quite wonderful about you wearing nothing but your skin and my diamonds. You're quite spoiling me on our wedding night."

"Oh, but—" Another hiccup escaped her, and she clapped her hands over her mouth in mortification.

"Have you had much to drink?" he asked more seriously.

"A bit," she admitted, then hiccupped again.

With a sigh, Adam moved away from her and poured her a glass of water. "Drink this. Slowly."

She did, and the hiccups soon vanished. "I'm terribly sorry, Adam. I was so fretfully nervous."

"Nervous?" He rubbed her shoulders. "Whatever could make you nervous?"

"Well, *you* do, of course," she said. "I mean, the thought of sharing a bed with you, that is . . ."

"You're afraid of the marriage bed?"

Her robe slipped off one shoulder as she took another drink of water. Adam reached up and gently pulled the robe back up over her shoulder rather than down, for which she was grateful. Her breasts felt strange and tingly, and her nipples had pebbled in the chilly air. She would be embarrassed for him to see that.

"It's silly, I know, but Gillian and Caroline said it might hurt, and I'm really not so brave as you think I am. But I will do my duty." She lifted her chin, wanting to make him proud that she was ready for whatever came next.

Adam had been smiling until she said *duty*. Then his open, soft expression faded, and he grew reserved once more.

"There will be no *duties* fulfilled tonight. You need not fear me—for now, at least."

He swept her up into his arms and carried her to bed. Then he pulled her covers back and laid her down beneath the sheets.

He bent his head and kissed her forehead. "Sleep well, lady wife."

The wine was taking its toll upon her, but she reached out and caught his hand as she settled deeper beneath the bedsheets.

"Adam," she sighed.

"Yes?"

"Stay. Please . . ."

She wanted to feel his body close to hers, to see what it was like to share such an intimate space with him throughout the night, to feel protected and cherished in his arms as she slept.

"You truly wish that?" he asked.

She nodded and yawned.

"Very well, lady wife. I see that *you* are the one who

must be obeyed." If he hadn't said this with a chuckle, she might have been worried she'd somehow upset him. The bed dipped as he removed his waistcoat, boots, and stockings, and then he lay down beside her.

She moved closer to him after a moment, wanting to know what it felt like to sleep with a man. As she nestled into his side, she decided that it was quite nice to lie peacefully with one's husband.

⚜ 7 ⚜

Adam was awake before the sun, and he held his wife in his arms for a long while. He was bemused as much as disappointed that he had not been able to bed her. Last night, when he'd found her in her bath wearing nothing but her coronet, he'd been overwhelmed with his desire. But the fear and surprise in her eyes had given him some measure of control. He was determined to protect her, shelter her, even from himself.

He had tucked her into bed, but he hadn't expected her to ask him to stay. As muddled as she was by the wine, which she'd clearly had too much of, she still wanted him to stay with her. It had been years since he'd had a mistress. Ever since John's death, he had done his best to keep intimate relationships out of his life. Now he had a wife, and it felt quite splendid to have her warm, soft, curvy body lying against his. His little Letty.

He brushed some loose curls away from her face and took his time examining her features in the pale predawn light that filtered in through the windows. He thought of how she'd called making love her wifely *duty*. That had wounded him, but he reminded himself that a woman's first time often came with pain, and he could not begrudge her that natural fear of the unknown. She had no knowledge of the pleasure that came after. Once he had her trust, he would escort her through that first time and hold her until the pain passed.

He realized that he was going to have to seduce his wife, something he'd expected to have to do before marriage, not after. At least he had ample time and opportunity while they remained at Chilgrave.

Adam eased out of bed before tucking the blankets back around Letty. He then exited her bedchamber and returned to his own. He hadn't removed his clothes from last evening, and now his shirt was rumpled. He'd just stripped out of his clothes when his valet entered.

"Good morning, my lord." Helms's genial smile greeted him as he bent to retrieve Adam's trousers and shirt from the floor.

"Good morning." Adam next set about shaving and then dressed in fresh clothes.

"Did you have a pleasant night, sir?" Helms asked.

"Well enough, though not as well as a man would

hope for his wedding night." He had always been open with his valet, and by his reaction Adam could tell the man had something to say. He nodded, letting him know he could speak freely.

"Mrs. Oxley was concerned, as was Mrs. Hadaway. It seems Lady Caroline and Lady Morrey got a bit deep in their cups last night."

"Yes, I discovered as much last night," Morrey sighed theatrically. "Wish me better luck today in wooing my tender bride."

Helms gave an amused look. "Luck be with you, my lord."

Adam ate breakfast alone, reviewing some letters Mrs. Hadaway had placed on a tray near his seat. As he was about to leave, Caroline slid into the dining room, shielding her eyes from the bright morning sun streaming through the windows. She winced as he quite purposefully dropped a fork on his plate.

"Helms was right. Both you and Letty had too much wine."

"It was my mistake. We were talking, and the matters being discussed were of such a nature that I feared I needed a bit more than usual to wash away the memory of our talk. Not that it succeeded."

Adam sat up straighter. "What did you talk about that so upset you?"

"I told her about John. She needed to know the truth, all of it. I know that you planned to tell her yourself, but part of his story is mine to share."

"Of course, Caro. You're quite right. You have as much right to share the story as I do. In many ways, he was more a part of your world than mine."

His sister's face grew pale. "Was Letty very frightened by what I told her? I woke up this morning feeling guilty, wondering whether or not she thinks differently of you now." Caroline sank gracelessly into a chair opposite him.

"I don't believe she thought very much about that last night. She was rather more concerned about the marriage bed."

"Oh . . . Adam, you didn't do anything, did you? She wasn't herself last night."

"Of course I didn't. You know I would never behave so boorishly."

"I didn't believe you would *knowingly*, but I wasn't sure if you could tell. The drink snuck up on me an hour before I went to sleep, and I feared it might have been the same with her."

He smiled a little. "She was hiccupping when I went to see her. That told me plain enough that the woman was not herself."

"Hiccupping? Oh dear." Caroline rose and collected a plate from the sideboard, then explored the foods still hot inside their chafing dishes.

"I think I'm going to go riding," Adam said. "If you

see Letty, ask her if she would like to go fishing with me this afternoon."

His sister stared at him. "Fishing? You want to take her fishing?"

He grinned mischievously. "Yes."

"It has clearly been a long time since you last wooed a woman. Most women don't want to be taken fishing. She'd rather have you read her sonnets while you picnic on some lovely hill. You are mad," Caroline said.

"Though this be madness, yet there is method in it," he replied.

"Do not quote Shakespeare to me this early in the morning."

He bent to kiss her forehead. "Very well, I shall wait until luncheon."

❦

LETTY STIRRED AWAKE SLOWLY, HER MIND FUZZY. HAD she gotten married yesterday? It all seemed so fantastical that for a moment she thought it had been a dream, but it did not take long to realize she was not in her home, but at Chilgrave Castle. She pulled the blankets off her body and saw no blood upon her thighs or the sheets.

Her eyes fell to the coronet on the bedside table, and it all came back in a rush. Sitting in her bath with that diadem on her head, giggling and hiccupping when her husband had walked in on her. Him lifting her up and putting her to bed. And he had stayed . . . but now her bed was empty. She slipped out of bed and went to the windows that overlooked the land beyond the castle walls. A figure riding a white horse was barely visible in the distance. She sensed that it was Adam, though she could not be sure.

"Morning, my lady," Mina greeted as she entered the bedchamber.

Letty greeted her lady's maid before turning her gaze back to the window. The figure was gone now, having vanished into the woods.

"His lordship had breakfast and rode out. You may dine at your leisure, my lady."

So it *had* been Adam. She wished she had gone with him. She enjoyed riding immensely, and it was not so easy to ride in London, where sidesaddles were required and ladies could only move at a sedate pace. Out in the country, she was free to ride as she liked. With her father dead and her mother ill, Letty had had no one to check her wilder impulses for many of her formative years. James had no issue with her riding astride or riding fast.

"Mina, could you have my riding habit set out? I should like to catch up to my husband."

"Certainly." Her lady's maid helped her dress in her dark-red riding habit, a lovely gown that had a loose train but also split skirts. These skirts would allow her to ride astride rather than sidesaddle. Madame Ella had raised a brow at the unique request when Letty had ordered it, but she had complied with the change in design.

Letty hurried downstairs, stopping only to grab a few biscuits to nibble on while the groom settled a horse for her.

Caroline emerged from the drawing room. "Letty? Are you going out? I believe Adam assumed you would sleep in after last night. He said to tell you that he wished to take you fishing."

"Well, I'm still tired, but I couldn't stay in bed. Fishing, did you say?" That was unexpected, but she wouldn't turn down the opportunity to be outside while the weather was so fine. Once the cold set in, she could cuddle up all winter and read books by the fire. "I saw Adam riding, and I thought I would join him."

"He rides quite far, sometimes several miles," Caroline said, her eyes clouded with concern. "Perhaps you would like to wait for him to show you around the grounds?"

"Nonsense. I have an excellent sense of direction." She hugged Caroline and rushed out the door to meet the groom a footman had summoned for her. He held the reins of a lovely black mare with dainty ankles. A proper saddle, not a side saddle, had been prepared per her request.

"This is Lizzie, my lady. Short for Elizabeth. She's the

queen of the Morrey stables." The young groom beamed with pride as he stroked the horse's neck.

"Oh, she's lovely. What's your name?"

"I'm Robbie, my lady." He offered his cupped hands, and she placed one booted foot in them as he hoisted her up.

"Thank you, Robbie."

She wielded her crop gently, tapping Lizzie's flank so that the black mare trotted down the bridge across the water. Once she was across, she steered her horse in the direction she had seen Adam riding. She did have a natural sense of direction, so she had no trouble discerning that he had ridden almost straight north. She followed the natural paths, noting where the grass was trampled across the field, and once certain of her course, she sent the horse into a gallop.

Letty laughed in joy as the wind rushed through her hair. There was nothing more freeing than being on the back of a galloping horse. No one could stop her, no one could see her, judge her, or cage her. She was free.

A dozen minutes later, she slowed her horse to a canter and then a trot as she spotted Adam ahead of her. He was galloping his horse across a distant hill almost perpendicular to her path. She pulled back on the reins and watched him for a moment, admiring the way he controlled his beast, urging it to turn sharply, then suddenly skid to a stop. A thought occurred to her. Was he practicing this type of horsemanship for fun—or for reasons related to his life as a spy? It would no doubt come in handy to be able to halt a horse that quickly and turn so sharply.

Letty urged Lizzie closer as he took off in another sprint. She gave chase, deciding she wanted to test her skill against his. Adam's black cloak flew out behind him. He was halfway down the hill when he glanced over his shoulder and saw her in pursuit. He halted so abruptly that she shot past him, laughing at the expression of shock on his face as she surged by.

She looked over her shoulder and saw that he was now chasing her. The white stallion he rode thundered like an old medieval charger a gallant knight might ride. Letty kicked Lizzie's sides and leaned forward, reducing the wind resistance. Lizzie was indeed a fast creature.

"Come on, my lovely." She urged the horse onward, and they fled in delight at the thrill of being pursued by their male counterparts.

They sprinted down the rest of the hill and through a wooded glen with tall oaks that created a shimmery canopy. Out of the corner of her eye, she saw Adam had gained enough ground to come up alongside her, though he was not close enough to grab her. She kept riding, refusing to stop, and when she stole a look at him, he seemed equally minded to beat her. In the distance, the woods opened up into a field, and there were tall hedges in parts of the field.

"Letty, stop!" Adam called out.

Unbeknownst to him, Letty was a master jumper. "Catch me if you dare!" she challenged before taking the first hedge. She cleared it with ease. A moment later, Adam followed.

The field proved a dangerous set of jumps, but Letty crossed each hurdle with natural expertise. As she reached the end of the field, she halted Lizzie almost as sharply as Adam had halted his mount. But somehow he and his white stallion now stood at the end of the field, directly in front of her.

How the devil . . . ?

He looked furious. Was it because she hadn't stopped when he'd ordered her to?

Adam started his horse toward her. "Letty," he called out gruffly.

"Adam, I'm sorry. I was having too much fun. You saw that I had no issues jumping—"

He grasped her reins when he reached her and held her horse still as he glared at her.

"That's not the point. When I say stop, *stop* for God's sake. You don't know the land here, not yet. You could have run straight into the marshes. Lizzie would have broken her legs and rolled over and crushed you."

"Oh . . ." Letty bit her lip for a moment before speaking. "I've had that happen before."

Adam stared at her in horror. "What?"

"I was thirteen. My new pony was spooked by a barn cat in the yard. He reared back and fell on top of me. He didn't break his legs, thankfully." The memory was not a happy one. The pony had been uninjured, but she had broken her ankle and suffered the pain of having it set in plaster. She'd been miserable in bed for a full week until James and one of the carpenters in the village had made some crutches for her. Then she was able to hobble about the house a bit until the plaster was finally removed.

Adam continued to chide her. "Then you must know the danger of running a horse over ground you aren't familiar with."

"You forget, my lord, that even ground you believe you know can change with a single rainstorm. And no horse is ever safe, or perfect."

For a moment the two of them stared at each other, one stern, the other defiant.

"And there is that fire," Adam said as he cupped her cheek. She was still astride Lizzie, and he was upon his white beast, but for a moment Letty felt as though she were leaning up against him, all of the inner parts of her soul touching his. Then the spell was broken as the white stallion nipped playfully at her horse's neck. Lizzie shied away, and the horses moved farther apart, forcing Adam's hand to drop from her.

"Follow me." Adam waved as he nudged his horse into a walk.

Letty followed. They rode in a companionable silence for a long while, allowing the trees in the woods to whisper to them as the breeze played in their branches. The morning mist was now slowly fading as the sun began to burn away the clouds. The effect left sunlight rippling across their path, illuminating patches of mist, which glittered like diamond dust scattered on the wind.

Adam paused his horse at the edge of the woods. They were facing the field again.

"You see the land there, at the end of the distant hill? How the grass darkens?"

She nodded.

"Those are the marshes." He turned to her, as though needing to see that she understood the danger. She did. "Do not go there, no matter what."

She took her time studying the landscape, learning the patterns of the native meadowlands before they turned to marshes.

"Adam, why were you halting your horse so abruptly in the field?" She positioned Lizzie beside his horse again. "Before the chase?"

"I often practice maneuvers that help me to be better prepared."

"For your work."

He sighed. "Yes." He was silent a moment before adding, "I sometimes run into dangerous situations. I quickly learned that a man's skill on a horse could save his life and the lives of others. Being able to stop my horse where I need to, even at a full gallop, can be very useful."

She toyed with Lizzie's reins and stared at him hopefully. "Would you teach me?"

"I don't think—"

"Please. This marriage was to protect me because you believe I am in danger. You must realize the necessity."

"I plan to be your veritable shadow."

Letty arched a brow. "Even shadows fade when night falls. You must acknowledge that I should have some skills of my own. Isn't that a more intelligent course of action? If we are separated, wouldn't you prefer me to have some sense of how to deal with my enemies? If nothing else, it would allow you more time to hone your own skills."

Adam looked heavenward. "Am I ever going to win any arguments with you?"

With a devilish grin, Letty trotted past him into the field. "Probably not. But you can win *other* things." She had no desire to control him when it came to everything, especially those things she sensed he would control very well—like the marriage bed.

"Very well, I will teach you what I was practicing."

For the next half hour, Letty became more comfortable in the saddle than she ever had been before and was easily able to train Lizzie to slide to a stop. When she felt she had practiced enough, she slid off Lizzie's back and walked along the edge of the woods. Adam dismounted and tied their horses nearby to graze before joining her.

Letty circled around a large tree, unable to keep her eyes off Adam as he came behind her. His hands were behind his back, and his lean legs moved in a gentle rhythm as he watched her playfully hide from him behind the tree. Adam came around one side of it, and she turned, putting her back to the tree as he cornered her against it.

"I am sorry about last night," she said.

He braced a hand against the bark beside her, and his other hand settled on her hip. A flare of heat filled her lower belly, and a faint throbbing pulse came to life between her thighs.

Adam's grip over her hips tightened ever so slightly. "I was sorry too."

"Perhaps we can try again tonight?" she offered, both nervous and excited at the thought. He took a step closer, his body now pressing against hers. She was suddenly afraid, though of what she wasn't sure, so she attempted to move away. He caught her waist and pushed her back against the tree, deftly capturing her wrists with one of his large hands, pinning them above her head.

"Adam—what—?"

"Hush, lady wife. I have caught you, and now you are *mine*." His words sent that faint throbbing deep in her belly into a more frantic pounding within her. He lowered his lips to hers, but he didn't kiss her. His lips brushed over hers, moving along her jaw down to her throat, where he nipped the sensitive flesh. She cried out, her hips arching away from the tree. All because of what he'd done to her neck. She was a terrible, wanton creature, yet at that moment she couldn't find it in herself to care.

Adam's other hand parted her split riding skirts, gripping one of her thighs. He slid his hand between her legs, his strong fingers questing through layers of undergarments until he found her. She shrieked in shock as he stroked the folds of her sex.

"Hush, pet," he purred, and all she could envision was how a dangerous tomcat would pounce upon a trembling mouse and gently bat at it with its paw.

One of his fingers moved up and sank into her, pressing tight inside that secret part of her. Wetness flooded between her thighs, and she wriggled, unable and unwilling to escape. He kissed the shell of her ear as he pushed that finger in and out of her.

"This is a taste of what I will teach you, this dark yearning for something more. The *need* you feel to be chased and caught. To have me master your body." His words, carnal and wicked, confused and excited her.

"I don't—I shouldn't—"

"Don't lie to me, or yourself. There is nothing wrong with wanting this. You are my wife, and I your husband.

We may explore this together." Adam kissed her now, a ruthless, violent kiss that matched the sudden thrust of his finger.

Something was building within her, something wild and uncontrollable. It felt as though her body was changing, as though whatever was coming, once it came, would leave a mark upon her that would never go away.

"Keep touching me," she demanded, needing his skin upon her skin in whatever way she could get it.

"Let go," he urged between his hungry kisses. "Surrender yourself to me." His hold on her wrists tightened as he inserted a second finger inside her, stretching her to the point where it was nearly painful.

"Christ, you're tight," he groaned against her mouth.

She was tight, and upon hearing him say it, it was like a curse and a blessing broke whatever had been holding her together. She simply came apart, and a frightening, powerful pleasure rippled through her. She screamed, but the sound was drowned out as he covered her mouth with his.

Letty was consumed by him, their bodies pressed tight, her will and his bound by this dark, exciting energy that his wicked touch created. He kept thrusting his fingers until she was begging for him to stop, not because it hurt, but because she could not take any more pleasure. He slowed down, his hand stilling as he cupped her sex. Then he brushed a finger over the bud of her arousal, and she flinched at its oversensitivity. He rested his head against hers, their panting breaths mingling.

"That's it. Ride it out with me," Adam encouraged. "Don't fight it."

She melted, unaware that she had been holding herself rigid as her mind and body tried to process what had happened. As she relaxed, little aftershocks of pleasure came more freely.

"There now," he soothed her as he pulled his hand from beneath her skirts. She was embarrassed at the wetness coating his fingertips but gasped as she watched him slip them between his own lips and lick them clean. It made the throbbing between her legs return.

"You taste sweet, lady wife, and your eyes . . ." His voice was soothing as he gazed down upon her. He still held her wrists trapped in his hand, and she couldn't find it in herself to care. She was safe like this, safe in his arms and his control.

"I thought . . . I thought I might fall apart and I would never be put back together again. It was frightening," she admitted in a small voice.

His silvery eyes held hers. "That is the beauty of embracing your passion. You can fall apart, and I will always be there to hold you together."

"Is this . . . Is this how it always feels?"

He nuzzled her cheek and kissed her forehead. "No, not always. Not for everyone. But a good man should always do his best to make his bed partner feel this way.

It is only lazy men who do not." He released her hands then and gently rubbed her wrists, massaging them. "You and I are lucky. We have something many husbands and wives do not."

"What is that?"

"I understand your desires, what you need to 'fall apart,' as you call it. To reach your peak. And your needs are not like those of other women."

"They're not?" She attempted to move, but her legs buckled. Adam caught her and swung her up in his arms as he started back to the spot where they'd left their horses.

"You mustn't be ashamed, lady wife. Many men and women have relations only in a certain way, the woman lying on her back and the man on top, but that is only one way. There are *many* ways to make love, and I plan to show you all of them."

At this pronouncement, Letty fell silent, wondering what all those ways might be. Adam carried her to the horses and only set her down next to Lizzie long enough to help her up onto the horse. When she sat astride, his brows rose.

"I was raised to ride this way. I assure you, I am far safer seated like this. Do you wish to make me ride sidesaddle?"

"Not at all. It is indeed much safer and better for your back. I was only surprised that I hadn't noticed it earlier." He smiled wickedly at her. "I was focused on other things, I suppose."

"I use my skirts to hide how I sit." She showed him how the riding habit fell to one side, covering one of her legs and making it look as though she were sitting sidesaddle.

Adam eyed her appreciatively. "That's a clever design."

"Thank you." She waited for him to mount, then grinned at him. "Race you back?"

She took off before he had a chance to respond, and she heard his laughter as he chased after her.

8

"Please, you mustn't kill it," Letty begged Adam.

Adam's curved silver fishhook paused before it could pierce the wriggling worm. His wife gazed at him from the other end of the boat where they floated on the water of the moat that surrounded Chilgrave Castle.

"I fear that I must," he chuckled. "You realize that even if I don't hook him, he shall still be eaten by a fish?"

Letty sighed. "Then do it, but know that I am saddened."

Adam had to work not to laugh at her adorable, childish pout. He hastily prepared the worm and then cast the line far away into the water before handing the pole to her. She accepted it, and while he focused on his hook, he could sense her studying him. He pretended not to notice.

"Why did you want to take me fishing?" she asked.

"Why?" He cast his line out parallel to hers in the moat.

"Yes. It's not exactly the sort of thing a woman expects to do the first day she's married."

He leaned back comfortably in the boat, his fishing pole held in one hand. "Oh? And what did you expect?"

"I suppose I thought I'd be meeting with Mrs. Oxley, Mrs. Hadaway, Mr. Sturges, and the rest of the staff. Then I would start to familiarize myself with the account books, menus, and any other things that the mistress of an estate like Chilgrave should know." She said this with an air of confidence, as though she thought that was exactly what she ought to be doing instead of lounging about in a boat with him. Adam knew she had been raised for those duties, but she was still rather young to have that thrust upon her.

"There is plenty of time for that. I wanted you and I to have time to learn about one another."

"That is a good idea. We do barely know each other," Letty said. "I don't even know how you take your tea."

"With one lump of sugar. I like a hint of sweetness." He winked at her and was satisfied by the deep blush that claimed her features. She was sensual yet so wonderfully innocent too. She was no jaded courtesan faking coquettish smiles in a mercenary fashion.

"What about you?" Adam asked. "How do you take your tea?"

"With enough milk and sugar that you barely taste the tea." Her impish reply had him laughing. "But I do need to know more about you. The serious things, I mean," Letty insisted.

"And what do you consider serious things?"

"Well . . . Your family, to start with."

"Ah, the paterfamilias and such. Well, the late earl wasn't a bad man. He was a decent sort, but my mother died young, just after Caroline turned four, and Father turned to her lady's maid for comfort."

Letty nodded in understanding. "Gillian's mother."

"Yes. Caroline and I loved Gillian's mother, but when she became pregnant, she left. I didn't realize until I was much older that Father had sent her away. He paid for her and Gillian to live comfortably, but he feared my finding out about them."

"Why?"

"He assumed—wrongly, as it turned out—that I would be upset. I wish he had married Gillian's mother, to be honest. Society be damned. I would have liked for her to have been raised alongside Caroline and me. But my father discovered this truth too late. On his deathbed, he begged me to find them. By then, Gillian's mother was dead, and my father's solicitor had lost track of Gillian." Adam paused, his voice softening a little. "I found my sister, only to learn that I had already lost her to your brother."

Letty scooted closer to him in the boat. "She loves

you, even only knowing you such a short time. She sings your praises."

He smiled, his melancholy thoughts retreating a bit. "I wish I could say I deserved any such praise."

"Well, she believes you do, and Gillian is not a person to put her faith in someone undeserving."

"And what about you? What of the noble house of Pembroke?"

"Much the same as yours, I suppose. Father died when I was very young, and my mama . . . Well, she did not die young, but her mind faded away only a year or two after Father passed. In a way, James and I raised each other. That's what I like about you, that you and Caroline have a bond the way James and I do." There was a bittersweet ache to her words. Their lives were similar in so many ways.

"I think a sibling is a blessing and a comfort. I am fortunate to have two sisters now." He gave a gentle pull on his fishing rod, testing what he thought might have been a nibble on his line, but found no resistance.

"May I ask a more serious and sensitive question?" she asked, her tone carefully neutral.

"I am, in most ways, an open book for you."

That blush returned. "Have you had many mistresses?"

That question was entirely unexpected. "Well . . . Not many by certain standards. I've had four in the last ten years."

"Four," she said, and he wished he could read her tone. Was she upset? Jealous? Worried?

"I promise you that, as your husband, I belong to you now. I haven't had a mistress in the last two years, and I will not take one ever again." He braced his pole on the edge of the boat and leaned over to take one of her hands in his. Holding someone's hand was incredibly intimate. In some ways, even more so than what they had done in the woods this morning. Hands were the way people connected to the world around them, and holding those hands, linking them like this, forged a bond with her that he didn't wish to break.

She didn't pull away, but she didn't meet his gaze either.

"I feel rather silly and unworldly," she said at last. "Do I disappoint you?"

Adam had to bite his lip not to laugh. "I would prefer you to be exactly who you are. No wilting maiden, nor some seductive courtesan. I wish for you to be *you*, lady wife. I find an abundance of delight in who you are—the wild Amazon creature who rides astride better than most men, yet succumbs to passion in my arms, whose surrender drives me to fresh heights of madness. You need never worry whether I am disappointed. I'm quite far from that particular emotion when it comes to you."

Letty smiled, and Adam's heart fluttered as it never had before. It wouldn't have surprised him to realize he was in very real danger of falling in love with his wife. He was not complaining about it either.

"Now, will you permit me a similar question?" Adam asked.

Letty looked like a doomed criminal on a scaffold. "I suppose I must."

"How many men caught your eye before you married me? Any former beaux who might track me down and challenge me to a duel for you?" he asked.

She relaxed. "Only a few, but I doubt any would challenge you to a duel." She nibbled her bottom lip in a way that reminded him of their glorious moment of passion in the woods.

"Tell me about these men."

"There was Silas Wilson, the son of a doctor near our country estate. He was three years older than me. I thought him quite handsome." She shook her head. "He never looked my way. I was but thirteen, a child to him. I caught him in the stables with a maid from our house. They were kissing quite seriously. It hurt to see him like that. I remember running back up to the house, and I tripped, skinning both my knees. The doctor was seeing to our mother, and he took a moment to patch me up, asking what had caused a young lady to run so frantically as to trip. I remember just wanting to die of embarrassment. I couldn't tell him about his son. I still have the scars." She raised her skirts to show her knees, unfastened the ribbons holding one stocking up, and rolled the stocking down. She seemed entirely unaware of what she'd done at first, then gasped and flung her skirts back down.

"Heavens, I don't know why I did that."

Adam moved closer and put his palm on the bright-green gown covering her knee. "We are becoming more comfortable together. There is nothing embarrassing about that." He removed his cravat and pulled part of his shirt down to expose his throat. He traced a raised line near his collarbone. "You see this scar?"

She leaned forward, tracing the scar with her gentle fingers. "How did you get it?"

"I was determined to improve my fencing skills while at university. We had been practicing with protective-tipped foils. Another boy challenged me to fight with an unguarded blade. Thinking that the danger would heighten my senses and reflexes, I agreed. My presumption was *very* wrong. The other boy caught me with a thrust, and I bled quite terribly. One boy even fainted, much to the embarrassment of our fencing master, who returned in time to see this happen. We were both tossed out of fencing school. My father had to hire a private fencing master to teach me."

"Oh heavens, it is a fierce scar," she agreed, still tracing the spot. Adam caught her wrist in his hands, holding her close to him.

"Are you less shy of me now?" he asked, smiling.

She smiled back and nodded. "Yes. I keep thinking of

what happened in the woods as well. I fear I get a little silly whenever you touch me."

"I like hearing that," he said as he pulled her onto his lap. She gasped and wobbled until she settled across his thighs, her hands gripping his shoulders.

"The beauty of being so close in this boat means we can do whatever we please."

He dipped his head to steal a kiss. Her petal-soft lips parted beneath his, and he thrust his tongue boldly against hers. She was shy at first as she learned to match him and his actions. The need to have her, to dip her back in the boat and toss up her skirts, was strong enough that it made his hands shake. But her first time was not going to be here in a boat. He would control himself . . . eventually.

A sudden clattering disrupted their kiss, and they turned to see Letty's fishing pole tilting over the side as something tugged sharply on the line.

"Oh no!" She flung herself off Adam's lap and lunged forward to catch the pole before it went over.

"Letty, wait!" Adam shouted. The boat rocked sharply, and both the pole and his wife tumbled into the water.

There was a heartbeat where he froze, expecting her to come sputtering back up to the surface. When she didn't, he flung himself over the side after her, plunging into the greenish-brown depths, reaching blindly about the water for her.

Could she swim? He hadn't even thought to ask that before taking her in the boat. The moat was nearly twenty feet deep in some places. Not to mention the gown she wore would drag her down with its weight, and her skirts would make it hard to kick her way up to the surface. Terror spiked inside him, choking out what breath was still in his lungs. He kicked back to the surface and gasped for air, then plunged back down again. He wouldn't stop, wouldn't give up. He couldn't lose her, not when he'd only just found her.

He surfaced again, kicking his legs and staring at the surface of the water near the boat. No sign of Letty anywhere.

A second later, a hand shot out of the water, holding the fishing pole aloft like it was Excalibur. Letty's face came up shortly after. She spit out water and sputtered as she looked around for the boat, then, realizing he wasn't in it, swirled about in the water looking for him.

He stared at her, mouth agape. He had been so certain she was dead. Flashes of that night at the river had filled his mind—of Adam screaming John's name, searching the dark waters until he had lost all strength.

"Adam . . ." Letty spoke his name with concern.

"I didn't know if you could swim," he said. "You didn't come up."

Letty tread water, watching him with greater distress. "Well, I can. You don't need to worry."

"Don't need to worry? Letty, my dearest friend in the

world died in a river. I watched him vanish. I can't do that ever again." He kicked toward the boat and grasped the side. Then he hauled himself up and over.

She reached the boat and held the fishing pole out. He grabbed it and angrily tossed it into the boat before putting his hands under her arms and heaving her aboard. He was furious, he was frightened—he was a hundred different things at that moment as he curled his arms around her and held her to him. She didn't fight him, didn't pull away. She stilled and tucked her head under his chin.

"Never do that again. Never," he warned in her ear. "Please, God, never again."

She breathed and placed a kiss to his chest. "I'm sorry."

Adam held her for what felt like an age, not wanting to open his eyes. It was only when he felt the chill of the water settling on both of them that he came back to himself with an inward curse.

"We should get inside and change, or you'll catch your death." He reluctantly set her back on the bench so he could row them to shore.

She curled her arms around herself as the cotton dress clung to her. As terrified as he had been just moments ago, he had to admit how adorable his wife was, dripping wet like a kitten. But he couldn't shake the anxiety he felt over nearly losing her. As they reached the shore, he hopped onto the bank and heaved the tip of the boat up onto the grass before helping her out. She started to reach for the poles, but he shook his head.

"Leave them." He put an arm around her shoulders and kept her close as he walked her up the long stone bridge over the water back to Chilgrave Castle. By the time they reached the castle's main gate, Letty was shivering.

"Heavens, I don't think I realized how cold the water was."

"It's a deep moat. The water is quite cold, except in the summer months. Even then, the deeper one goes the colder it becomes."

"I reached the bottom. That blasted pole was resting in the silt. I had to feel around to find it."

Adam stopped them just at the gate and made her face him. "No fishing pole is worth dying for. I don't care if that blasted diamond coronet falls in—you will not go after it." He wasn't teasing anymore. He was still angry and frightened.

"I—I understand. I'm sorry, Adam. James taught me to swim ages ago, and I just didn't think."

"Protecting you is my responsibility. Please do not make it harder for me to do that."

Letty's face flashed a dozen emotions that he could barely trace before she nodded. "I won't do it again, my lord."

She started to turn away from him. This was a pivotal moment between them, and he knew he had to make the right decision or lose her growing trust. He caught her by the waist and spun her back into his arms. She sucked in a breath as her hands braced themselves against his chest.

"Never shut me out, Letty. We are in this together, and I do not want to treat you like a child. All I'm asking is that you trust me. Talk to me. No more leaping headlong into danger."

Her pained look faded as she offered him a tremulous smile. "I didn't think a moat qualified as danger."

"You would be surprised." He rubbed his hands up and down her back. "Quite a few dangers abound on Chilgrave lands, even for me. And I grew up here."

"I understand."

Adam lifted her chin so he could gaze into her warm brown eyes. "Are you angry with me?" he asked.

"No," she replied honestly. "Are you angry with *me*?"

"No. I'm angry with myself. You needed my protection, and I wasn't prepared. And now you're trembling, and I'm neglecting my duty to take care of you. We need to get you warmed up."

The main door opened, and Mr. Sturges met them.

"My lord!" The butler's eyes widened. He better than most knew that Adam's occupation came with many dangers, and he clearly thought something sinister had befallen them.

"It was just a little boat accident, Sturges. Not to

worry. Please have a bath drawn in my chamber. My wife and I need to warm up."

"Of course." The butler rushed away, while Adam escorted Letty to her room.

"Collect a robe and a chemise."

She turned innocent eyes upon him. "Am I not to bathe?"

"Not here. Not alone." Adam's voice was a little rougher than he meant it to be, but he was still fighting off his concerns and his desire for her at the same time.

How did other men cope when they married attractive strangers? Was he wrong to want to bed her so soon? He felt half-mad knowing he could take her in the bloody bath if she gave him any sign of approval. But he wouldn't. As his countess, she deserved to have a romantic setting for her first time. He owed it to her to make their first time as honorable and pleasant as possible.

"*Oh* . . ." That single syllable held the weight of a thousand unsaid words. She collected her robe and chemise and followed him to his chamber.

"Here, sit by the fire." Adam set her in the comfortable worn armchair he favored. He was glad Helms had thought to have a fire already going. September in England could be cold, and the lake water didn't help matters.

She sat, and Adam placed her robe and chemise on the bed before he draped a heavy woolen blanket about her shoulders. A parade of footmen arrived, carrying steaming buckets of water to the deep copper tub until it was full and steam curled up from its surface.

Once they were alone, Adam gently pulled Letty to her feet. "Come, let's get you warmed up."

"I suppose you've had much practice at undressing women?" Letty asked, her teeth chattering a bit.

"A bit, I confess, but this feels different. My hands are almost clumsy when I touch you. It's as though I must learn it all anew," Adam murmured.

"The cold water, no doubt," said his wife. His fingers did seem to be lacking their usual deftness as he fumbled with her laces. "First you must loosen the tied knot at the bottom, then work your way up." Her voice was a little breathless, but at least her teeth had stopped chattering.

As he drew the laces out, he let his fingers linger in places, touching her through the thin layer of the wet chemise she wore as he exposed her bit by bit while undressing her.

She stayed quiet as he undressed her. Both of them barely breathed now as pieces of her gown draped about her body and then fell away. Every bit of him seemed locked in those powerful moments where his heartbeat and hers seemed to match, the dampness of his hands touching her chilled body as he lifted the chemise off her. She was warming up now, a blush heating her pale face, and he wanted to bury his lips against her throat and inhale her scent, but she needed to be even warmer than she was now.

When at last she was fully naked and he had a chance to admire her lovely body, he nodded toward the tub.

"Get in." His voice was hoarse as he reminded himself that she was cold, and still a virgin. He was not a ravenous beast who would fall upon his wife like a wolf, no matter how much the baser part of him wanted to.

"You should bathe too," Letty said as she sank into the hot bath. "Before it becomes too cold." There was a subtle hint of seduction to her words, as though she was beginning to learn this game they were playing. He knew by the flushed look upon her face that she was feeling heady with desire. Seeing his sweet, feisty wife, wet in the hot bath just a few feet away, inviting him in, was too much for him to bear. His cock hardened, and his mouth ran dry.

"I'm not sure I can remain a gentleman," he warned.

"I don't recall asking you to be one." Her little wicked smile only made it that much harder to stay away. For a second, his mouth parted, but no words came out as he tried to think of a rational response to keep himself at a distance.

"Your first time with me should not be in a bathing tub."

Letty's adorable face was just visible over the tall side of the tub.

"Husband, you will strip out of those wet clothes and join me. *Now.*" She splashed a hand in the water. "There is room enough for two, *if* you don't mind being close to me."

Little spitfire. Adam stared at his wife in shock. Oh, how he adored her at this moment. With a grin, he began to undress.

"Very well, but you may get the rogue yet."

9

Letty held her breath as Adam began to remove his clothes. In that moment, she decided she loved nothing more than the sight of her husband undressing. It was like a performance, a beautiful, seductive one, how he unwound his neckcloth and let it flutter to the ground. He unbuttoned his waistcoat and shouldered it off, then pulled his white shirt out of his trousers and over his head. His bare chest was broad, accented by his muscles. He reached for the placket on his trousers, his arms flexing as he did so.

Heavens, the man is pure sin, and I cannot look away, Letty thought. She would finally see what Adam looked like completely bare of all his clothes.

"Oh, right, mustn't forget these." He stopped undoing his trousers and bent to remove his boots and stockings. He shot her a teasing look, obviously knowing exactly how he was torturing her with this delay. Letty clenched the edge of the tub as he finally went back to undoing his trousers. He pulled them down and kicked them off, and she stared at *that* part of him. He was not like the statues in the museum. He was far larger, and it was not lying down against his body but pointing toward her. *Dear heavens* . . . Her lips parted in shock as he approached the copper tub.

"Move forward a bit. I'll slide in behind you."

She scooted forward, and he stepped into the tub. The water sloshed as he eased down. He parted his legs and gripped her waist.

"Now slide back and lean against me."

Letty did as he said and closed her eyes, feeling his hard-muscled body behind her. The hair on his calves tickled her legs beneath the water. His breath, warm against her neck, sent shivers of delight through her. Her nipples pebbled, and her thighs clenched together. The once hot water now seemed tepid compared to the burning of her body. His hands stayed on her hips for a long time before they began to slowly explore her, first her inner thighs, then her lower belly, and finally sliding up to cup her breasts.

"You have exquisite breasts," Adam whispered in her ear.

"Oh?"

"Yes, quite perfect. See how they fill my hands?" He

let the weight of them fill his palms before he gently squeezed them. "It gives me wicked ideas."

"What sort of ideas?" Her breasts turned heavy at his touch.

"I would like to put you on your hands and knees facing the mirror, while I claim you from behind and watch these glorious breasts move freely as I thrust inside you." Adam's words painted such a sensual picture in her mind. So sinful. So *exciting*.

"Would you like that?" he asked before he bit the lobe of her ear. Sparks of arousal shot down her spine into her womb.

"You truly are wicked," she moaned as he pinched her nipples lightly. He then gripped her throat, gentle but possessive, while his other hand cupped her mound. He kissed her ear, followed by her cheek, before he thrust two fingers inside her. Her hips arched up into his touch.

"More, *please*," she begged, wanting to feel as she had in the woods when he'd pinned her against the tree.

"I'm happy to oblige," he said and began to move his fingers faster and faster. Her knuckles were white as she gripped the edge of the tub, her body strained by the building rush. But just before she felt she would fall off the edge, he slowed.

She wriggled, splashing water about. "No! Don't stop . . ."

He chuckled. "Are you ready to come apart again?"

She bit her lip and nodded.

Her wicked husband's warm breath fanned against her neck as he gave her what he'd promised. He moved his fingers faster, and she arched her back. Ecstasy exploded from her head to her toes. She collapsed back against him, her limbs quivering and her breath shaky.

Adam embraced her as she drifted down from the wild high of her passion. When she came to herself, she turned to see his face.

"And you . . . Does a man feel this way?"

"Oh yes," he assured her.

"How does one do it for a man? The way you touch me, I mean."

He laughed and leaned down to brush her cheek with his lips. "Curious creature. I like that. Grip my cock."

"Your . . ." She tentatively touched his shaft, which was surprisingly stiff, and he groaned. "Am I hurting you?"

He shook his head. "Now, wrap your fingers around it and move your hand up and down. Yes, like that."

Letty stroked him and followed his commands. Faster. Harder. Slower. He almost seemed to enter a trance, and she felt drunk on the thought that she held him in her power. This moment was bonding them together in the most sinful, wonderful way she could imagine. Then he called out her name, his body stiffening in the water. After a long moment, he relaxed, and she sensed he had found his peak, and she removed her hand from him.

He pulled her to his chest again and nuzzled the crown of her hair. "Let's get you out of this bath and into bed. You've had a most exhausting day."

Letty played with his chest, letting her fingers circled his flat male nipples and trace the lines of his collarbone. "As have you." He was a beautiful specimen of a man, and she felt wildly giddy at the thought that he was hers.

"Come, lady wife." Adam stood up in the bath and helped her. Then he fetched a cloth to dry them both before he gave her a fresh chemise and robe.

Letty finished dressing and wrapped her warm robe around her. She took her time studying Adam's bedchamber. Her own room, that lovely circular chamber, held a hint of wild mystery to it. But Adam's room felt warm and welcoming. The sturdy four-poster bed, the green satin wallpaper, the light walnut paneling of the doors and ceiling accented with gold moldings. This could be her new home. No, this *was* her new home. That other chamber would be a private space for her, but she wanted to enjoy this room as hers and Adam's.

"I think I shall stay here," she announced.

Adam pulled his banyan robe closed and eyed her with amusement.

"So you've made your decision."

"Yes. Assuming you'll have me."

He came to her, taking her in his arms before he

cupped her bottom and squeezed. "I *suppose* I can tolerate your nightly presence," he sighed dramatically. Then he swatted her derrière. "Now get in bed, wife."

Letty shot him a saucy grin. "Yes, my lord. As you please, my lord."

As Adam got into bed beside her and pulled her into his arms, he smiled at her with increasing fondness. "Yes . . . You certainly do please me."

⚜

CAMILLE WAITED PATIENTLY IN A PRIVATE ROOM AT A small inn in Spitalfields before she went to the connecting door and knocked lightly upon it. She and her master always timed her entrances perfectly.

"Come in, Camille," her master bade.

She stepped inside and was immediately surrounded by shadows as the crowd of seven men inside turned her way.

"Who is the woman?" one of the men demanded.

"Be at ease, Mr. Thistlewood. The woman is mine. Her pretty face keeps my temper at bay, does it not, my sweet?" he asked Camille.

She dipped into a curtsy and flashed a beatific smile at him and the men.

"Yes, master."

"She certainly makes me think of much better things than anger," one man dared to joke.

Her master silenced him with a look. "Now, if you are ready to discuss what matters . . ."

"We are, Mr. Garland," the man called Thistlewood said. "Please, speak."

Her master smiled coldly. "Until now, you've all stayed just out of reach of the noose. That is commendable, but at this pace, you will never achieve any results. That is where I should like to assist you. Sending your little rebellious letters to Whitehall is foolish. I want that to cease immediately. The best revolutionaries do not need to feed their sense of self-importance. They leave that for the rhetoricians who rally allies to the public front of their movement. But where sedition and treason are necessary, it must be carried out in the dark."

"What are you suggesting we do, then? Don't we need public support?" another man asked. "Rally the people and such? Otherwise, whatever we do won't matter. It would be like killing the king. Another would simply take his place."

Her master held a hand to his lips to call for silence. "The French successfully removed their dynasty."

The man arguing with her master shook his head. "But a loyalist king took the throne after Bonaparte died."

"And that man no longer has the Sun God status the French once believed their royalty held. He is mortal— he can be deposed or killed, his family and heirs wiped out by Madame Guillotine. The French people know they have the power now, not some man upon a false throne."

Amidst all this, Camille was not focused on her master. She had a job to do, which was to listen to all that was said and remember the faces of every man present.

"What you need to do is remove the king *and* the system that keeps him in place."

"How does one do that?" someone asked. "I am not against the idea, merely inquiring how one can achieve it effectively."

"By doing it all at once."

"All at once?" Thistlewood stroked his chin, his eyes thoughtful. "How could you ensure that?"

Her master leaned back in his chair. "The House of Lords. Parliament itself."

The suggestion was met with silence, but judging by their faces, the rebels didn't seem bothered by it. Rather they were contemplative, trying to see how this one stone could kill two birds.

Camille's master smiled again. "The king intends to make a speech to Parliament, you see, and when he does, we shall be ready."

"How do you propose to destroy Parliament? It's not as though we could march up to it with pistols in our hands. If I recall, Guy Fawkes tried this and failed."

"He did, but he didn't have the access to places and

people that I do. When it is time, I shall tell you how we will make Whitehall fall."

Thistlewood glanced around at his fellow rebels. "Very well then. We shall wait for your signal. But we will not wait for long."

"You will not have to."

There were murmurs of assent, and Camille, still in the shadows, studied each face, searching for any hint of falsehood to betray a deceiver in their midst. One man seemed more pensive than the others. He sat close to Thistlewood, not speaking as the others, who were now resolved on their course of action and had dissolved into small talk. It could be nerves, of course, but it could be something else . . .

"I will send a summons when we are ready to set the plan in motion," her master said.

One by one, the men slipped from the room until it was empty except for her master and herself.

"Well, my pet, what did you see tonight?"

She sipped a glass of wine and stole a bit of chicken from the plate her master had left out from his meal before she replied.

"Thistlewood and his men are loyal . . . though one concerns me."

"Which one?" her master asked.

"The one who never spoke. He sat next to Thistle-wood, perhaps to establish an outward show of his commitment. But he said not a word, even when his eyes would sometimes flash at what you said."

"Well observed—even I missed that." Her master handed her his glass of wine, and she drank before offering him a smile.

"You are pleased with me?"

"Very pleased," he assured her. "Are you ready for your next assignment?"

"Yes."

"You are to find Lord Pembroke's sister."

At this, Camille suddenly brightened. "Oh, monsieur, I forgot to tell you." She rushed into the adjoining chamber and returned with a newspaper that she'd come across that morning. She handed it to him, opened to the society column.

"Lady Society," he grumbled. "I never did learn who the damned chit was." He scanned the article. "Lady Leticia was married the day before yesterday?" His eyes narrowed. "To Lord Morrey." The name was uttered with an intimacy that piqued Camille's interest.

"You know him, monsieur?"

"I killed his best friend." The ferocity of his expression shocked her. She'd never seen her master look angered like that before. He fingered one of his cufflinks, a habit he always had when he was upset about something. Someday he'd rub the cufflink's surface off from doing that too often.

Camille placed a hand on her master's arm. "Is he like you?"

"Like me? No, he is just another English dandy who sticks his nose in places it doesn't belong," her master said calmly, yet Camille saw a strange fire in his eyes—anger that hid a deeper emotion.

"I will go, monsieur—"

"No." He caught her arm, holding her forcefully. "You'll stay and ease my temper." He shoved her toward the bed. She desperately tried to calm him, hoping that he would be gentle if she did not upset him. When he was in a good mood, he was the best of lovers, but when he was not . . .

"Please, monsieur, give me a moment to make you happy." She offered him her prettiest smile, and the hellish flames behind his brown eyes began to fade.

"Oh, my sweet French flower," he murmured. "You always know how to soothe my black heart."

She allowed herself a moment of relief. By God's grace, she'd escaped bedding the devil tonight.

CAROLINE TOSSED FITFULLY IN HER BED, KICKING HER blankets off until the chill air woke her. She sat up in the darkness, listening to the wind howl against the window-panes. Remnants of a dream trickled back to her. She had dreamed of John and the first time she'd met him.

She had been riding in the park with Adam. He had spotted a man astride a lovely brown gelding and had hailed him. She had been struck at once by the man's fair features, as any woman would, but he had none of the condescension in his tone that many men used when speaking with ladies. He engaged her as equally as he did her brother.

That had only been the beginning. Over the next year, he had paid calls upon her, brought her flowers, and walked in the garden with her. He had recited poetry that made her laugh or blush. He was a flirt, but only with her. His gaze never strayed to any other woman. She knew with certainty that she held his heart, just as he did hers. When the day came when he proposed, she accepted, knowing that her life would change forever.

She had simply never guessed that it would be with his murder, rather than their marriage.

She slipped out of bed and went to the vanity table. In one of the drawers, tucked beneath layers of ribbons, silver-handled hairbrushes, and diamond-studded hair combs, she found a gold locket that hung upon a fine chain. She smoothed her thumb over the locket before opening it.

Inside was a portrait of John. He gazed out from the tiny miniature, his solemn features so unlike the happy, smiling man she remembered. She held the portrait up in the moonlight to better view it.

"Why did you have to go out that night?" she asked the man painted in oil. "Why didn't you stay home?"

She placed a palm over her abdomen and drew in a deep breath. She had shared a bed with John only twice, but those nights had been sweet and wonderful. When she had discovered she was pregnant, she'd been overjoyed, but she'd kept it a secret from him, using clever gowns to hide her growing belly. She'd wanted the news to be a surprise on their wedding night. Perhaps if she had told him, he wouldn't have been so cavalier with his life. He might have thought more of his own safety, for the sake of his future child.

Caroline closed the locket and set it back in the vanity drawer. She went back to her bed and burrowed beneath the covers. This time she dreamt of nothing except hearing that single feeble cry of her newborn babe before it too faded into the dark.

A FIGURE LOOMED IN THE DARKNESS TOWARD ADAM'S bed. His face pale, his clothes dripping with icy water, as though he'd dragged himself from the depths of the Thames.

"*Adam,*" the figure gasped. "*Adam, wake up . . .*"

Adam stirred, fighting the lethargy of sleep. The figure reached cold, wet hands toward him.

"*You must wake. He is coming for you.*"

At last Adam surged up, gasping. "John?" But all signs of the ghostly presence were gone.

He steadied his racing heart and covered his face with his hands. Then he looked down at Letty, who lay beside him. She had half buried her face in the pillow, her dark hair billowing out around her. She was still fast asleep, undisturbed by him and the ghost from his past.

He stared at the dark corner of the room where he had imagined the figure of John Wilhelm.

"He is coming for you," John had said.

Adam wondered who his friend had been trying to warn him about. Who was dangerous enough to bring his friend from beyond the grave to deliver a warning?

🦋 10 🦋

Letty was finishing up her breakfast with Adam and Caroline when Mr. Sturges entered the dining room, a silver tray in one hand. He came over to Adam and held it out. There was a letter on top.

"What's this?" Adam asked.

"It just arrived by royal messenger." Mr. Sturges's reply held a hint of concern.

"Royal messenger?" Letty echoed.

"Yes, your ladyship."

"Thank you, Sturges." Adam took the letter from the tray, and Letty noted the royal seal upon it.

Adam used his knife to cut the wax from the paper and unfolded the letter and read it silently. Letty exchanged a glance with Caroline, asking her without words if she knew what it was about. Caroline shook her head.

"It's from His Majesty. He is summoning me back to London. Well, both of us." He looked toward Letty.

"The king? Why?" Letty couldn't even begin to imagine why the king would wish to see her.

"It seems that he desires to meet you and is curious about the woman I chose for a bride on such short notice."

"You are on favorable terms with the king?" Letty knew that most of the influential aristocrats met the royal family from time to time, but a personal invitation was still quite extraordinary. She'd had her debut a few years ago, but he wouldn't have remembered her from that night, not when it had been filled with dozens of other young women.

"Well, there is a story behind that—one I should tell you once we're on our way to London. We must leave immediately. He wishes to see us this evening for dinner." Adam cast her a smile, but she saw his thoughts were already distracted, possibly wondering if there was a significant urgency to the king's invitation.

"Tonight?" Caroline gasped. "Letty, we must pack your things at once and see if you have a decent court gown."

"I don't believe I have anything suitable," Letty fretted. A court gown was far more splendid than one's normal evening gowns.

"What about the one you wore the night of Lady Allerton's ball?" Adam asked. "Is that suitable?"

Caroline sighed. "Adam, that gown wouldn't do as a court gown. Letty, you and I are close in size—you shall take one of mine." Caroline rose from the table and the two ladies went to Caroline's bedchamber. "This one should do well." Caroline opened the tall armoire. She removed a gown and laid it out upon the bed for Letty to see. The crème satin creation was a vision, dusted with pearls like drops of moonlight.

"What do you think? I have not yet worn it, so it will not have been seen by anyone you meet."

"It's stunning! Oh, Caroline, do you mind? I don't want to take such a gown from you."

Caroline waved a hand. "It's yours. I do not believe I will be attending court anytime soon. Now, let's have Mina come and pack it up."

Within the hour, Letty and Adam were bundled up in their traveling coach and heading for London.

"Now, will you tell me why the king summoned you?" Letty was seated across from him—not because she didn't wish to sit beside him, but because it was easier to converse with him this way. Adam removed his gloves and toyed with them in his lap.

"I was stationed in Brighton a year ago. The king was at the Royal Pavilion. There were rumors of Napoleon escaping from Elba, and we were all on edge. None of us knew then that he would be dead in just a few weeks.

There was an attempt made on the king's life. I did my duty." He touched his ribs on the left side. "I took a blade here. Not deep, mind you, but in the king's mind, I was the only one who stood between him and death."

"I hadn't heard he'd been threatened last year." Letty kept herself abreast of the news by reading the *Times*, the *Post*, and even *Ackermann's Repository of Arts*.

"It was an incident that was kept quiet. There were few witnesses, and those who saw it were convinced to remain quiet. I believe that was the first time the king had ever faced death, at least in such a frightening manner, and it made an impression on him."

"I imagine it would." Letty fell into silence for a long while, her mind now filled with worries and concerns. They were headed back to London, a place they shouldn't go, where her life was more in danger, as was Adam's. But a king's command could not be ignored.

Adam was troubled too; she saw it in his distant gaze. After a while, she moved to join him on the seat. He clasped her hand in his, though she sensed his thoughts were miles away.

It was shortly after midday when they reached Adam's townhouse on Half Moon Street. There they met Mr. Shelton, the underbutler who handled the townhouse while Mr. Sturges was at Chilgrave.

"My lord! We did not expect you back so soon," Mr. Shelton said. He was close to Sturges in age, in his midforties, and he seemed quite as capable. Letty had not met him officially, but Caroline had told her about him before they'd left.

"I'm sorry, Shelton. It's quite unexpected. We require a quick luncheon, and Lady Morrey and her maid will need to be settled into their rooms."

"Yes, my lord." Shelton bowed and turned to her. "This way, my lady." He led her up the stairs to Adam's bedchamber. The servants quickly put away the clothes from Letty and Adam's valises.

Letty took a minute to familiarize herself with yet another new room. The past few days had been far too much for her in many ways. She had only just started to settle down at Chilgrave, and now she had a new house and new servants as well.

"You look quite exhausted, lady wife," Adam said as he joined her in the room. Mina and Helms quickly left to give them some privacy.

She sat back on the bed. "I am. It is silly, though."

Adam closed the door and came over to her at the foot of the bed. He was unbearably handsome just then. She was quite besotted simply looking at him.

"Are you all right? I understand it must be difficult to jump about like this."

"It is unsettling," she admitted. "But I am more nervous about meeting the king this evening."

"You need not be. The man is not perfect, but he is

decent as a monarch." Adam placed his hands on her shoulders and leaned in to whisper, "This evening after dinner, you and I shall finally have time to become better acquainted in our bed."

"That would be nice," she murmured.

He leaned in, kissing her in a way that made her head tilt back and her toes curl.

"Now, come down for lunch, and we shall rest a bit before dressing for dinner."

ADAM KNEW HE WAS BEING A LITTLE DISTANT. HE could sense Letty's concern growing during their lunch, and so he'd sent her to rest for a few hours before they had to leave. It had given him time to think, to plan, and to worry. The king's invitation couldn't have come at a worse time. There were a hundred things that could go wrong.

When she was ready, his wife appeared at the top of the stairs, and the sight of her stole his breath. She wore a gown of creamy pale satin with a gold underskirt and a glittering gold frill collar about her neck. Her capped sleeves were dotted with soft, shimmering pearls, and her bodice matched the gold underskirt. The design was not overly complex, yet the soft cream and bright gold, enhanced with the pearls on her fuller court skirts, had the most stunning effect. Her dark hair was piled atop her head, with a few loose curls escaping to rest against her cheeks and down the back of her neck. And there in the coils of her gleaming hair was the Morrey coronet.

His wife looked like a queen.

Letty paused at the bottom of the stairs. "Do you think His Majesty will approve?" she asked.

Adam swallowed and nodded. "He will. And I shall be glad Princess Charlotte is no longer with us to be envious of you."

"You think perhaps we ought to leave, so we might not miss dinner?"

Adam realized that he had been staring at her for quite some time now. "What? Oh yes." He escorted her to their coach.

⚜

AS CARLTON HOUSE CAME INTO VIEW, THEIR COACH joined a line of other conveyances that waited to drop their passengers off in front of the large palace doors. Carlton House was quite the sight when the king chose to entertain. The dozens of windows that faced the south side of Pall Mall were lit, illuminating the area like daylight. The vast structure was indeed a palace in all but name.

Having been here once before, Adam was accustomed to its extravagant opulence, starting with the hexastyle portico of Corinthian columns that led to a foyer. Some of the world's finest works of art hung upon the walls, already drawing admiring looks from other guests who had never been here before.

Letty kept close to him; she linked her arm through his as they followed the stream of guests inside. They entered a suite of rooms with its enfilade opened to allow for a long banquet table. Adam nodded at those he recognized. But when he glimpsed Avery Russell at the far edge of the dining room amongst a cluster of other guests, they barely shared a glance. They dared not acknowledge each other more than that.

"Adam, you devil," a familiar voice broke in. "How are you?"

Adam turned to see the Duke of Essex with his wife, Emily, at his side. Godric was a towering wall of muscle with dark hair and flashing green eyes that often sparked with a dangerous temper toward fools. It was said the violet-eyed beauty at his side was the only creature in the world who could tame him.

"Godric," Adam greeted. "We missed you at the wedding."

"I know. Damned pity to miss it. We were in the country when we heard that you were getting leg-shackled. I offer my belated congratulations."

Godric bowed his head to Letty. "Lady Morrey, it is a pleasure to see you again."

"Your Grace," she answered with a blush. Her gaze then turned to Emily, and the two women separated themselves from the men to speak.

"So, *married*. Never imagined you would do it," Godric said. "Pembroke said you weren't the sort to settle down."

How thoughtful James was to try to hide the real reason in conversation with others—not that it mattered. A number of titled men remained bachelors all their lives, with no concern as to who would be their heirs. He had not exactly cultivated that reputation, but James apparently thought he needed to, likely in order to protect his cover.

"Yes, well, when the right woman is thrust upon you, it is hard to say no." He watched his wife and the pretty young duchess, wishing they would stay safely away from the windows and dark corners of the room. Damnation, he was going to see assassins in the wings at every turn until he could end the threat to Letty's life.

"I agree with that. Marriage was an unexpected surprise for me as well. My little hellion thought she could refuse me too, until I finally convinced her otherwise. Damned curious thing to meet a woman who wanted me for *me* and not my title when she finally agreed to marry me."

"It's lucky you kidnapped her when you did, or else Pembroke may have married her rather than you."

"Do not remind me," Godric grumbled. "I was never

so glad as when he married. The man is a bloody saint, and all the women adore him. If only they knew he was a member of *your* wicked club. They would not think him so saintly then."

Adam laughed. "Even then, he is still a better man than the rest of us. Imagine how I feel having him as a brother-in-law."

Godric laughed. "Isn't that a sobering thought?"

The dinner gong sounded, and everyone began to pair up for dinner. Adam and Godric rejoined their wives and proceeded to the banquet table.

"You are up here." Adam led Letty toward the head of the table. A tall man in the finest clothes money could buy stood at the head of the table, and Letty gasped at the sight of the king.

King George IV was no longer in his prime at sixty years of age, but he still struck a dashing figure, if a bit rounder at the edges. The king had been raised a handsome, high-spirited boy, always bursting past the bounds of his strict upbringing. The man had spent much of his life alternating between indulging his passions and trying to please his parents.

"Ah, Morrey." The king beamed at them. "Finally, I meet the lovely woman who stole your heart."

Letty dipped immediately into a deep curtsy. Adam bowed.

"Your Majesty," they both replied.

"Thank you for the invitation," Adam said. "May I introduce my bride, Leticia."

The king studied Letty intently, missing nothing.

"You chose well, Morrey. Not only is she quite lovely, but there's a light in her eyes that tells me you do not have a dull life ahead of you."

Adam nodded and smiled a little. "I am most fortunate."

"And so am I. Tonight I lay claim to both your wife and Essex's." The king nodded toward the Duchess of Essex, who was being escorted to them by Godric.

"Indeed. You will find both of them good conversationalists," Adam promised and patted Letty's arm as he helped her into her seat.

The dining room was full of chatter as the courses began to arrive. Adam and Godric sat next to each other at the far end of the table near the hostess of the evening, Maria Fitzherbert, the woman the king had loved his whole life. Adam made polite conversation with Maria but kept his attention subtly trained on the opposite end of the table where Letty spoke to the king. Her face was animated by whatever she was saying. The king and Lady Essex appeared to be listening quite intently.

"I must thank you, Lord Morrey," Maria said, catching Adam's attention.

"For what, madam?"

"George told me what you did last year, and he is so

LAUREN SMITH

happy to meet your bride. You know how he feels about love."

"Indeed," Adam replied.

The king had been so in love with Maria that he had married her when he was underage. He was eventually forced to annul the marriage and unite himself with Princess Caroline of Brunswick, yet in his heart he'd always been loyal to Maria. Now that Caroline was dead, the king was living more freely in the open with Maria again.

When the dinner was over, the king relinquished Letty to Adam's care once more.

"Well done, Morrey, very well done. She's quite shy until one engages her, but then she flowers most beautifully. She's clever and brilliant, and if she weren't so clearly in love with you, I'd steal her from you."

Adam bowed to the king. "Thank you, Your Majesty." Adam felt some of the tension inside him ease now that his wife was by his side again.

Adam wondered if the king was right. Was she in love with him? He couldn't deny the stirrings in his own heart, but he dared not guess whether she felt the same. Indulging in those thoughts now might get them both killed if he were to become too distracted.

"You survived dinner with the king," Adam praised her.

Letty's brown eyes glimmered. "Did I?"

"You quite clearly won him over."

"It was rather frightening, to be honest, but Emily was so calm, and that made everything much easier. The conversation flowed quite freely, and I was glad to have a chance to speak."

Adam and Letty moved away from the guests still hovering about the dinner table. "And what did you talk to the king about?"

"Politics, mainly. You see, I believe—" Letty began, but her words died as Avery Russell walked past them abruptly, nearly knocking Letty over. He didn't stop, but kept moving, vanishing into the crowds.

"What the devil . . . ?" Adam was still looking at Avery's vanishing back when Letty slipped something discreetly into his palm. Recognizing the sleight of hand in play, he automatically tucked the slip of paper into his coat sleeve.

"Follow me." He escorted Letty into a small library off the main dining room. Once he checked to make sure they were alone, he removed the note and unfolded it.

They are looking for you both. Leave at once. Do not return to Chilgrave.

Adam cursed softly. Once he had relayed the message to his wife, he strode toward the fire and tossed the letter into the flames. Letty remained at his side, an anxious look marring her features.

"Adam, what are we to do?"

"Exactly what he says. Come, we'll get your cloak and have our coach brought round at once."

In a matter of minutes, Adam was lifting Letty inside the carriage. As he climbed in after her, he saw a footman's stare linger upon them too long before he turned and headed for the Carlton House stables.

It chilled Adam to the bone to know that even amongst the king's servants there were spies. And not the kind who protected the Crown.

CAMILLE SMILED AND FLUTTERED HER FAN AS SHE watched the English king laugh and hold court with his subjects. The man enjoyed hosting these simpering fools. No wonder her master wished to destroy him and all those who followed him. They dined while others starved. They laughed and danced, while only a few streets away women sold themselves to feed hungry babies and men worked themselves to death to feed their families.

"We must defeat the system from the inside out," her master had often said. *"We must bring it all down to build something better."*

The king approached Camille and offered her a rakishly charming grin. "Lady Halsey." The fool thought her to be English like all the rest. It was far too easy to act and speak like an English lady, and no one had ever questioned her pedigree, not when she acted so perfectly English.

"Your Majesty." She dipped into a curtsy, allowing the king to see her ample bosom in the dark-purple court gown she wore. It was so easy to distract men.

"A pretty widow. You have your pick of hearts to break tonight." The king laughed before moving on to greet the next guest.

Camille turned her attention back to a man with reddish-brown hair who wound his way lazily through the crowd. She saw him bump sharply into the very person Camille had come to find—the new Lady Morrey.

Camille flicked her fan up in front of her face to hide her shock as she saw the man holding on to Lady Morrey's arm. Lord Morrey, the hapless English aristocrat her master had so easily dismissed, was the man who'd foiled her attempt on Lady Edwards's life.

So . . . Lord Morrey is a spy. She gazed at the handsome Lord Morrey and recognized those gray eyes that had so captivated her when she'd glimpsed him briefly as he'd thrown himself between her and her target. He was as tall and well built as her master, an equal match. How had her master not known that this man was a spy? He was the farthest thing from a silly English dandy.

Camille noticed the slight adjustment Lord Morrey made to his sleeve a moment after his wife pressed her hand to his. The man was good, almost perfect, but she missed nothing. He'd received something from the red-haired man and had tucked it into his sleeve. A message.

If Lord Morrey had married Lord Pembroke's sister, it meant she truly was important, so important that Lord Morrey had offered her the protection of his body and his name permanently.

Now that Camille was certain of the woman's importance, she would be even more certain to end her life. Whatever advantage she brought to the English Home Office, Camille would see it erased. It would be difficult now that she knew Lord Morrey stood between her and her prey.

There was only one solution. They would have to be captured so that the information she required could be pried from them. And then they would be disposed of.

Camille motioned for a footman to come to her as Morrey and his wife left the room. The man was one of her agents who had gained employment in Carlton House.

"Yes, my lady?" the servant asked, hiding any hint of knowing her.

"Follow them. Take plenty of men with you. Once they are well away from London, you know what to do. Get me the information, and then take care of them. Make it look like a random attack."

The footman nodded before slipping away into the crowd. Camille returned to the party, smiling as she noticed the red-haired man's gaze sweep across the room, not pausing on her at all. She was as good at blending in as he was. She couldn't help but wonder, was this new spymaster, Avery Russell, the reason her master was acting overly cautious? And if so, she would have to learn all that she could about him.

❧ 11 ❧

Letty didn't like the tired, worn look in her husband's eyes. They'd returned to the town-house after the dinner at Carlton House this evening, and now Adam was seated at his desk, writing a few hasty letters while Mr. Helms and Mina packed their trunks again. Letty had changed out of her court gown into a blue velvet carriage dress for the long trip ahead.

"Where are we bound?" she asked Adam.

He finished writing a letter and rubbed the ink to blot it. "We're headed to my uncle's home."

"I wasn't aware you had any uncles."

"Just the one, and he's rather a character." Adam called Shelton, and the underbutler soon entered the study.

"Yes, my lord?"

"Take these. One is for Caroline and the other for Sturges. He is to deliver it to Mr. Walpole himself."

Shelton accepted the messages. "Of course, my lord. The luggage is packed, and the horses are ready to go, sir."

"Thank you." Adam stood and gently ushered Letty toward the door.

"Your cloak, my lady." Mina dropped a red velvet fur-lined cloak over Letty shoulders and gave her a matching muff to keep her hands warm.

"But, Mina, you aren't dressed to travel," Letty said in alarm. Her lady's maid glanced at Adam.

"Mr. Helms and I are to remain here, at his lordship's request."

She was to travel without a maid? She was to travel completely unattended? Was that even proper? Did she trust Adam enough to . . . Heavens, she had to, didn't she? They were married, after all, but she still didn't understand.

"Adam, why—?"

"I'll explain once we're on the road." Adam nodded at Mina and guided Letty toward the door. As she stepped up into their waiting conveyance, she glanced back at the London townhouse. She'd barely had time to become familiar with anything in her new married life. Not here and not at Chilgrave. Adam joined her a moment later and closed the coach door as he sat down.

Letty waited for him to explain, hands fisted in her skirts.

"I'm sorry to leave them behind, but it is safer. We will be traveling quickly, and it may be dangerous. The less we have to worry about and the less luggage we have, the faster we can travel. My uncle will have a maid to see to you when we reach Scotland."

"Scotland?" She'd only been to Edinburgh once when she was fourteen.

"Yes. My great-uncle Tyburn is my mother's uncle. He's quite young, close to my mother in age. They were very close growing up. He is a hardened Scotsman, but I think you will like him."

Letty leaned back in her seat to face him. "Adam, how bad is it?" She kept her voice calm, even though her heart was pounding.

"It isn't good. We were spotted at the king's dinner party. I had hoped to leave for Ireland, but under the circumstances, I'd rather get us safely to Tyburn's castle. He lives close to Ben Nevis, one of the tallest mountains in Scotland. We'll be safe there. French spies will be reluctant to brave the wilds of the north. The landscape is harsh and the people harsher, at least when it comes to strangers. The castle is even more of a fortress than Chilgrave."

Letty's head was spinning. This was no honeymoon —it was yet another desperate flight from danger. Fear settled in her belly, and it took a moment for her to speak. "Adam, will this ever be over? Will we ever be safe? I feel as though I might collapse."

Adam held her close against him. He brushed his lips over her forehead. "Rest, lady wife. Find sleep for a while."

Letty didn't think she could sleep, yet somehow she drifted off. When she woke sometime later, she was uncertain of how much time had passed. The coach had stopped, and she found herself alone.

"Adam?" Her heart leapt into a panicked rhythm as she pushed the coach door open.

Adam stood in the lamplight of a small coaching inn, his cloak billowing out behind him. She drew in a breath of relief at the sight of him.

"Are we stopping?" she asked, raising her voice a little.

Adam returned to the carriage. "Yes. It's been four hours. The horses need rest. We will spend the night and leave at dawn."

Letty studied the dark expanse above, which glittered with stars. "What time is it now?"

"After midnight." Adam caught her by the waist and set her on her feet, then escorted her inside. "Our luggage is already in our room." They climbed the creaky staircase to their room.

He took her straight to the warm fire in the fireplace and held her chilled hands close to it. Winter was coming early, it seemed. Adam removed his cloak and draped it over a chair. There was a polite knock, and he opened the door to admit a man carrying a tray of food and a pitcher of wine.

"Thank you, Mr. Bristow." Adam paid the man a handful of coins and locked the door. "Come eat, darling."

Adam set the tray of food on the table, and Letty eased into one of the chairs. Adam took the other. Mr. Bristow had brought roast beef, leek-and-onion soup, and wine, all of which was excellent. She was relieved to find that she and Adam could be together like this, not feeling the need for talk simply to fill the passing minutes. Not that she minded talking with him. She quite liked it, but it was nice to know she could have a companionable silence with him as well. Letty gazed in exhaustion at the fireplace a long while before she sensed Adam was watching her.

"Did you have enough to eat?" he asked.

Letty nodded. She'd perhaps eaten too much. She felt rather like a wild animal, uncertain of when shelter and food would come again.

Adam held out his hand and leaned forward in his chair. "Give me your foot."

"My foot?"

He chuckled at her reluctance. "Yes, your foot."

Letty extended one booted foot. Her suspicion must've shown, because he laughed even louder.

"Oh, my darling, you are quite precious in your skepticism." He caught her foot and set it on his lap, then unlaced her boot. He slid the boot off and took her foot in both of his hands and began to massage it. The sudden pleasurable touch melted every bone in Letty's body.

"Is that something they teach at the academy for spies?" she asked.

Adam had a wolfish grin on his lips, which sent flutterings deep in her belly. "No, this I learned a long time ago from a friend."

Letty briefly closed her eyes but soon opened them again. "Do you mean one of your mistresses?"

"Yes, but she was also a friend."

"Well, I send her my thanks. This is quite wonderful." Letty closed her eyes again and couldn't help but moan as Adam's strong fingers pressed into her tender foot, the tips of her toes, her ankle, and the arch of her foot in the most splendid way. She wondered what else he could do with those hands, where else he might put them upon her.

"Now, your other foot," he said.

Letty placed her other foot in his lap without hesitation, and he repeated the ceremony for her.

"I feel quite certain I would do anything for you just now, my lord," Letty said drowsily.

Adam chuckled. "I shall remember that. But for now, it's time for you to be in bed."

Letty grumbled a little as he removed her feet from his lap. She walked toward the bed.

"Lady wife." Amusement filled those two words.

She yawned. "Yes?"

"You are still dressed."

She glanced down at her gown and nearly groaned. She so desperately wanted to sleep.

"Here, allow me to assist you." Adam came up behind her and started to undo the tiny buttons down the back of her gown with an experienced deftness no doubt also acquired from his previous mistresses. For this, too, she was grateful. Within moments, her gown gaped at the back, and she was able to slide it off with ease and let it drop to the floor. She turned toward him and sat on the edge of the bed as he bent, lifted her chemise, and next removed her stockings.

"Adam, you must think me quite a silly, useless creature," Letty sighed.

He pulled the covers on the bed back, and she slid beneath them.

"Why would I think that?" He started to remove his own clothing.

"Because I cannot seem to stay awake like you can." She burrowed deeper under the blankets and watched her husband bare his beautiful, muscled body.

"My dear, you've been through quite a lot these last few days. Indeed, more than most men could handle. It would be well within your rights to dissolve into hysterics after this nightmare of a honeymoon. Hell, *I* might dissolve into hysterics if *you* don't."

The thought made her giggle.

Down to his smallclothes now, Adam joined her under the covers. She slid toward him, feeling more awake now as she realized that perhaps tonight he would finally claim her as a husband would his wife.

She rested her cheek against his chest, the heat of him emanating through to her and his heartbeat steady and slow. "Adam?"

He rubbed her arm, slow and soothing. "Yes?"

"I'm too tired to fall asleep. Will you tell me about your uncle?"

"Of course." His hand moved to her hair, stroking it.

"Is he frightening?"

"Frightening?" Her husband sounded confused.

"Yes, he is a Highlander? I hear some of them in the far north are still quite brutish."

"He isn't frightening, but he is fierce. Show no fear when you meet him, and he will love you in an instant."

"Will he?"

"I promise."

"What else can you tell me about him?"

"He has two sons close to my age. Angus and Baird. They resemble him in their height and brawn, but they have their mother's attractive features.

"Your uncle is married?"

"He was. His wife, Bonnie, died a few years after Baird was born. She was Tyburn's great love, and he never married again, though many a Scottish lass has wanted to be in his heart—and in his bed."

"You visit them often in the Highlands?"

"Not often enough. Caroline and I quite adore Uncle Tyburn. I hope you will too. We could visit him often if you do."

Adam rolled onto his side to face her. The candles on the bedside table created enough light to illuminate the outline of his body, making him look more of a shadow lover than a man of flesh and blood.

"Adam, I do not think I am so overly tired now. If you wish to . . ." She couldn't say the rest of the words.

"If I wish to what, my darling?" Adam's white teeth gleamed in the dim light as he smiled at her. It made her tremble with that balance of fear and anticipation.

"You know . . ."

"Say it. You must say *exactly* what you wish me to do." He brushed her hair back from her face. The gesture was so tender, yet so at odds with the intensity of his eyes.

Letty was so aware of his strength then, of the massive width of his shoulders, of how easily this man could do whatever he wished with her and how she would be powerless to stop him.

"I wish for you to . . . bed me." She was glad for the shadows that hid the wild blush on her face.

Without a word, he leaned in and kissed her. She fell onto her back as he moved partially over her. He took his time kissing her softly, and she delighted in the way his kisses created a fever beneath her skin. He unfastened the laces of her chemise and teasingly loosened the top so he could pull it down off her shoulders. He pressed loving kisses to each shoulder, then kissed her collarbones. She arched and gasped as he finally tugged the fabric farther down, exposing her breasts.

He fastened his lips over one nipple, sucking on it until she clawed her hands in his dark hair and writhed. Waves of heat moved from her head to her toes as she tried to focus on the sensation of his mouth at her breast, but she couldn't help but notice that his other hand was creeping up her inner thighs.

"Your skin is so soft," he said as he focused his attention on her other breast. As he sucked, he slid two fingers between her folds and drove deep into her. She squeaked in surprise as her hips shot off the bed.

He paused to look up at her. "Did I hurt you?"

She shook her head. "No, no. It just feels . . . like too much," she confessed.

"Ah, but there are better things still to come," he promised as he bent his head to her breasts again.

Her shaky legs parted for him, and he pushed the covers back on the bed, moving his body down so that he knelt between her thighs.

"Adam, I don't know if . . ."

"Hush, love. You must trust me." He lowered his face to her belly and kissed a path down to her mound. It so shocked her that all she could do was inhale sharply as he reached the hidden pearl at the top of her mound. He looked up at her then, their eyes meeting. "This, too, I learned from an old friend." His chuckle caressed her for but a second before he sucked it between his lips.

An explosion rocked through her, sudden and violent, so much so that she could do nothing but gulp for breath as he licked and sucked at that part of her body. As the sudden climax began to give way, she became aware of his mouth still on her mound, his tongue playing with her in the most sinful way.

"There," he said as he sat up a little. "You are relaxed, are you not?"

"I may never leave this bed," she sighed dreamily.

Adam gently gripped her thighs and pushed them wide as he settled between them and kissed her again, their bodies pressed chest to chest now. The weight of him was surprising, but welcome. She felt strangely safe with his body cradled by hers, yet the hard press of his shaft so close to her core was a little frightening as well. Such a curious thing, she thought, to feel so excited and afraid at the same time.

"I'm sorry, my darling," he said against her lips as he shifted himself closer to her and his shaft now pressed just at the edge of her folds.

"For what?" she asked a second before he drove into

her. Her twitching inner walls vibrated with panic as he breached her maidenhead. She cried out, digging her nails into his shoulder and biting her lip.

"Relax, my darling. Let your body adjust." He held still, and she felt too full of him, of everything. It was almost hard to breathe.

"Is that the worst of it?"

"Yes, but when I move in a moment it may sting. I'm sorry if it does." He sounded like he meant it, that he hated hurting her. Something stirred in her chest, something wonderful and full of light at the thought.

Letty tensed as he started to move. He cursed and stilled.

"Letty, sweetheart, if you do not relax, I won't be able to move."

"I don't know how," she admitted, then looked away in embarrassment.

Adam's lips came down on hers, kissing her, nibbling at her playfully until she started to giggle and her legs widened and her inner muscles eased their rigid tension.

Now when he began to move, it stung, but not so terribly as she expected. She felt oddly empty as he left her body, but as he drove into her again, his shaft now much like the arrow she'd been warned of, seemed to strike at the heart of her. How was that even possible?

He thrust over and over, the stinging fading away to something else entirely. Her lashes fluttered closed, but Adam commanded her to open her eyes.

"I want to see that sweet fire in your eyes as I take you," he growled. His domination of her in that moment took her to a frightening new peak. This . . . *this* was the thing he'd been trying to tell her about. The secret battle of wills and pleasures that was sacred between two lovers. It was not something words could ever describe. It was dozens of complex emotions woven into a tapestry of pleasure, domination, and surrender. Of trust on both sides.

In some wild and wondrous way, she was both fully present with him, their flesh becoming one, yet also lost in some land where a shadowy lord claimed her as his own. Adam was both of these male presences, and she was fascinated, addicted to it, and to him.

He drove into her harder, his hips flexing as she moved her hands down his shoulders to his buttocks, gripping him, feeling his raw power as he filled her over and over.

Now she was the one in control as she gazed up at him and thrust her hips up, crashing them together more fiercely. Then something miraculous happened— that blinding pleasure hit her at the same instant it hit him.

He roared her name hard enough that the walls shook. He grew rigid, the tendons in his neck standing out as he gave himself up inside her. She felt him, wet, hot, filling her. They clung to each other in the after-math, their bodies quaking.

Adam relaxed into her, his weight heavy but not unwelcome. Sweat dewed upon their bodies, and the chilled air of the inn began to cool them. He stirred long enough to pull the covers back up over them, but he remained inside her. He was not as hard as before, which left Letty curious, but she would ask him later to explain the mysteries of the male body.

"Now, I have finally claimed you." Adam let out a rough chuckle before he kissed her temple and rolled them both over so they still lay fused together on their sides, facing each other.

"Perhaps it is I who have claimed you?" she replied, feeling her body still twitching around his. A thought occurred to her that at first brought joy, then fear.

Adam brushed the backs of his knuckles over her cheek. "What is it?"

"What if . . . What if I have a child from this night?"

Hurt darkened his stormy eyes. "You do not want my child?"

"I do, but I worry about its safety. We cannot run forever, not if we want to raise a child."

Comprehension lit his eyes. "I wish I could say I would've pulled out of you and spilled my seed upon the sheets, but I don't think the devil himself could've stopped me tonight. For that, I am sorry. I can only promise that if we have a child, I will protect it with all that I am, just as I will with you."

His vow should have made her feel safe, but it didn't

erase the knowledge that they were still in danger, that any child she might carry may also face that danger. Letty burrowed closer to Adam. Her fear for the future would rob her of any decent sleep she might have before dawn.

❦ 12 ❦

Adam awoke as dawn crested the horizon. He tended to wake up exactly when he needed to, no matter how tired he was. It took him a moment to orient himself and remember why he was still holding a mostly naked woman—correction, his *wife* —in his arms. Her chemise was scrunched up around her waist, her lovely breasts on full display.

Adam pushed the covers off as he sat up and dragged his hands through his hair. Letty's virgin blood was on his shaft and thighs. He winced. He should have been tender and slow with her, not like a rutting stag. He had lost himself in her last night in a way he never had before. Deep down he had known it would be like this, that first moment he met her. It was as though part of him had recognized its other half, the part that would make him whole once more. Ever since he'd lost John, he hadn't been himself. Being with Letty was allowing him to recapture that joyous part of himself, the part that thrilled at being alive, and being in love.

She didn't know yet that what they had shared last night was extraordinary. It was truly a gift. Thoughts of their incredible joining soon led to thoughts of its possible consequences, such as a child. He had to find whoever was after Letty and put an end to the threat by any means necessary. He would not have any child of theirs put in danger.

With great reluctance, he dressed and woke his wife. She rubbed her eyes, stretched, and blinked against the pale morning light.

"Adam? Where . . . ? Oh." She realized then that she was naked and pulled the covers up over her breasts, her cheeks deepening to a rosy hue.

"Good morning." He sat down on the edge of the bed and cupped her cheek, unable to stop grinning. "How do you feel? Are you sore?"

"Sore?" She tensed and then nodded. "A little. Oh heavens, I'm so embarrassed." She tried to pull the covers over her head like a child. Adam laughed as he pulled them back down to see her face.

"You were magnificent last night. The best I've ever had," he promised her.

Her eyes grew round. "Truly? The best?"

"Most certainly." Adam wanted to tell her that the previous night had been more than he had ever dreamed, that it had been magical, but he was afraid such words would make him sound like a foppish schoolboy. "You'll have time to rest in the coach today. We have a long journey ahead of us."

Thankfully, a coach wasn't the best place to make love. He had done it in the past, but it was far from comfortable. The jarring of the road and the sudden unexpected dips in the holes were quite disruptive to moments of passion. Besides, she needed time to heal before he made love to her again.

"I'll see to the horses and check on our driver while you dress."

Adam left her to give her time to adjust. He imagined it might be a little jarring for her to wake no longer a virgin, with the remnants of her blood upon her thighs. He should've cleaned her last night, but they had been too tired to do much else but collapse. Now she would have some time to herself to adjust and prepare for the day.

The horses and the driver were made ready, and he returned to find Letty finishing the buttons on a day gown that she needed no assistance to put on. It seemed Mina had packed her bags wisely, with gowns that left Letty able to care for herself. He had hated leaving Helms and Mina behind, but it was safer for the two of them to travel alone.

He leaned against the doorway, watching her finish the last button on her gown, lost for a moment simply relishing that this woman was *his*. Even though they had been brought together under terrible circumstances, he was content. No, more than content—he was happy.

"Are you ready?"

"Yes." She gathered her long hair at the nape of her neck and tied it up with a rose-colored ribbon that matched her gown. She looked so much younger with her hair styled like that. More like a girl of sixteen than a married lady of twenty. It only increased his urge to protect her. She started to lift her valise, but he gently nudged her aside and carried it along with his own down to the coach.

The ride north took another two days as they left England behind. At night, they collapsed into bed at an inn, and despite Adam's desire, he didn't have the heart to stir Letty awake simply to satisfy his lust. Instead, he held her in his arms, whispering to her about his life, and she whispered back—sharing of themselves in matters of the heart and mind rather than their bodies. He grew closer to her, reveling in each moment that his wife opened her heart to him.

Letty was a woman who believed in love, the kind that made poets dream and lovers sigh. Yet she was not a silly girl with nonsense in her head. She was a true romantic, but he could tell she had tempered that longing for love some time ago, holding her deepest dreams within. He understood, in a way. The marriage mart was not always seen as a place for love. The very name announced the mercantile or even mercenary intentions some went into marriage with. It wasn't a place where love matches came often. Perhaps that was why she had passed two seasons without a marriage proposal.

As he watched her sleep in his arms, he brushed his fingertips over the curve of her nose and the winged arches of her eyebrows.

"Love will find a way through paths where wolves fear to prey."

She stirred at his recitation of Lord Byron's words but didn't wake. Adam continued.

"I have great hopes that we shall love each other all our lives as much as if we had never married at all."

"Adam?" she asked, her eyes still closed.

"Yes?"

"I do so like Byron. Do not stop." She moved a hand to rest above his heart, and something sweet and pure caught his breath as he held still. "Please."

"Heart on her lips, and soul within her eyes. Soft as her clime, and sunny as her skies."

She sighed dreamily. "I like that one. Tell me another."

"You are you and I was I; we were two, before our time. I was yours, before I knew; and you have always been mine too."

He thought back to the day when she'd first come to see him, to seek answers about Gillian. He had been struck by her then, and not simply for her beauty. There had been something else, as though she was a piece of him that had long ago been parted and had only just in that moment been brought together.

She had looked upon him with the same baffled recognition, but he had done nothing. He had been polite and kept his distance. Love and marriage did not belong upon a path to vengeance.

Adam settled back in the bed, resting his head upon the pillow as he watched the moonlight sweep over the room before the clouds covered it and drowned them in darkness.

I HAD A DREAM, WHICH WAS NOT ALL A DREAM.
  The bright sun was extinguished, and the stars
  Did wander darkling in the eternal space,
  Rayless, and pathless, and the icy earth
  Swung blind and blackening in the moonless air;
  Morn came and went—and came, and brought no day.

HIS HEART HAD BEEN CLOAKED IN A STARLESS SKY, BUT Letty shone through the heavy clouds, burning away at his harsh need for revenge. He could not hold on to his anger and hate, not when this woman held love out to him.

Someday he would face a choice—her or his duty.

By the third day, Letty was thoroughly sick of being in a coach.

"May we stop and stretch our legs soon, Adam? I am going mad being trapped for so long in here."

Adam nodded. He opened the coach window and told their driver to stop at the next inn which wasn't far. They were traveling roads that were familiar to him now, and Letty was grateful that he knew what stops they would be coming to soon.

"It won't be long. We'll have an early dinner at the Crown and Thistle."

Letty laid her head back on Adam's shoulder. She replayed the previous night in her mind, a small, secret smile hovering about her lips. To discover that her husband was a romantic at heart, that poetry moved his soul as it did her own, was a true joy. But it was possible he wasn't a man who enjoyed reading. Most rakes memorized bits of poetry to impress ladies; perhaps Adam knew only a few artful lines, rather than being a devoted reader.

"Adam, are you a great reader, or a man who prefers only sports and activities out-of-doors?" She considered herself rather balanced, enjoying the physical pleasures of riding, walking, and even fishing, though certainly not the part of baiting hooks. She also enjoyed reading books on a great number of subjects. She was not quite a bluestocking, at least compared to some of her friends.

"I enjoy both," Adam answered. "You did not have a chance to spend much time in Chilgrave's library, but when we return, I will show you."

"I would like that."

"We will be at Tyburn's home this night, and he has a decent library as well."

Letty lost herself in daydreams of the wild Scottish wilderness, of her and Adam riding across the heather-covered hills.

The coach stopped at the Crown and Thistle just after dark.

"Let's go inside and have a bit to eat." Adam instructed their driver to rest the horses. "We can stay an hour or so and then continue on our way."

They entered the small inn and found most of the tables were full of men and women, a few eating and drinking despite the early hour.

"Wait here. Let me see if I can arrange a private dining room for us." Most coaching inns had several rooms strictly for married couples dining alone, since gentle-born people usually did not sit down to dine amongst the lower classes. Letty honestly did not mind either way, but Adam had strode away so quickly that she could not call him back without drawing attention to herself. She already felt a bit on edge once they'd entered Scotland, knowing that the English were unwelcome, especially this far north. The last thing she wanted to do was draw the focus of a roomful of burly Scots.

Adam leaned against the bar and spoke with the innkeeper while Letty stayed put close to the door. The door opened, and several men came in. Pressed against the wall as she was, the men did not see her. They scanned the large taproom before their focus halted on one person—her husband.

Every muscle tensed as she feared they would turn and see her next. These men were here for her and Adam—they had to be. The group of men, seven in total, began to speak softly with English accents rather than Scottish. They chose one of the few empty tables left in the room. Adam turned and came toward her, surprisingly relaxed. Surely he wouldn't be that calm if he had seen them.

"This way, my darling. There's a room at the back for us." He escorted her past the table of men, with his arm around her shoulders. Letty kept her chin steady, her eyes straight ahead. The second she and Adam were alone, she would tell him what she had seen. They entered a small room with a table and two chairs, which would have been cozy if it weren't for their current circumstances.

"Adam—" she began.

He held a finger to his lips as he locked the door. "Yes, this will be lovely, a nice quiet dinner," Adam said as if everything was fine, but he lifted one of the chairs and wedged it back under the latch. "I know you must be tired from all our travels," Adam continued as he went to the window and eased it open. Then he motioned for her to come over.

"This way," he whispered urgently, just as someone knocked loudly at the door to their room. "I'll boost you. Get outside and wait for me." Adam paused, a sudden fear in his eyes. "If we become separated, steal a horse and ride north on this road. It will take you straight to my uncle's land."

"No!" Letty's eyes burned. She was not going to leave him. The door thudded as something hard collided with it from the other side. Adam braced himself against the chair that held the door shut.

"There's no time to debate this. Go, now!" Adam hissed.

"I cannot leave you." Something inside her, something black and full of despair, feared that she might lose him forever.

"I'm not asking. I am ordering. You swore to me in that meadow by Chilgrave that you would do what I said when it matters. This is one of those times. Now go!" He nodded at the window as the door rumbled behind him with another resounding impact.

"And leave you to die? I made a vow too, not to part with you until death."

"And what if you are carrying a life within you, a life

we created? You must put that life above mine. Do you understand?"

Letty's hands went to her abdomen. She didn't know if she was pregnant or not, but he was right—if there was even a chance, that life had to come above all else. It was a choice she had never imagined making—Adam or the child she might be carrying.

"*Please*," Adam begged as another impact against the door shook him.

She rushed to him, kissing him fast and hard as she whispered, "I love you." Then she dashed to the window and scrambled through it, dropping to the ground. Almost instantly, hands seized her, one clamping over her mouth.

"Got her!" someone snarled in triumph. Letty screamed against the gloved hand before she was shoved facedown into the earth and the weight of a body crushed her back.

"Bind her hands," someone snapped.

She felt rope wrap around her wrists, but rather than struggle, Letty stopped fighting and went still. Her sudden lack of movement momentarily confused the men who'd grabbed her.

"You crushed her, you fool. We need information first."

The weight holding her body down vanished. The sound of men scuffling behind her told her that now was the time to run. She surged to her feet and dashed for the stables a few yards away. The door was open, and she rushed inside. The coach driver was sitting up in a corner, eyes closed as he rested with their horses.

"Mr. Marin?" She seized his shoulder and tried to rouse him, but Mr. Marin's head fell back, exposing that his throat had been slit from ear to ear. The dark-blue cloth of his coat had hidden the blood that now coated her hand. His body slumped sideways and fell to the ground with a thud. Letty tripped as she backed up a step and fell on her backside. She stared at the lifeless body. An innocent man had died because of her and Adam.

"Check the stables!" a voice growled from nearby.

Letty leapt to her feet and searched for a hiding place. She climbed up the ladder to the loft, even though she was sure they would check there. One of the flat beams stretched across the middle of the barn just above the loft space. She hoisted herself up and scooted along the massive beam. She was just small enough that if she tucked her dress and cloak tight about her and pinned her arms on either side, she might go unseen from below. She closed her eyes as sounds warned her that the men were searching for her.

"She has to be here. She has nowhere else to go," one of the men said.

"She's not."

"Check the loft and every stall."

Horses huffed and shifted in their stalls as the men

tore through the stables. The ladder leading up to the loft creaked, and Letty held her breath. Her heart pounded loud enough in her ears that she almost couldn't hear any other sound beyond it.

Keeping her balance on the beam, she dared not open her eyes, lest they see them glimmering in the dark from below. Hay rustled and boards groaned beneath the weight of a man just a few feet below her. She could smell him, a hint of gunpowder and sweat. Her nose tingled, threatening a sneeze.

"Come on down from there, Jordan. She ain't there. We've got him. He'll know where she ran off to."

Relief swamped Letty at these words. Adam was still alive. And as long as he was, she wouldn't give up. She had to get down and steal a horse to find Uncle Tyburn and his sons.

I will save you, Adam. Hold on.

The two men searched the stables once more before leaving. Letty stayed still, counting until she felt several minutes had passed before she dared to move. It was far more difficult getting down from the beam than it had been getting up, but she managed to land on a pile of hay with only a small thump. She waited again, ears straining for any sounds of men nearby. She searched the shadows but saw only horses poking their heads out of the stalls.

She chose a small horse, one that looked young and fast. She stroked her hand down its nose. It flared its nostrils and eyed her with defiance before tossing its head.

"You won't let them catch us, will you?" she asked.

The beast, a dark-brown horse with a white stripe down the length of his nose, huffed as though offended by the question. Letty retrieved a bridle from the peg on his stall and fitted it to the horse. Then she slipped inside and saddled him.

She guided the horse out of the stall and mounted him. The stable door was still wide open, and she didn't want to take a chance of being grabbed if she walked the horse out before getting on its back.

She leaned over the horse's neck and whispered, "Run, my darling, *run!*" She kicked his flanks, and the horse shot through the door and barreled into the woods skirting the road.

"There she is!"

Letty hissed a curse that would have made Adam blush. She kicked her heels into her horse's flanks and bent low over the beast. The road was close, and as soon as she reached it, she gave her horse more rein, allowing him to run even faster. The thunder of pursuing hooves behind her was like the rumble of a distant and terrifying storm. If they caught up with her, all would be lost.

Letty studied the road ahead, afraid that her horse would stumble and roll, but she couldn't slow now, not for anything.

She chanced one look back and saw at least two men on massive horses behind her. Those brutes could keep up with her on an open road, but perhaps not in the woods. It would be a risk to stray from the path on terrain she wasn't familiar with, but what choice did she have?

"Hyah!" She slapped the loose reins against the horse's sides as she veered sharply toward the woods on the right of the road.

The dense Scottish forest offered a dark and dangerous path, but Letty and her horse were small and quick. They dodged clumps of thistle bushes and skirted heavy copses of trees. One of the riders got close, his horse heaving alongside hers. Letty's horse turned and snapped at the bigger horse's neck, the sound so vicious that it made an audible snap.

"You little—" The man reached for Letty's arm, but his horse screamed and pulled away.

There was a *crack* as something struck her arm. Letty flinched but didn't take her eyes off the wooded trail.

"Don't slow," she told the horse, hoping that somehow he could understand her.

The woods swallowed up the man behind her, but she didn't slow, didn't stop, didn't look back. She sent out a prayer to any magic that might still linger in the woods that she needed help.

Show me the way to Tyburn's land.

Moonlight seemed to illuminate the path ahead, and Letty swore it must be her terror and exhaustion blending into each other because she strangely trusted the light and let her horse follow it.

The woods eventually thinned and soon stopped

altogether. Now it was only open land before her. In the distance, the mighty, dark shape of a mountain was black against the moonlit sky.

It's Ben Nevis.

Between her and the mountain was a dark stone castle. The horse made it halfway down the drive to the castle before he slowed and stopped. His sides heaved, and foam frothed at his mouth as he struggled to catch his breath. Letty slid out of the saddle. Her numb legs threatened to give out beneath her. She leaned against the horse, tears streaming down her face.

"You did it, my darling thing—you did it." She hugged his neck, soothing the beast until he began to calm.

"I must go on without you." She kissed the stripe on his nose before she raised her skirts and ran toward the distant castle.

Her lungs burned, and her feet felt like shards of glass had pierced the bottoms of her boots, but she didn't stop. She ran up the steps of the castle and pounded her fists against the door.

"Help!" she screamed. "I need help! Please!"

The door opened beneath her fists, and she tumbled inside.

"Ach, what the devil?" the man grumbled. "Some mad *Sassenach* screaming her bloody head off. Ye'll be raising the dead next."

Letty struggled to her feet, her eyes adjusting in the dim light.

"Please . . . my husband. Need Tyburn."

The tall man with reddish-brown hair stared at her. "Ye need Tyburn?"

She nodded. "Adam . . . my husband . . . captured . . ." She was breathing faster now, and her head felt lighter. "Said to . . . find Tyburn . . ."

"Adam Beaumont is yer husband?" the man asked.

"Y—yes." She wobbled, and the man caught her by the arm to steady her, causing her to screech as pain blossomed in her left arm.

"Christ, lass, ye are bleeding." The man held up one of his hands. It was soaked in blood.

"Oh . . ." She slumped to the ground and lost consciousness.

Some time later, Letty became aware of voices arguing. She opened her eyes, finding three brooding Scotsmen peering down at her. The face in the middle had hair streaked with silver and more lines around his eyes and mouth.

"Uncle Tyburn?" she asked, her voice cracking.

"Aye, I'm Tyburn. Who are ye, lassie? Angus said ye mentioned my nephew, Adam."

"He's my husband." She tried to sit up on the couch she lay on, and Tyburn pushed her back down.

"Husband?" Tyburn exchanged looks with his two sons. "What happened to ye? Ye are bleeding. Looks like a scratch, thank God." He nodded at her arm. She glanced down in a daze to see that her gown's sleeve had been cut off and her upper arm had been lightly bandaged.

"We were coming to you. Adam thought it would be safe, but they found us. Attacked us at the inn . . . Adam told me to escape. Dear God, we don't have any time. They'll kill him!"

"Who?" Tyburn demanded, a dark gleam in his silver eyes.

"We haven't the time. We must go back and rescue him." She started to rise.

"Ye are no' going anywhere, lass," Tyburn said. "Ye lost a bit of blood, and ye canna even stand on your feet."

Something inside Letty began to burn, an inner fire that was too hot to control. "I'm going back, and you all are coming with me. Now get me my bloody horse!" she shouted.

The three men stared at her for the span of a heartbeat before they leapt into action. The one named Angus rushed from the room, and the other two helped her to her feet.

"Which inn was it, now?" Tyburn asked as they walked toward the entryway.

"The Crown and Thistle. The men who took him were English. There were at least six of them, maybe more."

The younger man, Baird, grinned. "It's been a while since I've crushed a few *Sassenach* skulls—no offense intended, milady." He offered her a charming, bashful smile after his rather bloody statement.

"None taken. That is precisely what I expect you to do." She winced as they stopped on the stairs. Angus came riding into view with three horses behind him.

"Ye are certain ye can keep up?" Tyburn asked her. "There is no shame in staying here. Ye are injured. That was no mere scratch you took getting here. It looks like ye were shot, but the bullet grazed ye."

She looked up into the older Scotsman's face. "Adam sacrificed himself for me. When I left, he was still alive, and I will not leave him. Not after . . ." The most important words she had ever wanted to say turned into a sob, which she choked down. She straightened her shoulders. "We must ride—*now*."

"I dinna know who ye are, lass, but I already like ye." Tyburn gave her uninjured arm a gentle squeeze and helped her mount her horse. He was a large, fierce creature with a dusting of feathered hairs on his hooves.

"Is he fast?" she asked Angus.

"Aye, milady, fast and mean. Ye'll be safe atop him. He'll hold up a mite better than the one ye rode in on. That poor beast is resting in the stables."

She didn't care about being safe, only that he could rival the wind in speed. Tyburn and his sons leapt into motion, and she followed behind.

Please hold on, Adam. We're coming.

⚜

ADAM HELD THE DOOR AS LONG AS HE COULD, BUT THE moment Letty vanished over the windowsill, the intruders crashed through the door, busting the latch right off. He leapt for the window, but he was dragged back into the room. He allowed his body to go limp, and the men who held him stumbled with his sudden weight. For a brief second, he was free. He rolled up onto his feet and struck out at the nearest man with a punch that would have felled even the fearsome Lord Lonsdale. Adam spun to deal with the other man in a similar fashion, but he stopped short when he saw the pistol in the man's hand.

Never in his life had he felt more the fool. He was so far north in Scotland, he had dared to relax his guard. He'd assumed they would be safe this close to Tyburn's land, and he'd left his pistol in their coach. All he had was a small, flat blade tucked in his boot, too far out of reach.

"No sudden moves, eh?" the man warned.

Adam stared at him, not saying a word. The man he'd hit slowly came around as two more men entered the room. None of them held Letty captive, however, so he could only pray that she'd escaped. He studied the men, assessing whether he might be able to take them all on at the right time. They weren't hired men from rookeries, not entirely. Those men usually tended to be unshaven, gruff, and the smell that came off them would be enough to subdue a man on its own. These men were clean shaven, decently dressed, and were certainly doing well enough in their current line of work to look as they did. That meant whoever they worked for was successful too.

"The woman escaped. Jordan and Derek are searching the stables. She can't have gotten far."

The face of the man who spoke was familiar, but it took Adam a moment to recognize him. With his tall build, light-brown hair, square jaw, and deep-set eyes . . .

"I remember you," he told the man. "Carlton House. Dressed as a footman. Whose lapdog are you?"

The man's black eyes hardened. He flexed his hands menacingly. "Take him to the stables and string him up."

Adam decided to see what sort of men he was dealing with. "You would dare do that to me? I am a peer of the realm, the Earl of Morrey."

The faux footman looked aghast. "My humble apologies, sir. String him up *politely*, lads." None of the men seemed intimidated, so they all knew what kind of business they found themselves in, which didn't bode well for Adam.

Two of the men grabbed Adam by the arms and hauled him through the back door of the inn and out into the night. Luck had abandoned him. If he had been taken through the main taproom, he could have called for those loyal to Tyburn to come to his aid.

Another man rushed out of the barn. "Gent, the woman rode out on a horse a few minutes ago. Sayer and Marley went after her."

"Good, they'll catch her," Gent said.

Adam burned Gent's face into his memory. Though he was clearly in charge, he worked for another. Adam was left with little time to puzzle out who, however, as he was shoved against one of the wooden posts inside the barn, his coat and shirt ripped from him so he was bare from the chest up. His hands were bound, and the rope was tossed over a beam above his head and pulled tight, stretching him up until he was forced to stand on the tip of his toes. Pain lanced down his body, but he held his scream deep inside.

One of the men pulled a coiled whip off a nail on a nearby post, and Adam closed his eyes. This wasn't going to be easy. But he would hold his tongue for king, country, and most importantly, Letty.

"I don't expect you to tell me where she went," Gent said with a casual menace. "You'll need some convincing first." Gent nodded at the man behind Adam who held the whip.

"Five lashes to start," he ordered.

Adam allowed his body to relax, knowing that any tension in his muscles would only add to the pain. It didn't make the moment any less brutal when he heard the whip whistle through the air a split second before it struck his back. He hissed and arched in pain, waiting for the next strike. The blows seemed to last forever. When the man finally stopped, Adam's mind had grown foggy with pain.

"Now—I think you are ready for some questions." Gent grabbed Adam's head by his hair and jerked his face up from where he'd let it drop against the beam to rest.

Adam blinked, trying to master the pain radiating through him.

"Where's the woman?" Gent asked.

Letty's face appeared so clearly in his mind that it shocked him back into a stronger mental state. He would not yield, not if her life depended on him.

"We won't leave much of a corpse behind for anyone to find if you don't talk, and we'll still get the information we want. Now where's the woman?"

Adam blinked again. Pain radiated from his back in heavy waves. They would probably flay him open by the end. But he tried not to think about that; he forced his mind onto Letty. She must be on Tyburn's land by now, if she had stayed near the road. He prayed she was safe. So long as the men who'd gone after her didn't return triumphant, he could hold out hope.

"I do like it when someone makes it hard to get what I want." Gent's cold smile made Adam's stomach turn.

"Another five lashes. Pain is a special friend of mine." The whip cracked even before Gent finished speaking.

Adam shouted with each blow. The men took turns whipping him, but Gent's frustration was beginning to mount. Adam could see him pacing the length of the barn, growling at his men to strike harder, before finally, annoyed, he called a halt to the lashing. Gent produced a knife and made sure that Adam saw it.

"I warned you." It was all he said before he started carving small lines in Adam's back. Adam hadn't been ready for that. He cried out at the pain. At some point, a flask was pressed to his lips. He tried to turn his head away.

"It's brandy. Drink," Gent commanded. "Drink, or it goes on your back."

Brandy. God, I could use that. He drank deeply until the flask was pulled away.

Adam had always been strong, even as a boy, but this was a hell unlike anything he'd experienced before. It was even harder not to think, to blink past the stinging sweat that poured into his eyes. He sagged in his bonds as time seemed to speed away, leaving him in a hellish purgatory as he languished against the post.

Suddenly, a sweet voice intruded upon his listless, drifting thoughts.

"My love . . ." The sweet voice spoke in his ear. "You're safe now."

"Letty," he breathed, hope fluttering weakly. "How . . . ?"

"I created a distraction, let loose their horses. I snuck into the barn to save you. It's all right now. Tell me where we can go to be safe," she pleaded.

His words slurred, and he tried to open his eyes but couldn't. "Not . . . here. Can't . . ." Why couldn't he open his eyes?

"Where can we go to be safe? I can't go on without you. They'll be back any minute. Tell me where I should go."

"Letty . . ."

"Yes?"

He saw her face in his mind, and then he heard his words. "You swore to me that you would do as I said when it matters." *Why did she come back?* "You shouldn't be here."

"But I don't know where to go. Tell me where I should go. Tell me." There was an edge to Letty's voice now. Something felt off.

He struggled to open his eyes again. His lashes fluttered, and he saw the face close to his was not his wife's, but a different young woman. The maid who had been serving drinks at the inn. Fire surged through his veins, and his muscles fluttered. Fear and rage rose within him, tempered only by the drug-addled confusion from the brandy. This wasn't Letty. He wouldn't speak, wouldn't say a word.

"Ask him again." Gent's voice cut through Adam's still-scattered thoughts. The girl caressed Adam's cheek.

"Please, husband, tell me where to go so I can be safe—"

"Gent, this isn't working," someone snapped.

The maid was shoved away. "Take the lass back inside and see that she doesn't tell anyone about this."

Gent loomed large before Adam. Adam stared back at him, quivering with pain and rage as Gent assessed him. Gent finally shrugged and looked at the other men nearby awaiting orders.

"We don't need him anyway. He's only a guardian. We'll find the woman's location some other way. Take him into the woods and finish him."

The rope around Adam's wrists was loosened, and he collapsed, his knees hitting the hay-strewn floor of the stables. Hands jerked him up and dragged him out into the chilly night. The cold Scottish breeze drifted into his face, making him more alert than he had been before. Soon he was released, his body hitting the ground.

"He'll be eaten by scavengers before anyone finds him," one of the men carrying him said with a dark chuckle.

"Still, take no chances. Cut his throat."

A foot pressed down on Adam's back, digging into his wounds. He cried out as the pain finally overtook him, only to hear the sound of an ancient Highland war cry, far enough away that it was perhaps more wind and imagination than reality.

She found him. Tyburn. Adam let go, knowing that Letty must be safe. She had a fire that burned in her, and if he believed in nothing else, he believed in that, believed in *her*.

⁂

LETTY FOLLOWED THE THREE HIGHLANDERS, WHO wore hooded cloaks as brown as the trees around them. Tyburn had shoved one of the cloaks in her arms when she'd dismounted.

"Use this as a shield. Curl up and cover yer body with it if someone comes. The men will not see ye. It is one of our Highland tricks, ye ken."

She had thrown the cloak about her shoulders and slunk behind them as they headed toward the barn. Angus held her back as the barn door opened. The four of them remained hidden at the edge of the woods to watch. Two men dragged a limp body between them into the forest.

She gasped and covered her mouth as she realized it was Adam.

Tyburn growled softly, the sound covered by the breeze.

"Dinna worry, lass," Baird said. "We will slay them to the last."

She didn't care about that. She cared only about her husband.

"Lass, doona be hasty now. Wait for my signal." Tyburn slunk off into the woods away from them.

"Stay here, milady. No matter what," Angus said as he vanished in the opposite direction.

Letty held her breath as she watched the two men drop Adam onto the ground. He did not move until one man put his foot on his back, and then her husband howled. She jerked, instincts demanding she run to him, that she attack the men who were hurting him, but she couldn't. Tyburn knew this land, and she had to trust him.

One of the men near Adam, the one who held him pinned to the ground, lifted his head, a knife laid against his throat. The sparse moonlight glimmered off the blade.

A sharp cry echoed across the forest, an eerie sound, like an ancient, angry wood spirit who'd been summoned into a flesh-and-blood creature. The cry came now from all around, and the sound turned darker and deeper, into a warlike bellow. That was when the three Highlanders attacked.

She would never forget that sight, their tall, ghostlike forms flying out of the shadows, converging on the two men. Swords sang and blades flashed in the moonlight as they cut through flesh and bone. It was over as quickly as it had begun.

Letty ran to Adam, gasping as she saw the deep marks on his back, the *flayed* flesh. She feared even touching him, lest she add to his pain.

"Laddie, can ye stand?" Tyburn demanded of Adam.

"Uncle," Adam moaned.

"Aye, lad." Uncle Tyburn's voice softened. "Ye canna move, can ye?"

"I can," Adam said, but even Letty knew that was a lie.

"Angus, Baird, find those bastards in the barn."

The two brothers vanished into the night. A minute later there were screams, but they were soon silenced before Angus and Baird returned.

"Go tell Aberforth at the inn that we need a wagon and hay."

Baird nodded and rushed off toward the Crown and Thistle.

"Who is Aberforth?" Letty asked Tyburn.

"The innkeeper is a friend. He owes me, given what happened to Adam under his roof." Tyburn looked toward Angus. "Help me with him."

Adam cried out as he was lifted up, and Letty couldn't help but cry as she followed. She felt helpless, useless . . . and Adam was in pain, possibly *dying*. She couldn't let herself think that.

Baird met them outside the barn, a wagon waiting for them. Tyburn and Angus laid Adam facedown in the straw to spare his flayed back. Letty climbed in beside him and clasped one of his hands.

"Adam. *Oh, Adam.*" She placed her hand upon his hair, careful not to touch him anyplace that might hurt. He was unconscious again, but he let out a small sigh.

"Ye ready, lass?" Tyburn asked.

"Yes."

"Good. Hold on. We stop for nothing."

Tyburn mounted the front of the wagon and slapped the reins over the backs of the two cart horses. Letty lay down in the hay alongside Adam, holding his hand and praying to any god who might listen to save him.

❧ 14 ❧

It was close to dawn by the time Adam was carried into Tyburn's home. Letty's entire body ached as she stayed crouched in the hay next to her husband. Baird rode for the doctor, leaving Tyburn and Angus to take Adam to a bedchamber on the ground floor.

Letty watched helplessly as the two Scotsmen laid Adam on his stomach and had a servant bring hot water and clean clothes. If only she could take away his pain, make him hearty and whole again.

"Please, let me do something," she begged Tyburn. She sat on the bed as a footman set the clothes and water on a nearby table.

"Aye, lass, if ye can stomach it, we need to clean the wounds so the doctor may see what must be done." Tyburn's voice was soft, a little hoarse, and his gaze was a blend of stoicism and pity—whether the latter was for her or for Adam she wasn't certain.

"I can handle it." Letty bit her lip and dipped a cloth into the water, then began to dab at the drying blood on Adam's back. She'd never seen wounds like these before. The way he'd been hurt . . . cut open . . .

"What did they do to him?" she asked.

"I canna say for sure, but these look like lashes from a whip." He pointed toward the lighter wounds. "And this . . . a knife, maybe?" A dark cloud of rage filled his face as he looked to Letty. "I would kill those men again if I could."

Letty gazed at Adam's face, pale and worn-looking. Thankfully, he remained unconscious through what she was doing. "I'm glad they're dead. God forgive me, but I'm glad." She continued to clean Adam's back. She worked in silence for a long moment, feeling the weight of the older Scotsman's gaze upon her as she worked. But she couldn't stop her actions. If she did, she might break apart.

"Milady, I think it's time you told me everything," Tyburn said.

Letty stared at her husband a long moment before she let out a sigh. She told Adam's uncle as much as she could, but she didn't share the extent of Adam's activities, only that he worked for the government in secret. Even so, she felt she was being too free with her husband's secret life; she wanted now more than ever to protect him, though it seemed it may be too late.

"I ken his secrets, lass. Ye doona have to worry about me, Angus, and Baird."

"This is all my fault, my lord."

Tyburn put a hand over hers, squeezing it gently. "It isn't. And ye are family, lass. Call me *Uncle* or *Tyburn*."

Letty sniffed. It had been a long time since she had felt safe, at least since her life had been turned upside down. Even with Adam injured, she believed that Tyburn could protect them both from anything.

The doctor soon arrived, and Letty waited, heart in her throat, as the old man muttered a number of choice curses while examining his patient.

"The wounds arna deep. If he can survive the next week without his body becoming inflamed, ye mayna lose him."

Letty crumpled into the chair beside Adam's bed, the fire gone out of her. Tyburn quietly escorted the doctor out to give her some time alone.

She stroked Adam's dark hair back from his face, her hand shaking. Whispering soft, silly things to him, she prayed he could hear her, that her words would reach him wherever he was. It stunned her that this dark, brooding stranger had become her world in such a short period of time. There was no denying it—she'd fallen in love with this man who spoke poetry late at night and carried deep secrets and heartache, yet made love to her with full, wild abandon and held her afterward as though she were the most precious thing he'd ever possessed. She couldn't lose him now. She couldn't.

"Adam, remember your vow," she whispered over and over until she lost her voice and succumbed to exhaustion.

ADAM DWELLED IN A TWILIGHT WORLD THAT SEEMED half fantastical and half memory. He chased the phantoms of his younger self and Caroline through the years of their childhood up until the time that he'd attended university. The world around him flowed like fresh watercolors as he saw himself joining the Wicked Earls' Club after his father had passed. He relived nights spent at gaming tables, laughing with friends and taking women to bed . . . and meeting John Wilhelm.

John entered Adam's dream world, his body almost glowing as he played his part in the charade surrounding him. Only now, Adam saw John in a way he never had before. John's once bright eyes had become weary, and Adam now clearly saw the sorrow in him that before he had missed. John stood on that fateful bridge over the river.

"We failed them," he said.

"Failed who?" Adam asked. Any moment now, he

knew John would be attacked and fall into the depths of the water below.

"A government that destroys the voice of its people is no government at all. It is tyranny."

It was an argument they had had before. The water-color world faded, and he was now inside one of the lounges of their gentlemen's club, Berkley's. John cursed and tossed his newspaper on the table between his chair and Adam's.

"What is it?" Adam retrieved the paper and glanced at the article on the main page. Adam recognized the names of the men.

"More sedition discovered. Traitors to be hung in four days."

"We failed them," John said. He raised his brandy to his lips and drank deeply.

"Failed who?" Adam set the paper down.

"Those men. They weren't dangerous; they wanted to talk. They did not pose a real threat. But because they weren't of the peerage, their philosophical discourses were deemed anarchist and seditious. Now those men will die." John leaned forward and buried his face in his hands. "It weighs upon me."

His blond hair gleamed in the lamps in the lounge, and he again had that glow about him, but Adam didn't know why he saw that now when he hadn't seen it before. After a moment, John lifted his head and met Adam's gaze.

"A government that destroys the voice of its people is no government at all. It is tyranny." Again those words filled the air of his dream like a mantra.

"John, you know that the opposite is true as well. You may dream of democracy, living in a world of equal voices and equal thoughts, but so long as men are men, there will also be good and evil in equal measure. For every dreamer, every philosopher, there are madmen and murderers. For every voice of reason, there is a cry of chaos. Perhaps those men were harmless, but we've seen others who are not. When angry men gather to scream their rage at an established force, it doesn't mean they are right. Not always."

This was something Adam had struggled with much of his life. He was a man born to a privileged life, while so many others failed to get by. If he gave away his lands and money, all of it, it would not be enough to help everyone. What was the answer? There was no logic in stealing the wealth of some to give to others. It was a temporary solution that faded quickly. No, the answer was more complicated, rooted somewhere in charity and increased opportunity for the betterment of all men, but they lived in an age where such things were not yet possible.

Perhaps someday things would change. Until then, he would watch and wait and support whatever might push toward that change. And he would also do his best to protect his king and his country without betraying the people of England. He did not always succeed, but he also did not always fail.

"I envy you, Adam," John said. "You bear the weight of your life easier than I."

Adam had not known then that John was a spy, or that he was in charge of catching men like this. At the time, Adam had been puzzled by his friend's concerns.

The memory of that evening began to fade. The last thing Adam could see was John's face darkening with creeping shadows until John vanished.

Then a soft light appeared, like a distant sunrise on the edge of his horizon.

"Adam?" Letty's voice seemed so close, but she couldn't be—she wasn't in the dark with him. The sound of her voice filled him with a bright, beautiful stirring in his chest. She belonged in the light, not here in the dark with him, not surrounded by death and chaos.

"Adam, please wake up," Letty begged.

Wake up? Was he asleep? He focused on moving, doing anything he could to wake. It felt as though his body were made of lead, lead that was on *fire*.

A hiss of pain escaped his mouth.

"Easy." Letty's fingertips touched his face, gently coasting over his forehead, then his cheek.

"Letty . . ." His voice came out like gravel.

"I'm here. You're safe at Tyburn's castle."

"How?" He pried his eyes open, and a pale light blinded him momentarily. Had they made it? Was he really at his uncle's castle? Flashes of Gent's sneering face made his body tense in pain. How had he gotten away?

"We rescued you. Your uncle and cousins killed the men who hurt you."

He focused his blurry gaze on Letty's shape close to where he lay. "All of them?"

"Yes. All of them."

"Good." His vision began to clear as relief swept through him.

"You should drink something." Letty's beautiful face appeared before him as she held a cup to his lips. He drank, but it wasn't easy.

"How long have I . . . ?"

"A week. Your wounds are almost healed. We've been putting salve on them to keep the skin from cracking open. You've healed much faster than the doctor thought, and you only suffered a fever in the first few days."

"My uncle . . ."

"I'm here, laddie. I heard yer wife speaking and thought ye must've woken." Uncle Tyburn's face appeared as he joined Letty and bent to see Adam better.

"Thank you, Uncle. My wife—"

"Is a damned good lass. Ye chose well. Even injured, she came back with us to fetch ye."

"Injured?" Adam tried to sit up and gasped in pain for his efforts.

"I'm all right, Adam." Letty gently eased him back down. "It was only a little scratch."

"A scratch from a pistol," Tyburn said. "She's a tough lass. She didna let me or yer cousins have a say about her coming with us."

Adam, too weak to move, sighed heavily. "Yes, she has quite a fire in her. One I am more thankful for each passing day."

"As ye should be." Tyburn chuckled. "Now, I'll help ye up, but ye must eat some broth and drink a bit of water."

Adam nodded, knowing the pain would be great, but he should try to eat. Tyburn lifted him up, and Adam held back a cry as his back burned with invisible flames.

"Here." Letty scooted closer to him and held up a bowl of soup. She started to lift a spoon to his mouth to feed him as one would a child.

"I can do it." He took the spoon from her, but in his haste and desperation he knocked it out of her hand. It clattered to the ground.

"Oh, I should fetch a clean one." Letty's face turned red as she rushed from the room.

"Well, that was nicely done, ye daft fool," his uncle said.

"What?" asked Adam.

"The lass wants to help, and ye didna let her."

"I should let her spoon-feed me like some child? Uncle, if I do that, she will never see me as a man again. The last thing I can do is be weak in front of her." Letty depended on him to be her protector, and in that regard he was failing.

"Ye are damned lucky I know a bit about marriage. Now listen close. Being wounded is not a weakness in a woman's eyes, ye ken? But being cold, being cruel—*that* is weakness. Let yer wife feed ye, and then, when ye are healed, ye will be the man she needs, the one who trusted her to take care of ye when ye needed her. Trust me, laddie. *That* matters to women. It should bloody well matter to ye too."

Adam was silent a long moment. "Perhaps you are right."

"Of course I am."

Letty returned then, a clean spoon in her hand. She glanced between the two men before approaching the bed and handing Adam the spoon.

Adam looked at Tyburn, then turned back to his wife. "Actually, it might be better if you did feed me, if you don't mind."

Letty's unease vanished. She smiled and took the spoon back, as well as the bowl, before she eased down on the bed beside him.

"I'll be back to check on ye soon," Tyburn said. "Letty, call if ye need anything."

Letty blushed again as Tyburn left. "Thank you, Uncle."

"Uncle?" Adam asked.

"He insisted. It seems I am worthy enough to be considered family."

"Come closer." She scooted nearer to him, the spoon still in her hand.

"Do you really wish me to help you?"

"I do. I'll only end up dropping the thing again, in my state. I appreciate your aid in the matter."

For the next several minutes, she helped him eat. He put aside his pride and focused on the relief he saw on Letty's face as he finished the broth. Tyburn was right, damn him. Letty seemed happier that she'd been able to help—not because he was weak, but because she needed to feel useful. And she was. She was *more* than useful. He would have died if she hadn't been able to reach his uncle and cousins.

"Thank you, Letty." Adam covered one of her hands in his. "You saved my life."

She blinked and turned away. He reached up and turned her face back toward him.

"Please, look at me."

She did, and he saw tears clinging to her lashes like tiny diamonds. "You must be furious with me. I put you in this position. You are in danger because of me."

"You can be so silly." He said this teasingly, but she

bit her lip, her eyes watering even more. "I was in danger long before I met you."

He brushed her lips with his thumb. "Letty, *I'm* the reason you were hurt. You are in danger because I put you there, not the other way around."

"But I followed Lady Edwards," she insisted.

"That was her decision to let you. She could have stayed in the ballroom and left her hair alone. She chose to risk your safety."

Letty still didn't meet his gaze. "But you had to marry me, and—"

"Would you like to hear a confession, darling wife?" he asked.

"A confession?"

"Yes. A dreadful confession. I'm not sure if you can ever forgive me."

She waited as he drew in a breath.

"I could have said or done anything I wished to avoid marrying you. The men who saw us kissing were friends of mine. No one would have called me out on that, not even your brother. He knows what I am, what I do. And the others—well, they would have let things go as I wished, in whatever direction. Not one of them would have breathed a word about what they had seen. You see, I let the situation justify my secret desire to have you. I was the one who wanted it, wanted *you*. I am the villain, my darling. Do not hate yourself—hate me, if you must."

"Hate you?" she echoed softly. Her face was so adorable in that instant. "I do not think I could ever hate you, and perhaps that is exactly my problem. I fear I like you far too much."

"You *love* me far too much," he reminded her. He hadn't forgotten what she'd said just before they had parted that awful night at the inn.

"I do." Her smile sent flutters of excitement through his chest.

"And I love you."

She finally met his eyes, such hope burning in her gaze. "You do?"

"How could I not? You are everything to me." He almost told her that she mattered more than his need to avenge John. He wouldn't deny it, but she didn't need to know that she had at one point been vying with vengeance in his heart. All she truly needed to know was that he loved her, and she came before all else.

He leaned toward her, his lips brushing over hers as he tried to show her what she meant to him. That delicate kiss stole his breath in a way no kiss ever had before. It was a kiss of love, of undying devotion, and a promise of *always* being there for her, in whatever way she needed.

When he moved back a few inches, he saw her eyes were closed and she was smiling dreamily. He leaned back against the headboard, and fresh pain sparked in him as the spell of that perfect kiss faded. Letty opened her eyes and swept a fretful look over him.

"You should rest." She helped him back down on his stomach, and then she applied more salve to his wounds. He had to focus his energy on healing as quickly as possible. He had a terrible dread that this was far from over, and he had to be ready to face whatever came next.

15

Letty and Tyburn walked together through the gardens inside the courtyard of his castle.

"Has it really been two weeks?"

"Aye, lass. Some say time passes differently here in Scotland." He patted her hand where it rested on his arm. "A kind of magic, ye might say."

They paused as she caught sight of Adam and his cousins standing on an open patch of grass, holding dull practice swords in their hands. Adam was taking turns sparring with both Angus and Baird.

He'd lost much of his weight and still looked far too thin, but his wounds had healed and were now only angry red raised marks. The last few days he'd taken care to work his muscles, and he'd spent much of his time outdoors, walking, riding, and now sparring. Angus and

Baird were being careful with him, and she could tell Adam wasn't pleased.

"You're hitting like a child, Angus," Adam shouted.

Angus muttered a curse but didn't fight back any harder.

"And you, Baird, since when do you fight like a babe?"

"Ye are still healing, ye daft fool!" Baird shot back. "Ye want to end up back in bed?"

Letty tensed as Tyburn gently removed her hold on his arm and then walked toward the trio. He held out a hand to take Angus's sword, and the two brothers moved back to let their father face Adam. Letty stood next to Angus and Baird and did her best not to panic. She didn't like Adam trying to fight so soon.

"I willna go easy on ye, laddie," Tyburn promised. "Let's see what ye are made of."

Adam lunged for him, and the two met in a ringing clash of steel. Tyburn pressed on, blow after blow striking Adam's sword until Adam stumbled and fell. Tyburn held the blunt blade to Adam's throat.

"Ye need to give yerself time, laddie." He offered a hand to Adam. Letty noted the look of pained resignation on her husband's face.

"I don't have time, Uncle. You know that." Adam accepted his help, and Tyburn pulled him to his feet.

"A smart man knows 'tis better to heal than to train through pain."

Adam sighed, his shoulders drooping. When he saw Letty, he flinched. She empathized with his reaction. Tyburn had been counseling her on what Adam was going through, how he had suffered and felt so weak, not just in body, but in spirit. Letty hated that he felt that way. All she could see was his strength.

"Baird, Angus, let Adam have some rest. The man should have some time with his wife." Tyburn shot them a knowing look, and the three vanished into the gardens.

Letty stopped next to Adam, who idly swung his dull practice blade at his feet. "How did they do that?"

"Do what?" Adam asked.

"That vanishing thing. I swear it's some sort of Highland magic. They seem to just vanish at will."

Adam chuckled, and the sound warmed her heart. She hadn't heard that sound in quite some time.

"They have trained themselves to move that way, to use their surroundings to hide."

"Well, I would certainly enjoy that talent if I had it," she said, then put her arm on his shoulder. "You are doing so well, truly. I know you are frustrated, but you mustn't be."

He shrugged, his smile vanishing. "Not well enough for my liking."

"If I had been hurt the way you had, I would likely still be lying in bed and moaning dreadfully."

"You wouldn't," he said quite meaningfully.

"No? How do you know that?" she asked.

Adam gently caught her by the waist with one hand and touched her arm, the one that had its own angry red scar.

"Because you took a bullet and kept riding. I doubt you would have been in bed long."

Letty reached up, her fingers brushing his where the scar lay beneath her gown's sleeve. "It was only a scratch. I thought a tree had hit me—"

He was smiling again. "Yet it *was* a bullet, lady wife. Just accept your heroic actions."

She pretended to grumble at this, but secretly she was delighted at his playful response.

They walked through the gardens in silence until they found their way into a maze of hedgerows at one end of the courtyard. Over the last two weeks, they'd found themselves in a new dynamic as husband and wife. After all that had happened, there had grown a deep foundation of trust between them, a kinship born from shared danger and sacrifice. Each night she had lain beside him in bed, her body pressed close to his, comforted by his presence. But he hadn't touched her, not in the way a man touches his wife when he wishes to make love to her. He was still healing, of course, but she feared that perhaps something was holding him back. She didn't want anything between them, not ever again.

"Adam . . . ," Letty began uncertainly.

"Yes?"

"It's been three weeks since, well . . . We . . ." Even after all she'd been through with him, she was still too embarrassed to discuss sex.

"Since what?" A soft, knowing light in his eyes coyly mocked her.

"Since we made love." There, she'd said it. "I know you have been healing and that you still are. I . . . Heavens, I guess what I wish to say is that when you feel better, I am ready to resume such activities." That didn't sound nearly so romantic as she had hoped—it sounded practically contractual. She still wasn't sure how to speak of such things.

He turned her face toward him, and she tilted her head back to look up at him.

"You are a darling, wife. Splendid, delightful, charming, desirable. I don't think I deserve you. In fact, I *know* I do not." He kissed her then, a petal-soft kiss that spoke of love and all its many heartfelt yearnings before their mouths broke apart.

"Tonight," he promised.

"Tonight," she agreed, shocked and relieved that so important a detail in their lives had been so easily agreed upon. Tonight, she would have her husband back.

EDWARD SHENGOE ENTERED A SMALL INN ON THE outskirts of London. The taproom was nearly empty, save for a few drunken regulars. The past few months, Edward had been following Arthur Thistlewood and his rebel band from small inns to pubs as they met to discuss their plans to overthrow the government.

His assignment was to watch, wait, and when necessary, tell those above him what the rebels intended. If the plans were deemed dangerous, the men would be apprehended and tried for their crimes against Crown and country.

Edward removed his coat and hat as he met the bartender's gaze. The man paused in pouring ale into a mug to nod his head toward a door that likely led to a back room. Edward nodded in return and went inside. Thistlewood was already there, as were the mysterious Mr. Garland and his female associate.

"Greetings." Thistlewood gestured for Edward to take a seat. Edward sat near Thistlewood as the other rebels arrived. Edward had a moment to observe Mr. Garland and the woman. They had approached Thistlewood's group, somehow knowing how to find them. Edward had first wondered if they may be employed by the Home Office like him, but it became clear after that first meeting that whoever Garland was, he was not one of Avery's Court of Shadows.

Edward hadn't been a spy for very long. He had been recruited by Avery Russell after the previous spymaster had died, but he knew the look and feel of spies trained by Russell, and Garland was not that.

Avery Russell believed in the purity of their purpose, and he instilled that sense of loyalty to the Crown in his recruits. He was not a man who could be bribed, nor was he a man who would let others use him for their own ends. It was said that the former spymaster had fallen because he had let his private life collide with his work for the Home Office. It seemed Avery was determined not to let that happen to him.

Edward focused back on Garland, who stood, counting the men in the room.

"We have a week before the king addresses the House of Lords," Garland said.

The woman beside him faced the other rebels, watching them. Her coquettish expression was only there for show, but what a show it was. If Edward hadn't been good at reading people, he might believe what they wanted him to think, that this woman was Garland's mistress. But she was so much more than that.

If there was one thing Avery had taught his spies, it was that women could be as dangerous and as effective as men in the world of espionage. Sometimes even more so.

"What exactly is your plan, Garland?" Thistlewood asked. He leaned forward in his chair, resting his elbows on the table as he listened.

"You all know of Guy Fawkes. We spoke of him at the last meeting." Garland leveled a gaze at the man who had mentioned Fawkes the first time—he had also implied that the plan to destroy the government was doomed to fail.

"Yes, and I assume that you mean to do what he was unable to?"

The room was thick with anticipation as they all waited for Garland's response.

"Yes."

"How will you manage this? The grounds are constantly patrolled, as are the tunnels, I'm sure." Unlike the others, Thistlewood was not afraid to question Garland. Edward kept his mouth shut. Questioning the plans of rebels was the easiest way to expose oneself, so he stayed silent and listened.

Garland began to pace the length of the floor as he spoke. "I have acquired access to the tunnels to and the tunnels beneath Westminster, I have men on the inside who will help us put gunpowder at the four corners of the foundation beneath the room the king will speak in at seven o'clock, *and* I can time the kegs to blow the moment he begins his speech. Men will need to be there to light the charges."

"How do you know you won't be discovered?" someone asked.

Garland smiled. "Unlike Fawkes, I am one of the few who knows of the existence of these *particular* tunnels. No one will see us. No one will stop us."

Edward had to school his features into an emotionless expression. He had believed—or rather, *hoped*—that when Garland had spoken of destroying the government that it had been more of a boast than a full plan of action. But to kill the king and everyone in the House of Lords? Anarchy would ensue. Edward studied the other men in the room, seeing only excitement on their faces. The woman, however, watched him the way a cat would a mouse.

You must be a clever creature, but so am I. He gazed back at her, letting lust fill his eyes. He wanted her to think that his focus on her was for her beauty and no other reason. A moment later, she blinked, surrendering to him in their battle of stares. She turned her focus to another man.

"I know these are trying times for you all. Good men suffer under the yoke of the rich who oppress you. Now is finally the time when you will have your chance to change that. You will each receive instructions the afternoon of the king's speech. Follow your instructions exactly, and I assure you, we will succeed."

Edward and the others stood when the meeting came to an end. There was no time to wait. He had to contact Avery. Edward retrieved his hat and coat and slipped on his gloves. His skin prickled as he felt the stare of the woman as he made to leave.

He'd been marked.

She suspected he was not loyal to Thistlewood's

cause. Fear began to eat away at his usual confidence. If she told Garland anything, Edward knew his days—perhaps even his hours—were numbered. He followed the others into the taproom, careful not to rush away. They spoke quaint, false pleasantries in front of the landlord as if they were all old friends simply meeting for dinner and ale. Then one by one, they said their goodbyes and left.

When he was finally able to walk outside, he mounted his horse and rode like the hounds of hell were upon his heels, because something far worse was on the horizon.

CAMILLE WAITED UNTIL THE LAST MAN LEFT THE private dining room before addressing her master.

"It's him, monsieur. The one who worried me last time."

Her master reclined in his chair and watched her. "You are certain?" He appeared relaxed, but that was when he was at his most dangerous—when he was still, when he was studying someone.

"Most certain."

"Then I shall follow him. When I find his den of spies, I will do what is necessary."

Of that, she had no doubt. Camille saw the shadow of

death in his eyes. Death and something else she didn't quite understand. Remorse? The devil didn't have remorse, and this man was more devil than anyone she had met.

LETTY SIPPED HER WINE OVER DINNER TO HIDE HER laughter as Angus and Baird teased Adam mercilessly. The two Scotsmen were close to Adam in age, and it was clear that their shared history was long and loving. Letty was full of gratitude for that. Her husband and Caroline deserved such a loving family. It was a pity Scotland was so far away from Chilgrave Castle.

"Ye have to listen to this, Lett." Angus caught her attention.

"No, no, not another tall tale, Angus," Adam warned with a chuckle.

Angus winked at Letty. "There's nothing tall about it. Now, Adam was visiting, along with Caro, who was but a wee bairn back then. Baird and I convinced Adam to ride over to see the MacDougals, a few miles west of here."

"Oh Christ, no," Adam groaned.

Angus hushed him. "So he rode over to the MacDougal lands—they have a manor house, ye ken."

Letty leaned forward and nodded, propping her chin on her hands as she listened.

"And old MacDougal had a daughter, a pretty lass with red hair like a winter fire."

"And a temper to match," Baird added.

Adam reached for his wineglass and downed a large portion of it.

"Every man within twenty miles was in love with Nellie MacDougal, but she had eyes for no man, at least none who wanted her. It was rumored that she loved a man from the Lennox clan, but the Lennoxes and the MacDougals had a feud at the time." Angus settled into his chair, smugly enjoying the attention. "So I dared Adam to steal a kiss from her—mayhap more, if he could."

"You know, this really is not the best story for my *wife* to hear," Adam warned.

"Do go on, Angus," Letty encouraged with a grin.

"Well, he rode up to the front door of the MacDougal castle and asked to speak to the fair, fiery Nellie. We all expected him to return home with a black eye or a sore jaw."

"What happened?"

"He was alone with the lass for nigh on an hour. None of us know what happened, but the next week, Nellie married that Lennox lad, and nine months later the clan feud was ended when their bairn was born. Nellie named the child Adam." Angus chuckled as Letty stared at him, stunned.

"You mean . . ."

"Aye, lass," Angus laughed.

Adam drank his wine again and glowered at Angus.

Tyburn cleared his throat. "I think Letty has had enough of yer tales, Angus. The hour is late, and we all ought to be in bed."

"Agreed." Baird and his father rose from the table, and then they stared at Angus, who grumbled and stood as well.

"Goodnight, lassie," Tyburn said to her and nodded at his nephew before Adam and Letty were left alone.

For a long moment, Letty and Adam sat in silence. Then Letty said, "What *really* happened in that hour you spent alone with Miss MacDougal?"

Her husband took another sip of his wine. "You don't think that I seduced her and fathered the next laird of the MacDougal clan?"

Letty hesitated, but not because she thought he had. "No, I don't. It does not seem like something you would do. Not that you aren't capable of seductions," she offered. "You're quite dangerous at it, but I know you. That young woman's virtue was safe, I am sure of it."

Adam offered a soft, bittersweet smile. "How well you know me, lady wife. Yes, I went to Nellie's house that day in order to stop Angus and Baird from teasing me. They can be quite relentless when they set their minds to something."

"I can see that. Still, they adore you and Caroline,"

Letty replied. He needed to know how much he was loved, in case he didn't feel it clearly himself.

"I forget how blessed I am. Even after all that Caroline and I lost, we are more fortunate than many others."

"So you went to see Nellie . . . ?" Letty prompted.

"I took tea with her, and we spoke about love, but not in the way she had expected. She had expected me to try to seduce her like the other young men who lived nearby. Instead, I asked her about where her heart lay. She told me about her young man, and how she was afraid to seek her father's permission to marry him. I then asked for an audience with her father, the laird himself. He had not been aware of my visit with Nellie."

"What happened?"

"I told him that she wished to marry the Lennox boy. She was right about him—he wouldn't allow it. I then explained that his entire household had been aware of my rather lengthy, private meeting with Nellie and that it was in her father's best interest to approve her marriage to the man she loved or else I might let it slip that I had been with Nellie. Of course, should such a thing happen, I would do the honorable thing and marry her."

Letty was stunned. Adam had risked marriage to a woman he didn't love just to help her marry another? "How did you know that he would agree and not actually make you marry her?"

Adam grinned. "Because Scots will always band

together against an Englishman, especially one acting as smug and superior as I was that day. MacDougal would rather have his daughter marry a Lennox than a bloody Englishman."

Letty giggled. "Oh, Adam, how wonderfully clever. You are perfectly splendid. You know that, don't you?" She got up and came around the table to slide onto his lap.

He held her waist and gazed at her. "You think so?" There was a vulnerability in this powerful, brave man, and she loved that he showed that soft side only to her.

"I do. It makes you rather irresistible." Letty massaged his shoulders with care.

"You don't have to do that," he said.

She leaned in to nuzzle his throat and inhale his scent. "Do what?"

"Treat me as though I might break. I'm not fragile." He tightened his hold on her waist until that familiar thrill surged through her. She embraced the rising passion inside her.

"I do not think you are fragile," she promised him as she nibbled on his earlobe. He groaned, the sound momentarily drowning out the crackling fire in the dining room.

"You don't?" he asked.

Letty smirked at him as she slid off his lap. "In fact, I think you're quite ready to catch me." She got up and backed away from him, flirting with a smile as she waited for him to follow.

❧

ADAM'S BLOOD SANG WITH DESIRE FOR HIS WIFE. HE had been afraid these last two weeks that he had lost something, something that he desperately needed. But now, seeing his wife with hunger and love in her eyes, he wasn't lost—he wasn't broken. His wounds had wrecked his confidence, his value in his own eyes, yet here Letty was, showing him that nothing had changed for her. She didn't see him as weak or damaged. She saw only *him*. It was a revelation.

He caught her before she could escape out the open doors. No doubt she had hoped to toy with him all the way up the stairs, stringing him along, but he would not wait that long. With one swift move, he swept her against the wall beside the door and pinned her there, a smile playing on his lips as he held her waist. Adam jerked her skirts up, and she gripped his shoulders as he freed himself from his trousers. Then he was inside her, relieved to find her ready for him.

She gasped as he sank deep and their joined bodies made a soft *thump* against the wall. She curled her legs around his waist as he braced one hand on the wall beside her head. His other hand covered her mouth. Letty gripped his shoulders tight, clinging to him.

She whimpered in protest, but then he began thrusting into her in earnest, and her cries of pleasure were muffled against his hand. They collided together like two burning fuses glowing in the dark as he claimed her there in the dining room. She closed her eyes, and he continued to pump himself into her, each second more exquisite than the last. She arched her back, her inner walls clamping around his shaft as she reached her climax and he followed her in his own pleasure a second later, his body relaxing against Letty's. They stayed locked together, her legs around his waist for a long moment as they both caught their breath. He removed his hand from her mouth and replaced it with his lips. Her legs started to slide down the backs of his thighs as she relaxed.

She sighed sweetly, and her hands wound into his hair, holding him prisoner for her kiss. God, he had become addicted to this woman in a way he'd never imagined. He wanted to stay inside her forever, to hold her in his arms until they were both old and gray and had lived a full life together. She was his beginning, his end, his everything.

When their mouths broke apart, he pressed his forehead to hers. "I love you, lady wife." He stole another kiss as he gently let her legs drop to the ground and withdrew from her body.

"That was magnificent," she purred as he held her in

his arms. "Perhaps you could show me that again in our bedchamber?"

"I would be delighted." Adam fixed his trousers while she dropped her skirts back into place. Then he escorted Letty upstairs, a foolish grin on his face as he took his wife to bed. A long while later, as he lay half-awake, he realized that he had not thought of John or his desire for vengeance even once in the past several days.

16

Edward Shengoe slid off his horse and handed the reins to a groom waiting outside a townhouse in Grosvenor Square. With a furtive glance, he rushed up the steps into the house. He didn't bother to knock. This was no normal house, after all. A butler greeted him, and Edward handed the man his hat and coat.

"Evening, Mr. Bradberry."

"Good evening, Mr. Shengoe." The butler nodded. "The others are waiting for you in the library."

"How many are here?" he asked.

"Six, counting you. Mr. Russell has not yet arrived."

"Good. I will speak to them." Edward had sent a summons to all of them within minutes of returning home. He had sat down at his desk and written out a codicil to his will before speaking to his butler and housekeeper. It was perhaps a tad pessimistic to plan for so dark a fate, but something about tonight had warned him that darkness was coming, enough to sweep across the land. He had to be ready for whatever came, even his own end.

Edward paused at the doors to the library, holding his breath. The moment he told the others what he knew, it would make the threat that much more real. At last, he squared his shoulders and opened the door. The tall windows of the library, now dark with nightfall, still glowed from the firelight. During the day, the stained glass would send patterns of brilliant colors upon the floor.

One of the five men in the room turned to greet him. "Evening, Shengoe."

He nodded at the man who'd spoken. "Jackson." The five men all stood to face him, each close to his own age, and all somber as he began to speak.

"In less than a week's time, Thistlewood and his men will attempt to blow up the House of Lords while the king delivers his speech."

"Tell me you're joking," one of the men said.

"I wish I was," Edward sighed. "To make matters worse, I believe that I was marked this evening."

"Were you followed?" another asked.

"I could not tell, but it would be safe to assume I was. You are all at risk, and for that I'm sorry. You know now what's at stake. You had best leave and find safety."

The men exchanged looks. "If what you say is true, we are needed here. We won't run."

"I'm glad to hear you say that." A man's voice came from behind Edward, and his blood turned to ice. He knew that voice. Garland. "It will make what I must do much easier."

The tension in the room was thick enough to smother Edward as he slowly turned to face Garland. The man held a pistol. Behind him stood more than half a dozen others. Beyond them, Bradberry's still body lay on the ground, his blood staining the floor red.

Edward reached for his pistol, tucked in the back of his waistcoat, but Garland had already fired. The report deafened Edward as the pain surged through his shoulder.

The men of the Court of Shadows rushed into action. Edward stumbled out of the way and ducked as Jackson fired over his head. Garland dove to the side, and the bullet felled one of Garland's men standing right behind him. Edward managed to pull out his pistol and leaned against the wall as he took aim at one of Garland's men.

It was the end of the Court of Shadows, and Edward was glad Avery was not here. With luck, he would learn the truth in time and stop the fall of Whitehall.

Avery walked up the steps to the townhouse that he'd purchased through an agent in secret, which then had become a refuge for the spies under his command. While he'd kept their missions separate, the men all knew this was a safe spot, a haven to come to when needed.

So when Avery had received the urgent summons from Shengoe, he had known it had to be something terrible. Avery slipped inside the house without knocking and was surprised to find Bradberry wasn't anywhere near the door. This fact alone instantly put him on guard.

The wall sconces had been doused, and all was quiet and dark. He peered at the darkened staircase that led to the bedchambers upstairs. He should have heard discussions coming from the library or the drawing room. At the very least he should have heard the muted whispers of maids working upstairs. Instead, there was only silence.

He started toward the stairs, but stopped and knelt by the banister at the base of the steps. There was something on the floor. He pressed a gloved fingertip to it, and the tip of his finger came away coated in blood.

A chill of dread crawled up his back. While it was always possible he was wrong, he was already certain of what had happened here. He walked toward the library and eased the door open. He thought he had prepared himself for what he would find, but he was wrong.

His best men, loyal and true, lay dead throughout the library. Brave Jackson was slumped against the leg of a nearby reading table, a pistol resting in his hand. Trevor had collapsed in a window seat, a knife plunged into his chest, though one of his attackers lay dead at his feet.

The rest of Avery's friends were in similar positions. The destruction of the room made a blood-soaked tragedy play out in Avery's mind. He looked toward the fireplace. Shengoe lay inches from it, a trail of blood showing clearly that he had dragged himself toward the fire as he lay dying. Avery gasped in shock as Shengoe twitched, his half-glazed eyes still holding a faint light in them.

"Shengoe, my friend. I'm so sorry . . ." Avery rushed over and crouched down beside him, his throat closing as he struggled to calm himself.

His hand was stretched out, blood-coated fingertips pointed toward something on the floor. Words had been drawn, patterns, clearly by Shengoe with his own blood on the floor.

Whitehall will fall. The rest was too smeared to read clearly.

"What's happening?" Avery asked Shengoe. As he listened for Shengoe to respond, he examined the man carefully, assessing his multiple wounds. There was nothing he could do to save him.

"King's . . . speech . . ." Shengoe exhaled, his last breath trickling away in an eerie death rattle. Avery could have sworn Shengoe's last word was "fox." But what could that mean?

Whitehall will fall . . . King's speech . . . Fox . . .

Although Whitehall was no longer used for the government, the name still stood for England's ruling bodies. The warning suggested that the current government was in peril. The question was *how*. Whatever was being planned was but a week away. That was when the king would speak before Parliament, particularly before the House of Lords.

Avery could stop the king from speaking, but that meant the plotters would slink back to the shadows, and the next time they made their move they would have no warning. No, the risks were too great. He had to find a way *now* to stop this.

Avery closed Shengoe's eyes with gentle reverence. The weight Avery carried upon his shoulders had grown tenfold.

The embers of the fire were still burning. They glowed a deep orange, and the white bits of charred wood were as pale as bone. Avery reached for the poker and stoked the fire, not even sure why he did except perhaps out of habit. A numbness swept through him as he felt the loss of his men so deeply that it almost killed him.

But the tragedy went much further than the death of his friends; it was the death of all he had worked toward as England's chief spymaster. His reforms and ambitions for the Home Office had been undone in one fell swoop.

Hugo Waverly had to be laughing from his watery grave. While Waverly's hubris and lust for revenge had cost him his life, it had not left the nation in so vulnerable a state as it was right now. The irony was, only Avery and the killers would know that. While his lesser spies and informants would all still be in place, these men had been the linchpins that held his newly remade network together. He couldn't begin to imagine how he was going to rebuild now, or whom he could trust.

It was no wonder that Waverly had kept his men at arm's length. Every man in this room tonight had been a friend, and they were all dead. And who else could he blame for it but himself?

Shengoe's urgent message still echoed in Avery's mind. He'd warned that Arthur Thistlewood was being coaxed into violent action by someone. Until now, Thistlewood and his men had been men of words and little more. Whoever had pushed them toward this had to be the one responsible for what had happened tonight. Avery had to protect Whitehall, or else his friends' terrible sacrifice would have been for nothing.

He twisted the poker in the fire again. The reflection of the white marble fireplace was like polished glass. A shadow of movement flickered in that reflection. Avery had a second to spin around, raising the poker like a sword, ready to defend himself as a blade arced down toward him.

Sparks flew from the clash of metal and iron. A brutishly tall man with dark eyes glared at him from the other side of their crossed weapons. Avery leapt back, swinging the poker at the man's chest. The man barely dodged out of the way before he swung his sword again.

Like a man possessed, Avery battled him until the old fire poker broke beneath the other man's onslaught. Before the man could regain his footing, Avery shoved one of the bookcases over so that it came crashing down on top of him. The man cried out as the heavy oak shelves filled with books crushed him.

Panting hard, Avery approached the man who lay half-buried and moaning in agony. By the way his face was turning reddish-blue, Avery guessed the man was being suffocated by the weight of the bookcase.

"Who do you work for?" Avery demanded.

The man shook his head, a stubborn set to his features as he contorted, trying to free himself.

"Who?" Avery snarled.

The man shook his head again, still trying to free his arm. Avery saw too late the pistol the man pulled out before he fired. Sharp pain struck his shoulder as he fell back on the ground. He put pressure to the wound and raised his face to the man. Sightless eyes met his, and the pistol fell a few inches to the floor.

Avery's head fell back, and he breathed deeply

through his nose as he fought off the pain. He was alone. His most loyal men were all dead. He had no choice but to seek help elsewhere. He needed Adam Beaumont back in London.

"Avery?" A feminine voice cut through his thoughts. He struggled to sit up, just as he heard the woman cry out.

Caroline Beaumont knelt by his side and lifted him up, but her gaze quickly focused on the bodies of his men.

"Lady Caroline...why are you here?" he asked, pain still making it hard to think.

"I saw you on the street and I wished to speak to you about Adam and Letty...and oh... Avery, what's happened?" she cried out, her eyes stark with terror.

Avery shook his head. The last thing he needed to do was involve Lady Caroline in this matter, or tell her of the danger he would soon have her brother face. She'd suffered enough when she'd lost Lord Wilhelm. "I can't—"

"You will. Come on, let me assist you." Caroline put an arm around his waist and helped him stand. "You need a doctor."

Avery allowed her to help him. Lord knew he needed it.

She had a coach waiting outside, and one of the footmen who'd accompanied her leapt off the coach to help them.

"Do you have a horse stabled nearby?" she asked.

"I never ride. Too easy to be seen." He collapsed onto a seat inside the coach. Caroline told her driver to take them home.

"No, not yours. My brother's," Avery insisted. He would need Lucien's help, now more than ever. Horatia and her sister were in Brighton, and they'd taken Horatia and Lucien's little son with them. It would be safe. Lucien could offer Caroline protection if they needed it, and perhaps more.

"Very well." Caroline gave the driver the new address and then closed the coach door. She put pressure on Avery's shoulder using a handkerchief she'd pulled from his waistcoat.

"Avery, tell me what happened."

His hands shook as he tried to remain calm. He was losing blood. His eyelids were too heavy to keep them open. Caroline slapped his face. Hard. Despite the magnitude of everything happening around them, Avery still managed to be offended by this, and he glared at her in shock.

"Talk," Caroline said firmly. "It will help you stay awake."

"One of my men sent me an urgent message. He'd infiltrated a group of men plotting treason. I arrived late to the meeting."

"And they were the ones who . . ." Caroline's voice softened.

"Yes. I'm sorry you had to see that, my lady." Avery closed his eyes again, but he was in less danger of falling asleep now.

"You believe your man was exposed and followed?"

He nodded. "It is the obvious explanation. Before you arrived, I fought a man who'd stayed behind. They knew I would be coming."

"You know what the men are planning?" she asked.

"To attack Parliament, the day the king makes his speech to the House of Lords."

"What sort of attack?" Caroline pressed.

"Whitehall will fall . . . King's speech . . . Fox . . ." Avery repeated Shengoe's final clues. "That's all I know."

"Fox?" Caroline's eyes narrowed. "Like the animal?"

Avery puzzled over the possible interpretations. "I don't know. A fox in the henhouse, perhaps? An inside man? An assassin? But it's not just the king they're after. Whitehall will fall . . . Foxes burrow . . . A tunnel?" He shook his head, having hit a dead end.

Suddenly Caroline gasped. "Tunnel. You don't suppose he must mean Guy Fawkes? F-A-W-K-E-S? The gunpowder plot."

Avery's eyes widened. Could it be? He considered the possibilities, then cursed. "Yes, that must be it."

"How does that poem go again?" he asked her.

REMEMBER, REMEMBER!

The fifth of November,
The Gunpowder treason and plot;
I know of no reason
Why the Gunpowder treason
Should ever be forgot!
Guy Fawkes and his companions
Did the scheme contrive,
To blow the King and Parliament
All up alive.
Threescore barrels, laid below,
To prove old England's overthrow.
But, by God's providence, him they catch,
With a dark lantern, lighting a match!
A traitor to the Crown, by his action,
No Parliament mercy from any faction,
His just end should be grim . . .

CAROLINE'S VOICE ENDED IN A WHISPER. SHE LOOKED at Avery. "They mean to blow up Parliament?"

"It is the only way a small band could kill both the king and the lords at the same time, but how?"

"Are there tunnels beneath Westminster?"

"No doubt, but they would be secured, patrolled, even sealed off."

"Perhaps there is a fox in the henhouse after all?" Caroline suggested.

"So we must assume they have access, regardless." Avery was speaking more to himself than to her.

"Do you know of anyone who might have the architectural plans of Westminster?"

"Actually, yes," Avery said as the coach stopped in front of Lucien's townhouse. "My brother. He enjoys architecture, and I know he has a copy of the plans for it."

"The same brother whose house we just arrived at?" Caroline straightened as her footman opened the coach door and helped her out. She and the footman then braced Avery on either side as they helped him up the steps to Lucien's townhouse. When the butler answered, he took one look at Avery and cried out.

The butler shouted up the stairs, "My lord, come quickly!" He then called for one of Lucien's footmen to go fetch the doctor.

"What is it?" Lucien appeared at the top of the stairs nearby.

"Evening, brother." Avery chuckled.

The blood drained from Lucien's face.

"Avery? What the devil?" Lucien met them at the bottom of the stairs and relieved Caroline of her burden. "Follow me," Lucien urged the footman who held Avery's other side. Avery was half carried into the drawing room and laid on a fainting couch. But just as Lucien began to ask questions, Avery slipped into unconsciousness.

CAROLINE SLAPPED AVERY'S FACE HARD WHEN HE passed out. Lucien shot her a startled look.

"What? It worked before!" she protested. "And we have no time for politeness." Unfortunately, it did not work this time.

"Do you have smelling salts?" Lucien asked her.

"My lord, do I *look* like the fainting sort?" She tried not to take offense, but the implication still riled her.

"Apologies," Lucien muttered and told his butler to fetch some. "Lady Caroline, what happened to my brother?"

Caroline explained that she'd been riding through Grosvenor Square when she saw Avery walk past her in the other direction. She'd been wanting to speak to him about Adam and what else they could do to catch the spies who were after Letty and her brother, so she decided to turn around to wait for him. Her coach headed back the way she'd come, and she'd guessed that the only townhouse she was unfamiliar with was the one he must have entered. Her guess had been right. But after a short time, she'd worried that perhaps he wouldn't come back out, and her matter was urgent, so she'd decided to knock. But when no one answered the door, she'd realized it was slightly open. Every instinct in her had warned her to be careful as she entered the house in search of Avery.

She explained the horrific scene she'd come upon, the murdered men and Avery wounded on the ground. She relayed all this calmly, but when she caught sight of her shaking hands covered in blood, she realized how taxing all this had been on her, and she sank into the nearest chair.

"I told him a hundred times he would get himself killed." Lucien stared at his brother with a lost look.

"He has nine lives," Caroline said. "I've never seen a man with so much luck as he."

"Well, one day it may finally run out." Lucien went silent as the doctor arrived.

Sometime later, the doctor was done and Avery was bandaged up. The bullet had been removed and sat in a bloody mess of cloths in a bowl. Only then did Caroline and Lucien draw a joint breath of relief.

"My lord . . . Your brother mentioned you might possess the architectural plans to Westminster?"

Lucien turned to face her. "I do. Why do you need them?"

"Because . . ." Caroline twisted her hands in her gown. "The men who attacked your brother plan to blow up Parliament, like Guy Fawkes."

"Guy Fawkes? Bloody hell." Lucien looked heavenward. "What fools are these?"

"Dangerous ones who were serious enough to kill all the men who worked with Avery."

"What of your brother? Is Morrey still at Chilgrave?" Lucien asked.

"No, he went to Scotland to keep Letty safe. They're at Uncle Tyburn's castle near Inverness."

"Oh, yes. That is indeed a safe place. We almost couldn't get Ashton Lennox's wife out of her family's castle in Scotland. We practically had to storm it to even have a conversation." Lucien was trying to tease her, but she didn't feel at all in the mood to laugh.

"We must send someone to bring Adam back. As much as I do not want him in danger, we will need him. Avery cannot do this alone."

"He won't be alone," Lucien replied grimly. "I'll send someone north immediately."

Caroline nodded. "If you can fetch the architectural plans for Westminster, I shall watch over your brother."

Lucien stood, and Caroline took his place on the edge of the settee. "You saved his life," Lucien said quietly. "I owe you a great favor, Lady Caroline. Name it, and whatever it is shall be yours."

Caroline smiled. "Thank you, my lord, but what I desire, you cannot give."

When she was alone with Avery, she held out a hand to take his. If only someone had been able to save John. Adam had been too late, and that moment had made him become a spy as well. It was only a matter of time before her brother's luck ran out. Adam and Avery were both men who lived on borrowed time.

❧ 17 ❧

The rider came just after dawn on an exhausted horse, carrying an urgent message. Adam and Letty were in the drawing room with Tyburn when one of Tyburn's footmen rushed inside.

"What is it, lad?" All three people present in the drawing room stood.

"A messenger, my lord. From England. He says he has an urgent message for Lord Morrey."

A pit formed in Adam's stomach as he and Tyburn exited the room to speak with the messenger. The man who stood in the entryway looked travel weary.

"I am Lord Morrey," Adam told the young man.

"My lord, Mr. Russell said you must return to London at once." The young man gazed at him with fearful eyes.

"What? Why?"

"I was told to tell you that the fifth of November should never be forgot. That was all he told me, that and to come to the Marquess of Rochester's home once you reach London."

Adam frowned. "The fifth of November?" The implications there were worrisome indeed.

Tyburn pointed toward a door that led to the castle kitchens. "Thank ye, lad. Why don't ye go to the kitchens and eat. One of my staff will show ye to a room where ye may rest."

"Thank you, my lord." The young man left them alone.

"Well, what does the message mean?" Tyburn asked.

"Remember, remember, the fifth of November, the gunpowder treason and plot . . . It's a reference to when Guy Fawkes and his coconspirators attempted to blow up Parliament."

"My God," Tyburn said as he and Adam exchanged glances.

"I have to leave for London, now."

"But ye've barely had time to heal," Tyburn argued.

Adam rolled his shoulders and winced at the tight, scarred skin that pulled at him, but the pain was dull rather than sharp.

"Avery needs me. If he summoned me back from Scotland, then he has no one else left." As he spoke, his chest suddenly tightened with panic. The Court of

Shadows—something must have happened to them. "May I have use of your fastest horse?"

"Of course. But—"

"And me," Letty said. "Can you have the little black gelding saddled for me?"

Both lords turned to look down at her.

"No," Tyburn said at the same instant that Adam said, "Absolutely not."

Letty held up a hand in silence and kept both men from speaking further with an imperious look. "Husband, you would have been dead if not for me and that horse I stole from the Crown and Thistle. And I have as much right to defend my king and country as any of you do."

"But what of our child?" Adam argued, hoping to use this tactic to make his wife stay safe a second time.

"My menses came this morning, so the only life I risk is my own."

Adam pulled her into his arms. "And that is already far too precious a thing to risk."

She pushed back against him, a fierce scowl of rebellion on her face. "You will not talk to me sweetly and hope to convince me to stay here. If you go, I go. It is that simple." She escaped his arms and rushed up the stairs.

Adam, his arms held out empty of her, stood staring after her.

"As much as she deserves protection, that is a woman

who can take care of herself. Perhaps she should go." Tyburn sounded more thoughtful now.

"And if we both end up dead?" Adam growled.

"Then at least ye are together. Trust me, as a man who lost his wife and could not follow her to the land beyond, I would say that surviving without her was the hardest thing I've ever had to do. If not for my sons . . ." Tyburn turned away, not finishing the sentence.

"Please have our horses readied. I'd better make sure she knows we can't bring anything with us."

Adam headed up to the chamber he and Letty shared. She wasn't there. A young boy was bent over her trunks.

"You, lad. Have you seen Lady Morrey?"

The boy spun around with a very girlish giggle. "Perfect—even you didn't recognize me." Letty beamed at him from beneath the brim of her cap.

"How did you change so quickly?" Adam asked.

"A woman has to have some secrets, doesn't she? Come, we have no time to waste." She took his hand and led him from their bedchamber.

They were met at the foot of the grand staircase by Angus, Baird, and Tyburn, all dressed for travel.

"Uncle?"

His uncle smiled. "Ye didna think ye would be going alone, laddie?"

"But what if you can't—?"

"Keep up? Aye, we can. The horses are ready."

Adam followed his uncle and cousins outside. Four tall horses had been saddled, and the fifth horse was shorter than the others—a fierce little black gelding that danced about in anticipation. Letty rushed past Adam to the little horse and wrapped her arms around its neck.

"She's going to ride that little creature?" Adam asked Angus as she approached the little black beast.

"That little creature is the beast who saved yer life. Nearly killed himself outracing those bigger horses. He's fast. While ye were healing from yer wounds, Baird and I were seeing to him. He has the speed of the devil himself."

"I'm glad she's riding him, then." Adam walked over to his wife and assisted her into the saddle. "Are you ready?" he asked.

She nodded, and the serious look upon her face made his last argument for her to stay at Tyburn's home die upon his lips.

"Very well," Adam said as he mounted his horse. He glanced back at his wife, uncle, and cousins.

"Lead the way, lad!" Tyburn commanded.

Adam dug his heels into the horse's flanks. They rode as one toward an uncertain future.

IT TOOK THREE DAYS TO REACH LONDON AND THE Marquess of Rochester's townhouse. Letty had been there once, shortly after Horatia had married the marquess. She shouldn't have been surprised that they were to meet there; Lucien was Avery's older brother, after all. Adam hurried up the steps and knocked on the townhouse's door. An older butler met them.

"We're here to see Lord Rochester."

"Ah, yes. Do come in." The butler stepped back to let everyone inside. "The war council is waiting for you."

"War council?" Angus muttered to Baird, who shrugged.

"'Tis England," Baird said, as if that explained everything.

"This way." The butler led them toward the library.

Letty and Adam entered first,and saw a group of men all huddled about a table. She recognized the men as they turned to see who had arrived. Lucien, the Marquess of Rochester. Along with Godric, the Duke of Essex; Cedric, Viscount Sheridan; Charles Humphrey, the Earl of Lonsdale; Ashton, Baron Lennox; and Jonathan St. Laurent.

Relief nearly overwhelmed Letty. These men were known in certain circles as the League of Rogues, and their exploits were quickly becoming the stuff of legends. If there were men able to rival Avery's spies, it was this group of men. They parted to reveal Avery, whose left arm was in a sling.

"Welcome to the fight, gentlemen," Avery said with a

wry smile. Then his gaze drifted to Letty. "My lady." He nodded respectfully at her.

"I hope you don't mind, but my uncle Tyburn and his sons, Baird and Angus, insisted on joining me."

There were quick greetings before Adam and Letty joined the men around the reading table.

"Adam, I'll be brief. Arthur Thistlewood and his men are planning to destroy the House of Lords while they are in session for the king's speech. We have but a short time to place ourselves in the tunnels below Westminster and stop the gunpowder kegs from being lit."

Letty studied the pages of architectural plans laid out on the table and stepped back to allow Tyburn and his sons to see. She noticed Caroline seated by the fireplace, away from the men.

"Caroline?" She joined her sister-in-law by the fire. Caroline looked away from the flames to stare at Letty. She gasped.

"Letty? What are you doing here?"

"I came back with Adam. I couldn't let him come alone. What about you?"

Caroline pulled Letty into a chair beside her and then told her everything that had happened at the townhouse in Grosvenor Square.

"Dead? All of them?"

"Down to the last man. I fear the sight has left me rattled." She took Letty's hand into hers. "These are desperate and dangerous men, Letty. God help us all if they succeed."

Letty curled her fingers around Caroline's and squeezed lightly.

"But *you* saved Mr. Russell."

She nodded, that distant look back on her face. "And yet we may all die tonight."

"Then you should stay here," Letty said.

"Are you staying or going with them?" Caroline challenged.

"I'm going," Letty admitted.

"Then so am I."

"We must stay together, then." Letty and Caroline turned to listen to the men as they made their plans.

"We will need two or three men at each of the corners. I can only guess that is where Thistlewood's men will set the kegs and charges. We will access the tunnels through subterranean gates. Each man should be prepared to force the lock if they can't gain entrance, but once you get close to the corners, do not use a pistol. An errant shot could cause the very thing we need to prevent." Avery looked around at the men close to him. "Most of you are married, and some are fathers. No man will be judged if he chooses to stay behind. There are other ways you can help, should we fail."

This pronouncement was met with stony silence.

Avery cleared his throat. "Very well. The north corner shall be covered by Essex, Rochester, and Sheridan. South corner, Lonsdale, Angus, and Tyburn. East will be Lennox, St. Laurent, and Baird. West corner will be Adam and myself. Good luck to you all. And God save the king!"

"God save the king!" the others roared in reply.

Letty collected a pistol and a slender knife from a nearby table that had been covered with weapons. When she saw Adam tuck a blade into his boot, she did the same with her own. She still wore the trousers and waistcoat of a boy, and she had her hair down tight at the nape of her neck. She could run without the encumbrance of skirts. The last thing she wanted was to be a hinderance to Adam in a moment of crisis.

They left Lord Rochester's home, and the assigned groups rode off on horseback.

Though they would not need to leave the city, the journey seemed to take forever. Letty's heart pounded as she, Adam, Avery, and Caroline finally reached the place where they could gain access to the tunnels. Westminster was only a short distance from where they stood now, huddled in the growing gloom.

Letty couldn't help but think of King George somewhere inside the building, the entire House of Lords patiently waiting for his speech. So many would die if they failed, and anarchy would soon follow. The importance of what she and the others were about to do made her tremble.

Adam tested the gate that spanned the mouth of the

tunnel, which formed a black cavern ahead of them. It seemed to go on forever beyond the iron bars of the gate. As Adam eased the gate open, he shared a grim look with Avery.

"What is it?" Letty whispered.

"The gate wasn't locked. Thistlewood's men are already down there. We must be silent. Everyone, stay close." Avery lit a small lantern and then nodded to Adam. "I'll hold the lantern so you can see ahead of you."

Adam nodded and headed into the darkness first, a pistol in one hand and a knife in the other. Avery followed behind him, then Letty and Caroline.

It was an eerie thing to descend into darkness with only a weak lantern to light their way. Water trickled along the floor of the tunnel as they moved up an incline deep into the bowels below Westminster Palace. The sound of water upon stone somewhere nearby echoed so loudly that it gave Letty a headache.

Letty looked back frequently to check on Caroline behind her. Her sister-in-law was pale and silent, her skin almost luminous in the dim light. Caroline was somehow even more silent than the rest of them. Something was weighing upon her mind, and as much as Letty wished to speak with her about it, she dared not.

Adam began to move more quickly, and the rest of them followed.

"We can't be far now," Avery whispered as they

reached the fourth crossroads of tunnels. Suddenly a faint sound came to them down the tunnels from the north. Shots, a cry, then silence.

"Oh God," Letty breathed. "It's started. Should we go and—?"

"We can't stop," Avery said. "We must trust in the others. They are on their own for a time. We must ensure that Thistlewood's men are stopped at our corner."

The eerie sounds of distant fighting began again. They continued through the dark tunnel, like a bad dream. After another minute, light appeared ahead from a distant lantern. Avery set his lantern down so that they might creep up on whoever was lurking in the dark.

"Are you ready?" Avery asked Adam so quietly that Letty almost didn't hear him. As the light ahead grew brighter, Letty saw her husband's silhouette more clearly. He was half shadow, half man, power radiating from him. It was as if the darkness he held inside him had been made manifest, the part of him she had glimpsed the night he had saved her and Lady Edwards.

Three men were pushing several kegs close together. There were fuses at the front of the grouping of the kegs, and one man was tying the bundle of fuses together to make it easier to light the batch all at once. It seemed the men hadn't heard the sounds they had heard earlier, for they did not seem concerned that their plot had been discovered.

Avery shifted, putting himself directly in front of Letty and Caroline, blocking the men ahead from view. Letty stayed behind him, but she removed the knife from her boot and waited. She would do whatever was necessary.

ADAM STILLED, HIS BREATH SO SLOW THAT HE INHALED only five times in a single minute. He needed to be invisible.

I am mist. I am moonlight. I am the smoke of an extinguished candle. I am the shadow you do not see, but only feel . . .

For now, only Adam would step into the light, while the others stayed safe in the dark behind him.

The three men were busy arranging the fuses around the kegs and didn't see him as he stepped into their circle. Adam tossed his pistol into the air and caught it by the barrel as he rushed toward them. The first man spun to face Adam, and he felled him with a blow from the butt of his pistol, then swiped at the second man with his blade. The third man dove at him, and they crashed against the tunnel wall. Adam growled and spun them around so he had the other man pinned. The man landed a punch on Adam's jaw, but Adam rammed his own fist into the man's gut, causing him to double over.

Someone threw an arm around Adam's neck, pulling him back, choking him. Adam shoved back hard, feeling the satisfying crunch of the assailant's ribs as they collided with the tunnel wall.

Avery appeared in his line of vision, a knife in his uninjured hand as he attacked one of the other men. Letty and Caroline ducked around the brawling figures, and Adam glimpsed them trying to undo the fuses around the kegs. Adam took down another of the men by driving his blade through the man's chest. The man crumpled at his feet when he pulled it out.

"Are you all right, Morrey?" Avery asked. He stood with one hand clutching his splinted shoulder. The other men they had been fighting were dead.

Adam nodded and wiped his blade clean.

Avery glanced back toward the dark tunnels. "Can you handle things here? I need to check on the others."

"We have it handled."

Avery vanished into the shadows, and then Adam turned to his sister and Letty, who were halfway done removing the fuses from the kegs.

"I can finish that." Adam tried to shoulder the ladies away from the dangerous explosives. "Why don't you both go back the way we came? It's a straight path to the outside gate."

"Actually, I'd rather go after Avery," Caroline said.

"And I wish to stay with you," Letty informed him.

Adam cupped Letty's face and stole a quick kiss as he held her close, but he wanted her and his sister as far away as possible from these blasted tunnels.

He turned to speak to Caroline, only to find the tunnel empty. His sister had gone after Avery.

"Blast and hell."

"She'll be fine, Adam. Avery will protect her." Letty declared this with such confidence that he almost believed her.

"Then I will escort you back to the gate."

Letty hesitated. "Fine, but only after we have dealt with the fuses—" She stopped talking, her face suddenly pale as she apparently saw something behind Adam.

The hairs on the back of Adam's neck rose as he felt something in the dark tunnel behind him.

"It's been a long time, old friend," the voice said.

That voice. Adam turned, careful to keep his movements slow. The faint light of the lantern beside the kegs illuminated the form of a dead man come back to life. Adam's heart stuttered.

"J—John?" He gazed into his friend's face. "It's . . . it's not possible."

For a moment he thought he saw some kind of empathy upon the man's face, but it was soon replaced with a dark cunning that Adam had never seen before.

"And yet, here I am." John held a pistol in his hand.

"You're the one behind this? You're the one Thistlewood was meeting?" Adam guessed.

"I am," the man said.

John stared at Adam with an intensity that made

Adam feel sick. This wasn't his friend—this was someone wearing John's face.

"He and his men simply needed a push to do what needed to be done."

"For two years I've *mourned* you, John. You were a brother to me. And now you do this?" Adam could barely think past the betrayal he felt at this moment. *John is alive!* But John was the man trying to destroy England's government. It was something not even his worst nightmares could've conjured up. Thank God Caroline had already left. She couldn't have borne this.

"You spent years avenging your own demons, Adam." There was pain layered in the fury of John's reply. "I spent years spying upon men who would not have done any real harm, and then I had to betray them. Innocent men died. Far too many of them."

"You think this is the answer? Burn it all down?" Adam kept Letty behind him and out of John's direct line of fire, given that he still held a pistol aimed at them.

"You don't think there are people ready to propose a better way? We could have a new government, a better one. One that serves the people instead of the other way around."

"They'd never get the chance. You always understood human nature better than anyone. There would be nothing but anarchy left in its place."

"Better anarchy than tyranny."

"You know that isn't true. Anarchy hurts those with the least power. The mobs who take to the streets will only truly hurt the helpless: the children, the women, the people whose lives depend on some regularity and safety. The shopkeepers who run their businesses that feed and clothe others—those are the ones you would hurt. You would see everything burned to punish those above you?"

"Those same men keep all men down simply because they were not born with the right name, or because they don't have enough money to deserve their notice. They deserve to be punished."

"You are a *fool* if you think what you're doing will solve anything." Rage built inside Adam like a gathering storm, with the wind drawing up black clouds into a violence that, once unleashed, would wreck all in its path. How *dare* John betray him, his king, and his country. Adam's hands curled into fists. He still held his knife, but it was no use against the pistol.

"I joined the Home Office to avenge you, John—to find your killers. Everything I did was for a *lie*."

"Always so damned noble. Now you know how *I* felt, Adam. Well, you need not carry your burden any longer. I killed the French agents who were after me long ago. It was the perfect way to disappear."

"What of Avery's men? You killed every last one of them. They were innocent."

"*Innocent?*" John laughed. "They were tools for the Crown, just like you. Their lives don't matter."

Adam drew in a steadying breath. "Every life matters, from the street urchins to the spies who perished at the townhouse in Grosvenor Square."

"We disagree, then." John suddenly looked to Letty, and his pistol shifted toward her. "Unfortunately, I must be done with this quickly."

"No. Let my wife go. She's not part of this."

"Not part of this? She's one of the best spies I've seen in years. I can't allow either of you to go free." John's voice was so cold, so hard, that Adam wondered if he'd imagined the John he'd once loved like a brother. Had that man ever been real?

"You fool, she isn't a bloody spy. It was all a mistake that night at Lady Allerton's ball."

Adam thought he saw brief surprise in John's eyes. "Why did you marry her, then, if not so she could continue her spying with a guardian in tow?"

"To protect her. Because I desired her as I have no other woman. You should remember what that's like. Or did you never love my sister at all?"

John flinched at the mention of Caroline. For an instant, Adam saw his friend, not this monster.

"*Please*, John, let my wife leave. She won't be able to find you or do anything to stand in your way. She's harmless."

Letty stepped up next to Adam, laced her fingers in his, and leaned against his shoulder.

"I'm not leaving. I'm here until the end, whatever it may be."

Adam's heart fractured. He had been right from the start about his wife, about her bravery and her loyalty. Adam squeezed her hand before pushing her away from him. "And that is why you must go."

John's voice grew quiet. "You were a good friend to me, Adam. I didn't want things to end this way. You joined the wrong side, but your heart was in the right place. You have your chance to leave, Lady Morrey. Go before I change my mind."

"Go, Letty," Adam commanded her.

His wife raised her chin and stood her ground. "You've failed, you know."

"You mean the gunpowder? Perhaps. The tide may yet be turned once I am done here."

"No, you've made an even graver mistake."

"And what is that?"

Letty moved closer to Adam, once more taking his hand in hers, linking her fate to his. "You forget that there are still noble men and women in this world. Those who believe in the goodness of man, not their evil. Even if you succeed tonight, you cannot win."

"I *can* and I will." John leveled the gun at Adam. "It's time we finish this."

A shot rang out in the tunnel, and Adam pulled Letty

into his arms, shielding her from whatever may come. He clenched her tightly, waiting to feel death steal him away from her.

John gasped and moaned. Adam opened his eyes to see John fall to his knees. Behind them a few feet away in the darkness stood Caroline, a pistol in her hand. She stared at John with a look of terror and disbelief. The pistol clattered to the ground as she rushed to catch John before he fell onto his back. Caroline cradled his head in her lap.

"Caro? What are you doing here?" John murmured. The hate in his features faded away as he gazed up at her.

"You forgot about me, John. About *my* love," Caroline whispered.

Adam's throat tightened. He held Letty close as he watched his friend draw shallow breaths.

"I never forgot," John breathed. "You were always with me. I wanted a better world for you." The sincerity in his voice was undeniable.

Caroline sniffed and wiped at her eyes with a balled fist. "Love and hate cannot dwell in equal measure. Somewhere along the way, you let me go to hold on to something else. But I held on to you, John. Even after our daughter died."

John coughed, blood coating his lips. "Daughter?"

"Yes. When I heard you'd died, I grew upset, and she came into the world too early."

"What was she like?" John asked.

"She was beautiful, with your fair hair and my eyes. I named her Elizabeth after my mother." Caroline stroked her fingertips over John's brow as if to try to smooth away his worries. "I wish you could have seen her. You would have adored her."

"Our child . . . ," John rasped.

Adam felt his own lungs tighten as if he couldn't breathe. He would've given John his own breath once.

"Now I must let you go," Caroline told John, her voice full of tenderness for a man who'd hurt them both so deeply.

Adam would never understand how she managed it. Love was a strange and wondrous thing, but right now it was pain *unimaginable*. Caroline had let love rule her heart, even when faced with John's betrayal. She was a better person than he was. He couldn't forgive John, not like Caroline was.

"Caro . . ." John's body was jerking as death began to creep in on him.

"Go find our daughter. She needs you now." Caroline bent her head to John's and pressed her lips to his forehead as he exhaled and went still.

Adam and Letty stayed motionless for a long moment. Adam stared at John's lifeless body. He had lost him again. The pain he'd expected to banish had only deepened, like tearing open a scar. Caroline began to sob, rocking John's body in her lap. His sister's grief shook Adam into action. He knelt by her and touched her shoulder.

"Shh, Caroline, it's over now."

She finally let go of John and stood up. Adam lifted his sister into his arms, and Letty carried the lantern. They began to walk out of the dark tunnels and into the moonlight to find Avery and the others.

EPILOGUE

Three weeks later

Christmas at Chilgrave was everything Letty had hoped it would be. The castle was full of friends and family. Boughs of mistletoe had been hung freely around the castle by the footmen, much to Mr. Sturges's disapproval, since not only Adam was taking advantage of the mistletoe, but the staff members were as well. Greenery covered every surface and twisted around every banister and pole. Everywhere Letty turned, there was light and laughter.

She couldn't believe that three weeks had passed since the king and Parliament had been saved. It had been a small miracle that Avery and the League of Rogues had escaped harm other than a few bumps and bruises during the scuffles in the tunnels with Lord

Wilhelm's men. They'd all been fortunate beyond belief which meant this Christmas was even more important to celebrate.

Once the king had been made aware of what had happened that night, everyone involved had been brought to Carlton House for a private audience where King George had expressed his eternal gratitude.

But not everyone had come through those dark events unscathed. Caroline had become more withdrawn than ever, and Avery, too, had grown distant. They, more than anyone else, had lost much in the last few months.

In the ballroom at Chilgrave, Angus bowed before Letty. "Milady? May I have this dance?" He offered her a courtly bow, and she accepted with a giggle. It was easy to forget what had happened with John when Angus and Baird were around to tease her.

The ballroom at Chilgrave was full of couples lining up to dance. The hired musicians struck up a lively tune. She danced in circles with Angus until Baird captured her for the next wild, twisting dance. The two Scotsmen had called for a jig, rather than yet another of the sedate numbers the musicians had been playing for the guests, and this now put them in the path of the other dancers.

"Oi! Watch out!" Lucien barked as Baird trod on his toes. His wife, Horatia, laughed and guided her husband safely out of harm's way. By the time the dancing paused for a brief break, Letty's feet had grown sore. She had not seen Adam for most of the night, and as the evening's festivities wore down, she began to worry. Adam had been distant the last few weeks. He'd been quiet, withdrawn, eating little and saying less. She found him on the terrace, looking out over the gardens in the courtyard.

"Adam, are you all right?" She shivered from the winter chill as she stood next to him.

He didn't immediately reply. He appeared to struggle to speak. "I can't stop thinking about that night. All this time, John was alive . . . I became someone I didn't want to be in order to avenge him, and then I became his enemy."

"What happened wasn't your fault. You couldn't have known what he was up to."

"But *why* didn't I see it? Why didn't I know?" Adam looked toward her, and then she tucked herself against him, hugging one arm around his waist. "And if I had known, maybe I could have steered him off his dark path. Maybe—"

"You couldn't have made him do anything he didn't wish to do," Letty said calmly. "He chose his own path."

Adam drew in a breath and let it out slowly. "I wish you could've known me. Before . . ."

"Before what?" she asked.

"Before I became what I am now. I am no better than John."

She turned to face him. "You're wrong—you are better. The things you do? You've always been motivated by helping others, not hurting them. The man I stood beside in the tunnels, offering his life to save mine, that's the man I love. *You* are a good man." She leaned up on her tiptoes and pulled his head down for a kiss. He slowly began to kiss her back, but she could feel the pain and guilt in his kiss.

"Adam," she whispered against his mouth.

He curled his arms around her waist and touched his forehead to hers. "Yes?"

"You must pull yourself out of this darkness. Do you understand? Not just for me, but for *him*."

"For who?" he asked in confusion.

She curled her fingers around one of his wrists and pulled his hand down to her abdomen. "For *him*."

"For him . . ." His eyes widened. "You mean . . . ?"

She smiled up at her husband. "Yes, and I've been dreaming that it's a boy."

The music from inside could still be heard where they were, and Adam seized her in his arms and twirled her around right there on the snowy balcony.

"Boy or girl, it does not matter—it's ours." He laughed, and the lines of sorrow upon his face began to fade a little.

"Do you like your Christmas present?" she asked him.

He chuckled. "I *adore* it, and you. We ought to celebrate, immediately."

Letty giggled as he swept her back to the ballroom, a protective arm about her shoulders. The guests were so enthralled with the festivities that none noticed Chilgrave's lord and lady as they snuck upstairs.

Letty giggled again as her husband closed the door to their bedchamber and flipped the lock.

"What was that for?" she asked. "I have no intention of running away—unless you want to chase me."

"Angus has a way of appearing where he shouldn't at the worst times," he explained. "Now, you said something about a chase?"

Letty gave him a good run about the room before he had her on her back on the bed. He leaned over and kissed her, taking his time to work his magic over her.

She gripped the edges of his shirt when he tried to pull away. "My lord, how you tease me."

"Oh? You don't wish me to . . ." He leaned in and whispered wicked suggestions in her ear.

"Oh, I quite *insist* you do that," she said with a sigh of longing.

He laughed and shifted down her body, removing and loosening her clothes as he did so. "I thought you might."

Letty parted her thighs and threw her head back as his mouth went to her mound. Adam tortured her until she was panting and begging for him to fill her. When he finally did as she asked, they clung to each other, their love and their excitement for the future pushing them toward the bright star of their release.

They made love sweetly, though it was no less thrilling than all the other times. Afterward, Letty settled against him, her head tucked into the cradle of his arms.

Adam brushed a hand up and down her back. "I don't deserve you," he said.

She rested her chin on his chest to look at him. "You're wrong,"

"Am I?"

She nodded. "Quite wrong. You deserve me and all the good things yet to come."

His eyes twinkled. "Is that so?"

"It is."

"Very well. I won't argue with you, lady wife."

She scooted up a few inches and kissed him, soft and sweet and with all her heart. "That would be wise."

❦

CAROLINE WATCHED THE SNOW BEGIN TO FALL FROM where she stood on the balcony of her room at Chilgrave which was directly above the ballroom. Music drifted up from below, but the warmth of the Christmas season failed to reach her.

For two years she had believed that John was gone.

All that had been a lie. She removed the small bit of silver from her cloak pocket and held it up in the moonlight: a cuff link with an antique coin as its face. She had given the pair to John as a gift shortly before he died. She had found this cuff link on the floor next to Avery when she had found him wounded at that townhouse in Grosvenor Square.

Somehow then she had known the awful truth—that John wasn't dead. But she hadn't wanted to face it. She had meant to go after Avery in that tunnel, but something had made her turn back. She had seen him, heard his voice, and before she could think she was lifting her weapon. And when John had threatened her brother and Letty, she had done what she had to, at great cost.

Caroline closed her eyes and cast the cuff link deep into the garden. She was done with love, done with dreams of a future with children and a loving husband. John had shattered that illusion. Perhaps, in some perverse way, she should thank him for that.

"Lady Caroline?" Avery's voice called out softly. He stood in the doorway leading back inside to her bedchamber.

"Mr. Russell," she greeted. "Why aren't you with the others?"

He stepped out onto the terrace with her. "I am leaving shortly. I wished to say goodbye."

"Oh?"

"Yes, I am needed back in London. There is much to

rebuild, and it won't be easy." He leaned on the stone railing, brushing a dusting of snow off the ledge. "I also have a lead regarding the woman who was seen with Lord Wilhelm and his rebels."

"There was a woman with him?" A fresh pain stabbed Caroline's chest. He'd said he'd held her in his heart all this time, yet he'd had another woman at his side.

"Yes, we believe she was both his mistress and a spy who worked as his left hand. She was the one who was tasked with hunting down Letty, and she led Wilhelm to my men."

Caroline pulled her cloak tightly about her as she turned away from the balcony railing.

"Avery . . ." She spoke his name, steeling herself.

"Yes, my lady?" He searched her face.

"Don't make John's mistake, or Adam's. Don't chase vengeance forever. It will not bring you the peace you seek."

He bowed his head without comment and left her alone. Caroline turned back to the snowy courtyard, wishing that she could feel something, *anything* aside from the numbness of her broken heart.

She was frozen—frozen forever.

THANK YOU SO MUCH FOR READING *THE EARL OF MORREY!* **Don't miss out on any of the other League of Rogues series by going HERE!**

Be sure you've signed up for my **NEWS-LETTER** and/or **BOOKBUB** so you don't miss the next League book and Caroline and Avery's stories.

Turn the page to read the next Wicked Earls' story **The Earl of Brecken**

THE EARL OF BRECKEN

J anuary *1819*
London, England

MADOC CRUMPLED THE PAPER AND SCOWLED FIERCELY at the roaring fire. He scanned the library of Brooks's, then squinted at the dark corners of the room, glad no one else witnessed his irritation. He and a close confidante were enjoying a leisurely evening in a private London gentlemen's club. They'd traded a profitable evening of gaming for a quiet place to talk and enjoy a decanter of brandy, when he'd remembered the envelope tucked inside his coat pocket.

"Bad news, Doc?" asked Kit, his dark eyes teasing as

he loosened the folds of his cravat with a finger. "It's rare to see such a storm darken your face. I'm accustomed to the jovial yet bland expression you've perfected."

He snorted with good humor at the Earl of Sunderland's observation. "Ha! My invisible armor protects me well. To answer your question, news from home is rarely good these days."

"Health or financial issues?"

Madoc tossed the wadded paper into the flames and watched the edges blacken and curl. "The solicitor informed me that he's still waiting for my annual income. He sent word to my father, who replied it would arrive forthwith. I suppose I don't need that stallion at Tattersall's."

"I could loan you the sum," offered Sunderland with a grin, his midnight hair gleaming in the flickering light, "but you won more brass than I did at the tables."

With a sigh, Madoc swirled the amber liquid in his crystal glass. "I couldn't care less about the money. I've got blunt enough from my, er, other *services*. It troubles me, though, that the sum has shrunk each year I've been gone."

"I can't imagine trouble with the estate. It's always turned out a good profit. How is the cantankerous old Welshman?"

"Mama's last letter described Father's health as declining. He's rarely left the grounds since his fall, and now he won't leave the castle."

Madoc remembered the accident like it was yesterday. Foxhunting had been his father's favorite pastime—
until he took a steep hedge that broke his back. The Earl
of Brecken hadn't walked in ten years. "He's so blasted
proud, didn't want anyone to see him as *less than a man*, as
he put it."

"How old is he now?" Sunderland asked. "Must be
nigh on sixty, eh?"

"Sixty-three last month." He rubbed the back of his
neck. "I believe a journey home is in order. Something's
amiss."

Sunderland grunted. "Are you presently *retained* or
free to go?"

He nodded. "The scoundrels are lying low for now.
My man, Walters, will keep an eye out for any new
activity or rumors and send word when I need to
return." Madoc cast another glance at the door. "Besides,
I'm long overdue to see my parents. I've managed no
more than half a dozen visits to Brecken Castle in as
many years. I've missed the wilds of Wales."

"I assume Brecken thinks you're still on a Grand
Tour?"

"Since my *person of interest* has returned to England,
the Home Office agreed I could tell my parents that my
adventures on the Continent have come to an end.
Though I hated lying, my first loyalty must be to the
Crown." He drummed his fingertips against the polished
wood of the arm chair. "I've been instructed that as an

LAUREN SMITH

indulged, unmarried heir, I will want to spend much of my time in London. Which is why I had you meet me at Brooks's rather than White's."

"I thought perhaps your travels had turned you liberal." Sunderland chuckled. "Wouldn't be the first aristocrat to sympathize with the masses."

Madoc gave a half-grunt, half-chuckle. "I sympathize with myself and getting back to life as it was before the bloody war. But no, since I need to be aware of murmurs on both sides of the throne, I need to frequent both clubs. To think the past four years, I've been dreaming of the humdrum but idyllic countryside, not the smoky dens of London. In truth, I'm tired of looking over my shoulder or wondering what's waiting for me in the shadows." Lifting his glass, the well-practiced smile returned. "Here's to no more spy rings and long, dull days of leisure. May I never take boredom for granted again."

Sunderland guffawed. "By all means, enjoy them if you can before you become earl. After that, your days may not be filled with intrigue, but you will certainly stay occupied. My estate, properties, and seat in the Lords demand much of my time."

His friend's statement gave him pause. "I hadn't really thought about the future, in that sense, but you're right enough. I've been trained for the title and know what is expected of me. Yet, having the responsibility solely on my shoulders scares the hell out of me." Madoc sighed. "If I fail an assignment, my disappearance will cause little harm. Another man will take my place, and the task will be accomplished. But making decisions that affect the lives of my tenants, people whose livelihood could be crushed by a man's whim..."

The earl nodded. "The obligation can be heavy at times, but it's our duty to maintain our inheritance, our family name. Those who tend the land and the animals, work within our abodes, are all an integral part of the system. Treat them fairly, and with the dignity they deserve, and you'll do well. It's that mutual understanding and common goal to make life better that will bond you to them."

"Blast, if you don't sound like my father. And a Whig." Madoc laughed. "Next you'll be telling me it's time to find a wife. Speaking of spouses, how is Grace?"

"Trying to ferret out a ghost that she thinks lives in the original stronghold of Sunderland Castle. The last time I ventured to that area, the hairs on my neck rose. My wife seems to think it's an ancestor." Sunderland laughed, his dark eyes crinkling. "Good God, I hope I don't have that effect on people. But if the days get too tedious for you, come to Sunderland Castle. We'll give you the whole north wing."

"No, thank you. I prefer an adversary I can see." Madoc studied his friend. "You still seem happy with the leg shackles. How long has it been?"

"Three years. She's my life's blood, I tell you. Flows through my veins. If you want some words of wisdom, the right woman completes a man." The earl finished off his brandy and set the empty glass on the polished side table with a *thud*. "Well, Doc, shall we have another or call it a night?"

"One more before I resign myself to the next role of prodigal son. Soon enough, I'll face my mother's wrath for not answering her correspondence. I almost prefer the dangers of espionage."

"Be careful what you wish for."

"And my father, if he still partakes, prefers whisky to brandy." He shuddered. "Good God, maybe I should I bring along my own bottle to preserve my sanity."

"Considering the countess's temper, I'd recommend a cask."

***

THE RIGHT WOMAN COMPLETES A MAN.

Sunderland's words echoed in his head. Madoc squinted against the early morning fog that swirled around the stallion's hocks and left droplets clinging to the top of his Hessian boots. He mentally sorted through the females of his acquaintance. None seemed to hold the kind of influence described by his friend. He'd met beautiful women, intelligent women, silly women, even a combination of these, but never had he considered even one of them indispensable to his happiness. Perhaps the Countess of Sunderland was an enigma.

Madoc shivered, pulled up the fur collar of his great coat, and adjusted his beaver hat. With a well-placed kick, he urged his horse into a canter. He wanted London far behind him. His luggage would follow, but he needed air and time to prepare himself mentally for the upcoming encounter. His last visit had been more like a stay in a mausoleum than one's boyhood home. His father's mumbled responses and lackluster eyes had not prompted any lively conversation—until the end.

"I've completed my final year of university. Are you sure you want me to leave again so soon?" Madoc leaned against the mantel, the smoldering peat in the grate hot against his riding breeches. The May sun poured through the floor-to-ceiling windows and mocked the thin, dour man wrapped in heavy wool blankets. Where had the Earl of Brecken gone? That man had been larger than life with a booming laugh, an iron fist, and cunning wit. A man his son had looked up to, imitated, his every action in the hope of gaining the glow of his father's approval. The kind of man who commanded attention merely by walking into a room. And therein lay the problem.

The silence stretched. Perhaps the earl had fallen asleep. His gaze fell on his father's bony fingers, clutching a shawl about his rounded shoulders, as if it were his last defense. Madoc swal-

lowed as his father's hazel eyes narrowed. The brown and green flecks, passed down to his only son, sparked with anger.

"Every young man needs to see the world. It's part of your basic education. Do you think I'm unable to manage my own affairs because I cannot walk?" rasped the earl, pushing back a limp strand of gray from his forehead. "Do you think the inability to use these feckless limbs affects my brain?"

"No, Father, but I believe it has affected your spirit." He went down on one knee and took a cold, papery hand between his warm palms. "Please, let me take you for a ride in the carriage, get out and see some of your tenants. Your soul is in this land. It would do you good."

"I don't need you to take me anywhere. If I wanted to leave my home, I'd do it," bellowed the old man with surprising volume. His shoulders slumped as if the admonishment had depleted what little energy he'd possessed. "Go! Enjoy your youth while you have it. Lady Fortune is a capricious, evil female. You never know how long happiness will perch on your shoulder."

Madoc's jaw tightened as he gave the earl a rigid nod and left the room. Why was he surprised? Delaying his response to the Home office, he had hoped for one last bid to bring his father back to the land of the living. By God, he'd tried. Now, he'd take the assignment with no remorse, working under one of England's most brilliant spymasters. At twenty-two, he was making a name for himself. The danger and intrigue made him feel alive, a welcome and vivid contrast to the quiet hills of the Welsh countryside.

His parents suspected nothing, assuming their son had come

from Oxford rather than Belgium. This "Grand Tour" would provide the perfect ruse to be abroad, his title gaining him entry into the right circles to mingle, charm, and... listen. Napoleon had been declared an outlaw and was wreaking havoc again. The Crown needed every available set of eyes and ears. It may be years before he was able to return. If he returned. Lord Risk was as fickle as Lady Fortune.

He stopped at the front door, his palm on the cold handle of the door as he looked over his shoulder, a final glance around his childhood home. An ancient castle with the countess's modern touch. The large receiving hall had been paneled with oak, the stone floor covered with narrow, polished planks, and the windows enlarged to allow more light. The furnishings had come from London by way of France and Italy, the earl sparing no expense for his new, young wife. Painted silks and satins hung on the walls and dressed the glass panes.

"Must you leave, Madoc? Can you not put off your trip for a year or so?" His mother appeared at his elbow, the familiar martyred expression creasing her face. Her slender fingers clutched his riding coat. "He was so looking forward to your visit."

Madoc snorted. "Mama, you know my passage has been paid. Father has been quite adamant that I go."

"You don't understand what he's been through, what it's like for him. He's bitter, that's all. If you stayed, he'd come round. I'm certain." Her onyx eyes watered conveniently, and she laid a hand on his cheek. Rays of light shed a halo about her black chignon, at odds with the growing venom in her tone. "Have

you become one of those dandies, then? Looking for pleasure and living off your father's money and good name?"

He ground his teeth, his jaw tense. "He's been like this for six years. My presence for a few weeks will not produce a miracle. I will obey my father's wishes, ma'am."

Madoc turned on his heel and stormed out the door. A chestnut gelding stood patiently waiting in the courtyard. He mounted and turned the horse to face the veranda, hooves and cobblestones reverberating in the warm afternoon air. "Good day, Mama." With a bow and sweep of his hat, he added, "Until we meet again."

FOUR YEARS AGO. FOUR LONG YEARS.

So much had happened in that time. He'd changed, lost his naivete, his youthful optimism. His skills belonged more to a soldier than a titled landowner. He had a relentless grip on a sword, excellent marksmanship, and a wicked right punch. He could go days without sleep. His superiors regarded him as the man with a seductive smile and honey-like charm that could distract top officials—or their wives—while correspondence was pilfered in their own libraries for secrets that could hasten the end of the war. He'd become the perfect chameleon, as comfortable playing a discontented foot soldier or a common thief in the rookeries as he was the polished dandy spending his father's fortune.

It had taken its toll.

Madoc trusted few people, rarely heard a conversation or request without discerning a hidden implication or ulterior motive, and was bone-tired. He wanted to sleep until the sun was high in the sky. Ride across his childhood estate, nod at tenants, and have no greater worry than balancing the ledgers and deciding which country dance or dinner to attend. It was time to begin his life, the life he'd been born to, the life that had called to him when he'd stepped onto English soil again. Yes, he was ready for the role he had only pretended at the last four years.

***

A TIRED AND DUSTY MADOC TROTTED TOWARD THE village of Breckenknock. He crossed the stone bridge, drew in a renewed breath as the clear water rushed and splashed under the arches. The slate mountains and snow-capped peaks seemed to be stacked on top of each other, as if a crowd trying to see over the next shoulder, and provided the perfect background for his brooding mood. Curiosity would greet him in the village. Waves and questions about the master when the tenants realized it was Lord Madoc riding through. A frigid wind whipped at his face, and he hunkered inside his coat.

He cursed himself for not waiting on the carriage

LAUREN SMITH

and his valet. It was demmed cold. The sun peeked out from a billowy, gray cloud. He squinted at brightness, his watery vision barely able to discern the outline of the small town looming in the distance. As he drew closer, Madoc blinked and wiped his eyes with his palms. Was he lost? Had it been so long since he'd been home?

He slowed his chestnut gelding to a trot and made his way to the square, taking in the dilapidated buildings. The main thoroughfare—that made him chuckle as they kicked up dust along the dirt and gravel road—was crowded with people buying last-minute wares from vendors closing up and hurrying home before dark. A growl in his belly reminded him he hadn't eaten since breakfast, but his mind was on the derelict condition of Breckenknock.

There were no inquiries or smiles. No hoorays or nods from the men. Filth trickled like a brown and yellow brook from the alleys and puddled near the street. Roofs were in disrepair and walls had been patched and re-patched. The tenants' clothes were worn and shabby. What in blazes was going on? His lovely village had gone to ruin.

"Good day," he called out to the blacksmith he'd known since a boy. "I've just returned home and can't help but notice..." He made a long sweep with his hand to encompass the sight before him. "What has happened?"

"Ask his lordship," boomed the man before ducking

his head and removing his cap. "Or the devil in his pocket."

"And does this devil have a name?"

"Aye, it's Caerton's son, Niall."

"He's taken over for his father, then?"

"He's taken... That's a true statement, to be sure." The man turned away and disappeared into his smithy.

"By God, I'll get to the bottom of this," Madoc yelled to the retreating figure.

Four generations of Caertons had managed the estate for the Earls of Brecken. The last time he'd seen Mr. Caerton, the old man had been in decline. Finding it difficult to maintain the physical responsibility of managing Brecken's vast holdings, he had begun training his oldest son, Niall, to replace him. Madoc had never liked him growing up. He remembered the boy picking a fight and cheating by throwing dirt in the other lad's eyes to win. Of course, that had been years ago. People change. He was living proof of that.

It got worse as he cantered toward the castle. The fields were overworked. At a glance, he knew there had been no rotation of land. Less fertile soil, less crops, less profit. Perhaps Caerton had died before he'd been able to instruct Niall in all aspects of management. He'd give the steward the benefit of the doubt until he had the facts. If the past years had taught him anything, it was that appearances could be deceiving. A mirthless laugh scratched his throat, thinking of the disguises he'd donned over the years.

Madoc kicked his horse into a gallop as he passed a paddock of thin plow horses. He was glad he'd come home. It was time to take over for his father and have a word with the Niall Caerton. As he clattered onto the stone courtyard, the butler appeared at the door. The smile and twinkle in his blue eyes belied the blond hair streaked with gray.

"Lord Madoc, it is so good to have you back." He held the door open for Lady Brecken, who rushed down the steps to greet him.

"Oh, my sweet son. The lord has answered our prayers. You've come home just in time."

WANT TO FIND OUT HOW MADOC MEETS MISS Evelina Franklin romance?

<u>Get EARL OF BRECKEN at major retailers HERE!</u>

OTHER TITLES BY LAUREN SMITH

Historical

The League of Rogues Series

Wicked Designs

His Wicked Seduction

Her Wicked Proposal

Wicked Rivals

Her Wicked Longing

His Wicked Embrace

The Earl of Pembroke

His Wicked Secret

The Last Wicked Rogue

Never Kiss a Scot

The Earl of Kent

Never Tempt a Scot

The Wicked Beginning

The Earl of Morrey

The Seduction Series
The Duelist's Seduction
The Rakehell's Seduction
The Rogue's Seduction
The Gentleman's Seduction

Standalone Stories
Tempted by A Rogue
Bewitching the Earl
Boudreaux's Lady
No Rest for the Wicked
Devil at the Gates
Seducing an Heiress on a Train

Sins and Scandals
An Earl By Any Other Name
A Gentleman Never Surrenders
A Scottish Lord for Christmas

Contemporary
The Surrender Series
The Gilded Cuff
The Gilded Cage
The Gilded Chain
The Darkest Hour

Love in London
Forbidden

Seduction

Climax

Forever Be Mine

Paranormal

Dark Seductions Series

The Shadows of Stormclyffe Hall

The Love Bites Series

The Bite of Winter

His Little Vixen

Brotherhood of the Blood Moon Series

Blood Moon on the Rise (coming soon)

Brothers of Ash and Fire

Grigori: A Royal Dragon Romance

Mikhail: A Royal Dragon Romance

Rurik: A Royal Dragon Romance

The Lost Barinov Dragon: A Royal Dragon Romance

Sci-Fi Romance

Cyborg Genesis Series

Across the Stars

The Krinar Chronicles

The Krinar Eclipse

The Krinar Code by Lauren Smith writing as Emma Castle

ABOUT THE AUTHOR

Lauren Smith is an Oklahoma attorney by day, author by night who pens adventurous and edgy romance stories by the light of her smart phone flashlight app. She knew she was destined to be a romance writer when she attempted to re-write the entire *Titanic* movie just to save Jack from drowning. Connecting with readers by writing emotionally moving, realistic and sexy romances no matter what time period is her passion. She's won multiple awards in several romance subgenres including: New England Reader's Choice Awards, Greater Detroit BookSeller's

Best Awards, and a Semi-Finalist award for the Mary Wollstonecraft Shelley Award.

To Connect with Lauren, visit her at:
www.laurensmithbooks.com
lauren@laurensmithbooks.com

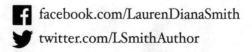 facebook.com/LaurenDianaSmith
twitter.com/LSmithAuthor
instagram.com/Laurensmithbooks